Covert Ops: Danger on the Island

I0654117

Steve Barker

GREEN CAT BOOKS

Published in 2021 by

GREEN CAT BOOKS

19 St Christopher's Way

Pride Park

Derby DE24 8JY

www.green-cat.shop

ISBN: 978-1-913794-25-5

ACKNOWLEDGEMENTS

Thank you to
Pauline Carter-Rapson
George James
Simon Munnery
Derek Barker
George Holland

for their help with this book

Contents

Chapter One - Another Day

It has been several months following the last mission on St Halb and not much excitement since. The gelt from the previous job came in handy, even manage to pay off all the arseholes who were demanding money from me. Even took a little R&R with a 30-day cruise around Asia.

For the rest of the dosh, I upgraded my caravan to a lodge. Even invested a substantial amount in what I believed a fantastic investment scheme called Sirius BTC, but like most things I touch, this turned out to be a scam run by a tugboat captain in Panama.

Like most people, I always needed more money, but I'm missing the thrill and danger of executing a mission, if the truth be known. Fortunately, Simon is arranging a potential job with somebody he met in his army days. Now I come to think about it, Simon appears to know a lot of the wrong type of contacts, or from our perspective, the right kind.

Oh well, almost lunchtime, and I'm bored and, for some reason, in a bad mood, so going to take myself down to the local tavern for a few wet ones, and being too lazy to cook food, grab a meal as well.

Unfortunately, the campsite facilities are closed for the winter, and with no access to my usual drinking establishment, I needed a new place on the island to frequent. On one of my many walks to ease stress levels caused by the bloody PTSD, I stumbled across a pub not too far to walk or, more importantly, stagger back home after far too much to drink.

The public house is set back from the road, with a sizeable patio section to the front which had several wooden benches scattered around the place.

On entering, the wooden bar is immediately in front of you, and what I love, a massive log fire off to my right surrounded by huge brown leather sofas that you could slouch in for hours.

More tables occupied by young couples and a small gathering of around six lads are off to the left. All appeared to be having a fantastic time, considering the amount of laughter coming from them.

Single men, either staring blankly at the array of bottled spirits lining the back wall or down at their half-filled glasses, crammed the bar area. Lucky for me, one space remained at the far right end, so I squeeze myself in and attract the barperson's attention. On the way into the place, I overheard someone call him Gary.

"Hi, Gary, a pint of John Smiths, please?"

"Sure, coming right up."

Turned around to go over to plonk my arse near the fire when I spot the young men had relocated to the sofas, bastards. The joint is packed with people having a terrific time, so only one thing for it, act like the rest of the men slumped along the bar and stare into empty space, while sitting on a barstool.

Been sitting minding my own business for 20 minutes or so, when I sense some person knock into my arm. Turning my head to the right, to discover one of the youngsters managed to squeeze themselves into the gap to my right. It must be his lucky day; he'd not spilt any of my beverage so let this go, for now!

Through the mirror on the wall, past the rows of neatly— positioned spirits, I watch as the cheeky fucker grabs my glass of beer, his second mistake. Then, still looking straight ahead, "Excuse me, mate, you will find that's mine!"

He finishes off the third and final mistake, "And what are you going to do about it, old man?"

I raise myself up on the stool, grabbing the back of the man's head with both hands, and slam his head with as much force as I could muster into the counter. Grab the glass and what was left of my drink from his blood-stained, limp body as it slipped to the floor.

"So you wanted my beer, well here it is," as I pour the remaining beer from the half-filled glass over his face. The man should be thankful; this helped wash the blood from a broken nose.

Turn to glance at his so-called mates, now shitting themselves, motionless on the sofas close to the fire.

"Want to say anything, arseholes? Good, I'm in no mood for this shit today." Suppose now I need to find another boozer. About to leave when Gary grabbed my attention.

"They deserved that; please come back anytime."

"Thanks, Gary, I will."

Then leave the pub and make my way along the high street in the direction of home, stopping at the food store to purchase a few pies, as that idiot in the drinking establishment prevented me from having the planned meal. Instinct found me looking in all directions as I exited.

To my right, the youths from the boozer were trying their best to blend into the crowd. To the trained eye, they stood out like spare pricks at a wedding. Maybe they found some courage near the bottom of a glass?

Not sure if they intended to jump me or not, so I enter another shop only to reappear seconds later. Yep, confirmed, they'd stopped again, but closer this time.

Now formulating a strategy in my head, I take the next left as I knew of a road that ran parallel to the main street. The plan was simple, come up from behind, taking them out separately.

Now sprinting as fast as possible, I head down the road; need the element of surprise. So turn left, then left again, and find myself behind the group. The man at the rear, by my reckoning, must be about five feet six inches tall and overweight for his size and age, I bet he is the one who ate all the pies.

Moved up fast behind him, fling my right arm tightly around his neck and drag him back into the side road. As I release my grip, I swing him round and land several hard, well-aimed punches to his face, knocking him to the ground.

The man's swollen tearful eyes stare up at me, as he pulls his legs in tight to his body. Then, with a trembling voice, "Please don't hurt me anymore. I'm just doing what the others wanted."

"OK, you fat fucker, if you can comprehend what's good for you, stay where you are for the next half an hour. If you come after me, I will kill you. Nod, if you understand?" With his eyes fixed directly on me, he nods. Right, time to take out the bloke who appears to be the instigator of this little episode of courage.

Work out that by the time I had finished with the fat boy, the other two would be past the place I initially turned left, so once again sprint down the back road and turn right at the end just as they pass, continuing their way along the high street—perfect.

I didn't have time to separate the pack, so I launch at the biggest of the two, the resulting force hurtling him to the floor, smashing his head vigorously against the concrete slabs of the pavement.

Not giving him time to recover, I plant several powerful kicks to his face and stomach, ending in him crying out in agonising pain while blood drips from the gash on the back of his head.

Then, expecting an attack from the other one, I turn on my heels to face him, but he'd run off into the distance.

My attention turns back to the man on the floor. "Want some more, you little fucker?"

The man remains motionless in silence, blood oozing between the fingers of his hands where his head rested on them. With no more response, leave the scene and head off home.

Reminded by the growling in my stomach, why I'd gone into the shop, I am still hungry, so remove the clear plastic package from my jacket's inside pocket. The cheeky fuckers squashed my pasty, but hey, food is food.

Due to the idiots, I left the pub a lot sooner than planned. So now, a simple case of what to do for the rest of the day. Might as well pick up several beers from the supermarket and make this a movie afternoon.

Right, the beer nicely cooling in the fridge, time to select a training film or, as some people call it, a war film. But, what is surprising, is what bits of information are available in these movies for people in my line of work. For example, many years ago, I learned how to make a lightbulb explode while watching said films. Trust me, the process is simpler than you might think. All you need is a syringe and a little petrol to make your own electrical IED.

Been slouched on the sofa acting like a zombie for several hours when the phone starts to sing its merry head off in the kitchen; one day, I'm going to learn to put the bloody thing next to me. Can't be bothered to move, so I let the irritating thing ring away. If it were important, they would call again.

Well, it must have been, as the annoying phone only shut the fuck up for five minutes before it rings again. Better remove my fat, lazy arse from the sofa and answer it, I suppose. Bet that it is Simon; he is the only one who calls back straight away.

Pick up the mobile, "Hi, Simon, how may I be of assistance on this lethargic afternoon? Or it would be if I didn't have to get up to answer the fucking phone."

"Well, good afternoon to you too, Steve! You should keep your mobile closer like most normal people. But, sorry, you are not normal, are you. Are you free to talk, or are you busy doing nothing sitting on your fat arse?"

"Always got time for you, mate. What's the problem?"

"No problem, Steve, remember a while back when I said a friend of mine has some work we might be interested in. Well, now it's become apparent that the task needs to be completed within the next few weeks, so when are you available to discuss?"

"Available any time, Simon."

"In that case, I will grab George, and we will pop over to the Isle of Wight tomorrow — can you pick us up from the ferry?"

"That's kind of you. So what's the matter, your polo donkey gone lame?"

"Second word is off, Steve."

Looks like today hasn't been a complete washout, now Simon has come up with more work. Now the boys are coming over, better sort out the spare rooms. Then take a look at what's happening on the food front. A glance in the fridge confirms my fears, empty, so now I'm going to have to go back to the shops.

On the positive note, it is now early evening, and many of the rude trolley pushers, you know the ones — aim right for you and barge you out of their way — ought to have done their shopping and gone home. That is because the older generation typically complete their buying early morning.

Shit, the place still appears to be busy, but nevertheless, I need to go in, there will be no time in the morning. Right, remember what one of your therapists, Steve Alexander, was constantly bleating on about — do your breathing exercises.

Stop about 20 metres from the door and take a long deep breath for seven seconds, hold it for five, then breathe out for the count of six; I do this 10 times before making my way into the store.

Once inside, I am confronted with the sight of shoppers busy rearranging boxes of goods on the shelves before reaching the back to find the longest best before date. I never understood the point of all this nonsense, as you didn't eat food in date order.

My plan to keep the arseholes away, is to walk with the basket sticking out from my right or left hip, depending on which row of neatly-stacked produce I intended to walk down. This worked, and I soon had everything I need, so I join one of the long queues at the tills.

Must have been stood carefully surveying everyone around and deciding which one to take out first, if any action is required — as they say, attack is the safest form of defence — when I sense someone's hand shove me forward.

Definitely not in the mood to take shit from anyone today, so I turn around to confront the brave idiot for some forceful negotiations with my right fist, ready to open the discussions. Whoever it is must have regretted their actions, as nobody appeared within about three metres of me, lucky for them.

Once home, grab a cold beer from the fridge, plonk my arse on the sofa, and get Alexa to switch on the TV. Overcome with the sudden desire for some light entertainment, so end up binge-watching A Touch of Frost, by far the best show David Jason ever made.

Chapter Two – Meeting

A quick gander down at Mickey, and the fact that the television had changed itself to the shopping channel confirms that I had fallen asleep on the sofa again. So remind me again who watches this crap at 04:00?

What's become routine recently, I'm now soaked with sweat from the night terrors, which seem to be getting worse for some reason. But at least I survived another night, so that is a positive note to start the day.

There is no point in trying to fall back to sleep, so head to the bathroom to complete the morning 3 Ss, Shit, Shave and Shampoo, followed by my morning gallon of coffee.

Switch on the TV back on as background noise. Nothing worse than sitting in silence, as this is when the brain and the escaped librarian start to ruminate over past events in my military career that caused my PTSD, something I've spent years attempting to avoid.

Still, plenty of time before I need to meet Simon and George at the ferry in Cowes, Isle of Wight at 10:30. Will be using public transport, so will not need to leave here until about 08:35. This gives me loads of time for the most important meal of the day, according to the Army, that is, and perhaps far too much coffee.

I have been on a health kick for a month, so my usual Weetabix receives the boot to be replaced with some type of healthy breakfast. Resembles hamster food to me, but someone said it is good for you.

Brekkie finished, and am about to depart for the bus when Simon calls.

"Hi Steve, it's Simon. We've missed the ferry, George needed to feed his battle-hardened Chihuahua. Will be on the next one and should be with you about 11:30."

"Thanks for letting me know. Slap the ugly bastard for me, and I'll be waiting outside the terminal for you."

"Sure thing, Steve, meet you when we disembark from the ferry."

Might as well leave now, as the last thing I need is to catch the 09:34 bus from Shanklin with all the freeloaders with their bus passes. No doubt it will be packed, and we all appreciate how much I love buses. However, it is not the mode of transport that is the problem. It's the people who don't understand how to sit quietly. Well, here is a news flash, everyone else couldn't give a flying fuck about your problems, me least of all, due to my lack of empathy.

Appears like my day is going the right way with three positive things this morning, woke up, didn't slip and break my bloody neck in the shower, and now I arrived at the Shanklin bus stop with only three people waiting.

An older gentleman around six feet tall, dressed in a long black coat, is standing next to the kerb. Inside the shelter, a young woman is bent over a small pink pushchair, making stupid baby noises to some two-legged pooing machine wrapped up warmly inside.

The only other person waiting, a young man who appears to be in his early twenties wearing blue jeans and a short brown jacket, leaning against the wall listening to music blasting into his ears via a set of headphones.

Must have waited no more than 10 minutes when a double-decker bus pulls up. Once on board, I pay the bored-looking driver before making my way up the winding stairs to the top deck and the back seat. This way, no idiot has even the slightest chance of sitting behind me and annoying me. I'm in a good mood and want it to stay that way.

The lush green hills of the Isle of Wight, with its occasional glimpses of the shoreline and views across the English Channel, quickly passes by. I take this time to reflect on the last mission on St Halb in the Caribbean, a task with all its twists and turns that reminded us that you could not trust everyone.

Take Sam as an example, someone we believed to be a person we could trust, who then turned out to be working with the drug gang the entire time. Then, of course, worst of all, the bastard Henry, the man who financed the whole thing, who not only double-crossed us but ran the complete outfit.

Wasn't all bad, we certainly had more than a few moments of fun and excitement, and we made some lifelong friends in Abbie and Derek. Plus, in our line of work, we made great contacts with Katie and Cody. That reminds me, better ensure Simon contacts her to find out if she has any connections over here. We may need some play equipment and objects that might go bang.

Brought back to reality by the shouting and uncouth obscenities from three youths now heading in my direction. Yes, I might have carried out some nasty things at work, but I can't stand the use of foul language for the sake of it, especially aloud. The trio stop halfway down and now occupy three seats, one each.

There was something else I hadn't noticed, when thinking about the last mission. An older couple now taking up a seat at the front of the bus, And a woman with several young children in tow sitting between the irritating idiots and me.

Deep breath, Stephen, bring the anger levels back down. They are not encroaching into your space; just disregard them.

Now that one of them has decided it would be good to play horrible screeching sounds loudly from his mobile phone, it is impossible to ignore the fools. This wouldn't be too much of an issue if it happened to be good music. But no, it's that annoying rap shite with lots of vulgar swearing that would make any average person blush. Glanced over in the woman's direction, she appears uncomfortable and tries her best to shelter her children by distracting them.

Feel the anxiety and anger boiling up inside me, but I manage to keep it under control for the moment. That is until one of the three youths sees me looking at them.

"Got a fucking problem, mate?" he rants.

Right, time to shut these annoying arseholes up. Rise from my chair with complete composure, scanning all three for any movement, and walk over. While closing in on the one with all the gob, I observe the other two on the opposite side to the gobshite, fidgeting uncomfortably in their seats.

"Good morning, gents, not sure if you realised other people are on this bus as well, including three young children, so we all would be grateful if you turned down that crap coming from your mobile and stop with the bad language."

"Yeah, and what you going to do about it, old man?" comes the instant reply from the gobshite.

No way would I let him get away with a second chance. So reach over and open the window while grabbing his phone with the other hand and tossing it out.

16

The young man tries in vain to object and starts to rise out of his seat. As he does, I plant a severe blow to his windpipe with my left hand resulting in him grasping at his throat with both hands, trying hard to catch a breath like it is his last.

Turn around to the other two, still sitting motionlessly, "You two got any comeback?" there is a short moment of silence. "Thought not." Walk backwards a couple of steps and press the red button on one of the uprights to indicate to the driver to stop the bus.

"Suggest you three remove yourselves and walk back down the road to collect your mobile phone. Then, maybe next time, you will think before annoying other people."

A few minutes later, the vehicle comes to a halt. Without saying another word, the trio rise from their seats and exit. The remaining passengers glance in my direction and applaud.

Isn't long afterwards that the bus pulls into Newport Bus Station. Right, that is the first of the two bus rides to East Cowes. Let's hope the next one goes more smoothly.

The second ride is going without a hitch. Arrive at the Red Funnel terminal with around half an hour to wait until George and Simon turned up. The passenger terminal is only small, with the ticket and coffee outlet on one side and rows of chairs and several tables on the other. The company had arranged a small counter stocked with rubbish that you don't want or need down the middle of the room.

The sad thing is that many people will still purchase the stuff because they either forgot to acquire a souvenir on the Isle of Wight or shut the brats up who are going on at them to buy a teddy bear dressed like a ship's captain.

Grab an Americano with milk from the coffee shop and plonk my arse down close to the window, where I can watch the ferry come in. A few people come and go, apart from that, the place is quiet, with only a couple of people waiting to board as foot passengers. I take a glance down at Mickey. The slow-moving hands of the clock face tells me there is just another 5 minutes until the ship arrives, might as well wait outside for the boys.

While standing, staring towards the vessel as 30 or so people walk down the gangway, some showing a neutral expression on their faces; these would be the islanders. Others with small children and supporting big-hearted grins, undoubtedly conned their kids and told them they are going abroad for their holiday. Towards the rear of the group, I spot Simon and George emerging from the ship's doorway. Behind them is a well-dressed man in black trousers, a blue pinstriped shirt and a grey jacket.

"Hi, George, glad you could make it. How's the battle-hardened Chihuahua?"

"Not too bad, he is thinking of going for selection with 22 Regiment in Hereford, Steve."

"OK, Simon, who is the gentleman with you?"

"Steve, I would like to introduce Mark. The CEO of Bashp Enterprises and the man we will be doing the work for."

"Great to meet you, Mark. Shall we leave and go back to my place?"

"Are you still on Shank's pony, Steve, or have you been brave and purchased a car?" asked George.

"The only place you would walk, George, is to the pie shop." I knew this wasn't the case, as he liked walking as much as I did, but I love winding him up.

"Now that would be true, Steve, apart from one thing, looking at your oversized gut, it would appear you ate them all already, fat boy."

Simon turned around to Mark, "Ignore these idiots. They're always like that."

"Now, gents, as for a vehicle, as you know, I do not own one for a reason. First, they can be tampered with while parked, plus easily spotted and tracked and lastly, any idiot can follow you. So for today, for your selection, there are two choices: bus or taxi. Because we have company, I would suggest we grab this red cab right here."

The taxi is a lot faster journey, with the advantage of no idiots to deal with. I try to keep the mission plans out of conversations during the ride back to my place, due to the unknown variable in the vehicle, our driver. Overall, the trip takes around 35 minutes and soon stops in the car park opposite my lodge.

"Don't panic, you tight arses. I'll pay for the cab." Then, turn to face Mark, "Not you, mate, you're a guest, I am referring to the two idiots sat next to you."

Open my wallet to take out the driver's money when a voice from the back pipes up. "Did you detect the creaking sound when he opened his wallet, George?"

"Forget that, Simon, the car is now full of moths!"

The thought of retaliation crosses my mind, but I decide against it. So instead, I pay the cabby and send him on his way. Then, to err on the side of caution, stand and wait for the driver to disappear into the distance. Can't be too careful, don't want any strangers seeing which of the neatly-lined row of brown lodges belonged to me.

A quick walk around the perimeter confirms nobody has been fucking about with my property while I've been away. The green leaf from the trees surrounding the lodge is still located between the door and frame. Used this because it would look like it accidentally got caught when I closed the door, to the untrained eye.

Once inside, Simon and George go straight to drop off their bags in their respective rooms. They have been here several times before, so they know where they are.

"Take a seat, Mark, fancy a brew?"

"That would be fantastic, thanks, Steve."

"How do you want it, NATO standard?"

"Not heard anyone call it that since I left the military, but yes, please, Steve."

The moment Simon and George re-enter the room, "Here you go, boys, three NATO standards when you're ready. Mark, would you like to elaborate on the task you would like us to undertake?"

"Will start at the beginning. Last year Bashp Enterprises successfully won a bid to provide the British military with a new optical sight and wind indicator, complete with specifically developed smart ammunition for trained snipers.

"What makes the equipment unique is that the shooter looks through the scope, picks the target, then presses a button on the side and the inbuilt software calculates where the best place to aim would be.

"The optics do this by considering the distance to target, wind speed, and weather conditions from a small device placed in front of the firing position. Specially programmed ammunition then follows the invisible laser from the sight and lands on the target.

However, the unique code ensures that just the military or anyone programmed into the system can use the equipment. Any questions so far?"

"You're the sniper in the group, George, anything you would like to discuss regarding the rifle?" I ask.

"Not yet, but I would love to handle one to gather more intel. Could that be arranged, Mark?"

"Shouldn't be an issue, should be possible to arrange one for you to look at in the next couple of days."

"That would be perfect, not sure how much you discussed with Simon and George, but can you please explain why and what is the problem and why you need our assistance in the matter?"

"Sure, it all started about two months ago when I suspected one of my employees, a man called Dennis, of taking company work home with him. As you can imagine, for security reasons, this is prohibited. This resulted in him being fired from the company.

"A week later, after a complete stock check, we discovered that 200 of the rifles are missing, including the smart ammunition. The frightening part is that several portable programming suitcases used to connect the shooter with the sniper rifle are also gone.

"Now, if these weapons got into the wrong hands, such as organised crime organisations, we might witness a lot of pointless deaths with no way of catching the people carrying out the killings, as they would be long gone once the round hits home."

"Thanks, Mark, but let us face it, there's always been shootings by gangs, and always will be, and in my opinion, let the fuckers kill each other. Knowing Simon and George, they would be considering the same thing as me. So Mark, can't help thinking you have another motive than solely removing weapons from the streets."

"Of course you're right, Steve, I do. The company is struggling financially, for the last year or so and is close to foreclosure. So need to keep this military contract at all costs. Where hence lays the primary issue. In three weeks, an inspection by the government and the army top brass will take place at the factory, and they will want to check the full inventory. This is why I would like you to recover the weapons as soon as possible, with extreme prejudice if you have to."

"OK, that's not a problem, Mark. Sure we can do that for you. One question, how does the establishment know what weapons should be on the property, or did you provide them with a list previously?"

Mark nods.

"A few more questions from me, and I'm sure Simon and George will no doubt come up with some too, but before we do that, if anyone fancies a beer, you will find them in the fridge. Fetch me one while you're there, Simon?"

"Yes, almighty one, anything else I can do for you, clean your boots or kiss your arse perhaps!"

"Now come to think about it, Simon, you can grab the biscuits as you're in the kitchen, sure Mark and George would love a cold one as well. Then for being a good manservant, you can take yesterday off."

After grabbing the drinks from the fridge and placing them on the small wooden coffee table situated in the centre of the room, Simon looks at Steve.

"Seems like you've repaired the table from the last time you threw the teddy out of the pram."

"Yep, twice."

The next 20 or so minutes are spent in general chat where we discover that Mark was Simon's squadron commander in the Queen's Royal Irish Hussards. Of course, I reminded them all the best regiment in the British Army at the time was, in fact, the Royal Green Jackets. George's argument that this honour went to the Grenadier Guards goes on deaf ears. After reminding him of the Guard's motto, 'if it doesn't move, clean it', I find myself dodging a barrage of empty beer cans.

A glance at Mickey on my wrist reminds me that time is getting on, so better turn the conversation back to business. "This may appear like a stupid question. How do you know Dennis is on the Isle of Wight, Mark." This is Something Simon told me a few days back when he called me a few days ago.

With a slow, careful motion, Mark puts the half-empty beer can down. "Now, this is a difficult one and a little awkward. A young man named Stuart, who happens to be a family member, left the same time as Dennis. After a week, he returned to me, asking for his job back as he disagreed with the group's activities and what they planned on doing with the weapons.

"Of course, I gave him his position as a computer programmer back within the company, mainly to maintain peace on the home front. He informed me that the hardware is being shipped from a small boatyard along the Medina River, not far from the Red Jet terminal in Cowes. Dennis also has a house in America Woods. Sorry, not sure where that is on the Isle of Wight, only been there a couple of times. Led to believe this is where the ammunition and rifles are being worked on."

I take a sip from my cold beer, "Thanks for that, luckily we know someone who lives here, me. America Woods is about a 15-minute walk from where we are, plus I think I know the location of the building you're talking about. Any other questions for Mark, gents?"

"I've got a few important ones. First, how many people are we expecting to encounter? Second, are they armed? Lastly, are they likely to put up any resistance, bearing in mind the weapons they own?" asked Simon inquisitively.

Mark turned to face Simon, "According to Stuart, about 20 men are working for Dennis. He believes that one of the men is an ex-US Navy SEAL, turned mercenary.

While speaking, Mark produces a beige folder from his briefcase and opens it. "Here is a photo of Dennis and his profile from our company file."

From what we can determine from the picture, using reference points such as the window he is stood next to when the photograph was taken, Dennis is about five feet six inches tall and has a slim build.

"If you cast your eyes over these pictures," Mark takes out two more photos from the folder. "These are the people believed to be working with Dennis. This man here, is the Navy Seal, and this one is Stuart."

"Where and how old are the photos?"

"Taken in our reception about two months ago, Steve. Nearly forgot, there is a picture of Dennis here on my phone," he continues, passing me the phone. "He nicked it one day, messing around. When he handed the telephone back, found a selfie of him. I forgot about it until just now.

Now when it comes to putting up a fight, I would say this is more than probable, as they are armed, and from what Stuart told me, guards are standing at the gate of the building in America Woods. Also seen several heavily-armed people in the boatyard."

"Thanks for that, Mark, especially the photos."

"No problem, Simon, I hope the information is useful. What about you, George, any questions for me?"

"One question, for now, as you've been to Dennis' place. Are you in possession of any drawings of the property that might help us?"

"Sorry, as for plans, no, but I did visit the place a couple of times. When I arrive home, I will draw a plan of what I remember. Will make sure I give you this when we meet with the rifle."

"Fantastic, thanks, Mark."

The beer is now passing through me, so need a piss. So got up and head off to the bog. By the time I return, the rest are helping themselves to more beers from the fridge. "If we are all finished here, I think we should wrap things up for now. Mark, will you be staying tonight for a few beers down the local tavern?"

"Would love to, but need to make a move back. Could you call me a taxi?"

Find the number of a local cab firm I had used several times before and give them a ring. "Good afternoon, Isle of Wight Taxis, how may I help?" comes the gentle female voice on the other end.

"Hi, I would like a cab from Parkdean Resorts, in the name of Mark," I wasn't going to give them my name. "We will be at the reception."

"No problem, we will be about 35 minutes."

The park reception area looks quiet, but I learned a long time ago never to trust what you can't see. Through the glass-fronted door, I spot a young woman sitting behind a grey metal desk, working away. That is what it appears to be. She might be surfacing the internet for all I know.

In front of reception and directly across the road stands a maintenance yard. The extensive brown wooden gates are fully open. Inside, parked to one side, are two electrical carts with several rows of seats and a white plastic roof. I've seen the staff using these for getting around the place. Observe for a few minutes for any movement of people; didn't spot any, but they must be around as the gates are open.

The taxi hasn't turned up yet, so I decide to stand off for a while. The ideal place to wait would be among the brand new caravans the park had for sale to the office's right. The area consisted of a gravel base on which stands five brand new homes ranging from £50,000 to £100,000, which all looked perfect as new things always do. The new caravan park opened up to the main road going through the estate at the far end, where we will hail down the taxi.

Been playing a nosey bugger and looking through the windows for about 10 minutes when Mark yells out, "Steve, the cab is here."

"OK, mate, before you go, do you have any more questions for us?"

"Nope, can't think of any at the moment."

"No worries then, Mark. I will arrange for Simon to give you a call in a few days, to arrange a time for a meeting on the mainland."

Once the cab disappears into the distance, I head off back to my place. When I arrive, the boys had relocated to the old wooden bench outside.

If I'm honest, it had seen more satisfying days and is looking tired. I will undoubtedly purchase a new one at some point. The seat is situated on the brown-coloured decking which surrounded the lodge on two sides.

"Here you go, Steve, a nice cold beer," George hands me a beer as I plonk my arse next to them.

Take a gulp from the can. "What do you think, gents, is this something we can do, and how long do you think we would take to be able to complete the task before the deadline in three weeks?"

"The time scale shouldn't be an issue as we are already fully kitted up, and unlike the last job, there is no need to travel to some far off land, and I've nothing else planned. What about you, George?"

"Same as you, Simon. Might as well stay until the task is completed."

Take another swig of beer, "Fantastic. This will, of course, take some planning; as they say, failure to plan is a plan to fail."

"Yes, we know, Steve. As you're the planner, we will make some scran while you come up with a basic idea on the mission," comes the reply from George.

"Thanks, gents!"

"You're welcome, so stop moaning and get on with it. Come on, Simon, you're the best cook among us. Saying that, I'm basing this on the fact Steve and myself are shite cooks."

Grab a notebook before going back outside, away from the two idiots now throwing food at each other. From what I can perceive, thinking logically, the task should be broken down into several phases.

First, we would need weapons, and this being the UK is not that easy. Will give Katie and Cody a call to discover if they knew of any contacts over here. Next, a trip to the mainland to meet with Mark and pick up the new sniper rifle for George. At some point, a visit to the boatyard in Cowes would be needed to determine how the operation worked.

Our principal target would be the buildings in America Woods. We need to spend some time watching any coming and going of people and vehicles. Once we are in possession of the plan of the place, a nighttime recon would be required, to establish where everyone might be located inside. It would look utterly stupid if we stormed the wrong room.

Finish jotting down a few notes when George appears, carrying two white round plates piled high with food. "Here you go, dig into this — freshly prepared by yours truly — battered fish and chips."

"Thanks, mate, but you forgot the mushy peas!"

"Perfect reason for that, Steve."

"Oh, yeah, what?"

"You didn't fucking have any in the cupboard."

At that moment, Simon appeared with a small plate consisting of half a fish and no more than five chips.

"See your eating habits haven't changed."

"Nope, still the same, Steve, plus I do not want to end up like you two fatties."

"While you're up, how about making a brew, mate?" I ask.

"What did your last slave died of again, don't tell me not doing as they were told. Fancy one as well, George?"

"Yes, please, Simon."

Scran finished, and the brew is going down well, so I grab my notebook and open it on the first page. "Been through the process in order and believe we need to break the mission down into the following components.

- Trip to the shops for goodies.
- The collection of any weapons and a meeting with Mark. Do you mind Simon giving Katie a call?
- A recon of the boatyard.
- A short observation to gain an insight into any movements from the building in America Woods, to learn habits.
- Once we are in possession of the buildings and yard plan, a closer inspection will be required.
- Possible ambush.
- The primary attack on the complex may also require an assault on the boatyard in Cowes.
- The recovery of weapons and ammunition.
- Method of transporting everything back to the mainland.
- Finally, the most crucial part, sort out payment.

Before we call it time on this day, are there any questions or input, gents?"

"What about transport, Steve, something we are going to need to start with?"

"Don't panic, Tanky, we would hate for you to have to use your legs to get anywhere. Will rent a car in the morning from the self-hire place in Lake. Got any questions, George?"

"Not at the moment, but will no doubt think of a few once we break the plan down into its individual parts, apart for one. As we all appreciate, you love making things go bang, got anything special in mind?"

"What can I say? You know me too well, George, I have several ideas which we will go shopping for tomorrow."

The rest of the evening is spent having a good laugh and pulling up a sandbag for some good old war stories about our previous missions, plus the ale is running as freely as the conversation.

As the darkness descend, a battery-powered lantern provides enough light to carry on until the small hours.

Look down at Mickey, who is telling me it is now 02:05, well past my bedtime. "I'm off to bed. I'll leave you to it, but remember we have an early start today, so will be kicking your sorry arses out of bed around 08:00."

Chapter Three — America Woods

Daylight has not yet penetrated through the curtains, which is a reliable indicator that it is still daft o'clock. Plus, for some reason, woke up with a mouth similar to that of a camel's flip-flop. How much did I drink last night? With my body on autopilot, head to the bathroom to relieve the growing pressure on the bladder; one of the disadvantages of not using the bog before turning in for the night.

Return to the bedroom and stumble around in the pitch dark until I find the phone to check the time. Evidence enough, the body won the morning battle between it and the brain. Now I remember I am now supporting a sparkling new timepiece strapped to my right wrist.

By pressing the button on the side, a fluorescent blue dial now told me it is 05:45. An evil grin starts to form on my face as the idea of shouting fire in a loud voice to wake the other two comes to the front of my twisted mind.

Someone must have hit me with a happy stick during the night as I decide on a different course of action. Will make the sleeping beauties a full English breakfast instead.

Twelve pork sausages cooking in the oven, and the aroma of thick-sliced maple-infused slices of dead pig gently sizzling in the frying pan filled the air. Next, slice the tomatoes and mushrooms; they will go in the pot once the bacon is cooked. To ensure this is the full-monty, remove the black pudding from the fridge and place them in a second shallow frying pan to cook through.

Not long before everything comes together, including six fried eggs, lay them all on individual serving dishes on the dining table and move on to 'operation: get your arses out of bed'.

Flick through my phone until I find the music I want and ensure the volume is turned up as loud as possible. Right, time for the lazy bastards to be woken up from their slumber.

Make my way along the corridor towards the bedrooms with my mobile playing Reveille at full volume and me shouting, "Hands off cocks and on with socks," I banged on their doors.

A half-coherent voice comes from George's room.

"Now that's not very nice, George. Does your mum know you use such language?."

Wait for a few seconds outside Simon's room, listening for any signs of life, none come. Time for 'operation: quilt snatch', fling the door open, grab the duvet and drag it off, and stand back with one swift movement. No way would I remain in striking distance; I know what a mean bastard Simon could be when he is abruptly woken.

The strange thing is, if we've been on a mission, they would both have heard me creeping down the corridor and be ready to pounce and beat the crap out of me.

Now, two of what can only be described as half-dead, bedraggled figures now enter the living room, one of which is covered in an old chequered blanket I kept for lying on when working under the lodge.

"Good morning, gents, glad you could join me."

"Do you ever fucking sleep, Steve?"

"Advantage of the bloody PTSD, George, only ever get a few hours sleep and within that wake up several times. To answer your question, I will sleep when I'm dead and at the final rendezvous point."

"Fair point, mate; anyone fancy a brew while I'm here?"

"Bring the whole pot over."

Grasping the jug of boiling water with one hand, George joins the others already sitting at the table, tucking into breakfast.

"Tell me, Simon, what time did you two idiots stop drinking last night?"

"Not long after you left."

Food consumed in short order, and the conversation soon turns to the plans for today.

"Once you two have sorted yourselves out, we need to go for a walk to America Woods for a quick recon of Dennis' place. Don't panic, Simon; it is not far."

"Do one, Steve, I don't mind walking—I just prefer to drive."

"Once back from the little outing, we will need to go Newport to do some shopping for the mission. Suggest we hire a car for the next few days, there is one a short distance from here on Osbourne Road.

To break up any money trail, we will split everything up. I'll make a list for each of us later. Plus, Simon, can you contact Katie and Cody over in St Halb, regarding any contacts over here where we can lay our mitts on a few extra weapons and things which might go bang."

"No problem, Steve, I will call her once we are back from our walkies."

Glance down at Mickey, who is telling me it is 09:05. "So let's sort ourselves out and be ready to go at 09:30; any questions?" Both George and Simon shake their heads.

Make sure I pack a small notebook and several pencils into my jacket pocket. Made the mistake of taking a pen once before on two day OP in the Falklands back in the '80s, wherein it chucked it down with rain the entire time, and the ballpoint wouldn't work. Taken a pencil instead since then.

Also grab my binos in case we need to stand off and scrutinise any area for a short time. This would depend on what is happening when we arrive.

Even though anyone we might meet in the woods wouldn't have any idea of what we are up to, my professional pride kicks in and I jump up and down a couple of times to ensure nothing in my pockets rattles in any way. Positive Simon and George would be preparing in the same way.

Dead on 09:30, we depart. After ensuring I trapped an old leaf in the door, lock up the place. In the Army, they taught you always to vary your route. So erring on caution, instead of walking straight down the concrete path leading from the front door to the road, turn left and walk around the back of the lodge.

Using the bushy trees which run along the road's side as cover, approach about 50 metres from my place. A small gap in the treeline which overlooked the car park gives an ideal advantage point. Not that I was expecting any trouble, but it is hard to break the PTSD hypervigilance habit.

The resort is now closed for the winter, so only a few cars are parked up. All empty apart from a black Audi. In the driver's seat sits a lone figure, looking out towards the lodges on the other side. Stand off for around five minutes before heading to the bridleway, which ran off the street as it turned right, making its way through the rest of the estate.

Once we reach the crossroads, we separate, merging into the background to ensure we're not followed. About to signal all-clear when the person we spotted in the Audi comes strolling down the trail. The man is wearing a blue pair of jeans and a short green jacket. Our friend stops in the centre of the junction before taking a quick look in all directions.

Glanced over to George, situated among the dense foliage waiting for the order to jump this person and beat the crap out of him, for no other reason than just for being there. About to give the signal when our new friend continues walking, lucky for him, in the opposite direction to where we want to go. We wait until he disappears out of sight before continuing our journey to America Woods.

Walked this route several times before, but mainly with my head firmly up my own backside, just putting one foot in front of the other. However, I will need to be more observant this time and keep a look out for potential ambush sites and alternative escape routes.

Been walking down the track for around five minutes, chatting away with Simon before turning to find out where George is, he must be at least 50 metres back along the path. Of course, this would be perfect in normal circumstances on a mission, but there is no need for such caution as this, only a preliminary observation.

"You OK, George, what the fuck you doing all the way back there, the speed you're walking anyone would think you're an ex-guardsman? Even the Donkey Walloper is up here."

"The second word is off, Steve, guess the first one. Anyway, not everyone walks at 140 paces to the minute or whatever you Green Jacket numpties walk at."

Isn't long before we arrive at the first of the two properties on route to America Woods. The first, a grey building situated to the rear of the grassed garden, that extends to the hedgerow. Located in the corner near the road but behind a populated row of green bushes, a small wooden chicken coop that might become an issue if we come this way at night and they start squawking their heads off.

Beyond the bend and immediately opposite a manmade pond, almost 140 metres and surrounded by short wild grass which came down to meet the water, stands an immense farm complex.

On one side of the sizeable cobbled area, the primary residence is made of red bricks, with expansive windows in all aspects. It isn't a problem, apart from the extensive one overlooking the tarmac road that traverses between the farm and the pond, and the one we need to traverse.

Another massive whitewashed barn, complete with double wooden doors, runs along the property's back. What looks like a stable conversion was taking place opposite the farmhouse. From what I comprehend from my current position, the whole complex appears to be surrounded on two sides by an eight-foot-high brick wall. A wide opening to the front allows access to the property. Didn't spot any gates or, of course, what lays behind the long barn block.

Parked up opposite the house, two black Land Rovers and a tractor in the far corner. From somewhere in the courtyard comes the sound of voices, but not visible from our current location. On the other side, the footpath leads to America Woods and is situated only 30 metres from the farm entrance.

Turn around to face Simon and George. "We can't stay here all day, gents. Anyway, we've still got the benefit of nobody around here knowing what the fuck we are up to. Let's go."

I am about to cross in front of the gate when George grabs my arm. "Look over there near the house. Is that not one of the men in the photos Mark showed us yesterday?"

"Fuck, you're right, mate. What is one of Dennis' goons doing here?"

"No idea, but let's keep going. As they say, the best place to hide is in the wide-open, plus with any luck, they will not know anything about us yet, much less what we look like."

"Good point, well made, George."

Once across the entrance with no issues, we make our way along the narrow, twisting dirt trail as it made its way through the open meadow, occupied by several cows minding their own business in the distance. Not the ideal route from a military perspective. The ground to the left of the path banked steeply up for about 30 metres — a perfect place for an ambush.

We would take the high ground if we come this way once the mission got underway, but this trail will do today.

Once we enter America Woods, we walk off the trail, which twists and turns as it mingles its way around the whole area.

"OK, gents, the building Mark told us about is another 20 minutes walk from here in that direction." I indicate towards the main trail that leads off up the hill to our left. "If you follow me, Simon, concentrate on the left, George, you do the same on the right while I'm watching our front. Suggest that we keep an eye out for possible ambush sites, escape routes, and hold—up positions."

Like dedicated professionals, the boys give a sufficient gap between us, with me leading off. Isn't long before we detect voices coming towards us from further down the trail.

After what we witnessed at the farm, taking no chances, I point to my right then dart off into the undergrowth without glancing backwards. Without hesitation, Simon and George follow suit and head for the bushes.

Two figures dressed in jeans, dark jackets and military-style boots soon immerge down the track, chatting away, oblivious to the fact three men concealed in the scrub watching their every move, ready to pounce if required.

Ensure they disappear before giving the others the all-clear signal. About to move when Simon cancels the order, he spots another person, this time coming from the direction of the farmhouse. As he passes, I spot something that makes me curse under my breath, something we hoped not to find.

The idiot is dressed in the exact same fashion, even down to the footwear. Shit, going on from what we just witnessed, the hired help are no local thugs but perhaps a well-trained organisation. Evidence now points to them using Dennis' place as a base for operations and the farmhouse, with this being the primary route from each location.

Need to make a decision... continue on our current route or divert to the tracks on the other side of the woodlands? If we stay on our present course, we can continue looking for ambush sites and be at the property within 10 minutes. However, this comes with the disadvantage of being spotted. The alternative route is slightly longer, with the possibility that no person would be coming this way.

Place my right hand on my head, as the signal for George and Simon to close in on my location to discuss our options. After a quick discussion, we will not use any, but take the extended and more demanding route straight down the middle, making most of the trees and bushes as cover. I want to check out one spot where the trail crosses a small stream as a potential ambush site.

The going is more challenging than it might have been through the thick, dense vegetation which filled the land between the two trails, mainly due to it pissing it down a couple of nights ago, making the ground soggy. Every step you take, sinking into the soft ground a few centimetres before the mud takes hold of your foot as you take the next step.

Never been happier to view an old wooded bridge in the distance. Turn around to check on the boys when George calls out, "You know where you're fucking going, Steve? Thought you chosen men are good at pathfinding, this mud is getting on my tits."

"Stop your complaining. The bridge is about 50 metres away if you're lucky, and nobody around may let you clean it. We know how you guardsmen like cleaning things. Besides, Simon isn't whinging like an annoying brat."

"Not yet, mate, saving it for when we get back to your place," comes the reply from Simon.

Stop short of the bridge, concealing ourselves among the foliage which ran along the edge of the trail. As bridges go, it isn't that big. In fact, no more than four metres by two metres and covered a moving stream running beneath. The reason for wanting to investigate this location is for a possible ambush site and its area layout.

On the opposite side to us, the ground slopes up for about 20 metres. Several closely-packed trees and bushes run across the skyline. This will make a perfect sniper's position due to the concealment it provides.

From what I fathom out from my current location, the position will provide a flawless view of the bridge and the track, as it leads uphill in a straight line for about 30 metres. Ideal killing ground. Will get George to check this out, as he is the marksman among us.

Considering what we witnessed this morning, this is an organised group and needs to be handled accordingly. There will be a good chance they will have done the same as us and recced the complete area. So Simon and I will examine the area for likely firing positions, not for ourselves but placing our minds in that of the attackers. This will give George the advantage, knowing where they may take cover to return fire.

Stand off for five minutes to ensure nobody is in the vicinity, signal George and Simon to close in on my location, to discuss the plan.

"Find a route up into the treeline, George, and locate a good shooting position and escape route." No point in telling him to sketch the target area, worked with him on too many missions, like the one in St Halb, and knew he would do this automatically.

"No problem, meet you back here in around 35 minutes."

"OK, Simon, if you take the other side and scan for potential positions where our friends will be able to return fire on George's location. Leave this side to me. The target building is over that ridge, roughly another 100 metres away, so be careful and not expose yourself."

"Roger that."

The ground on my side comes complete with a side trail leading off to the right, through a massive patch of metre-high brown ferns covering the whole area to the top of the hill. The issues here are that it may not be visible from where George is located and will have to wait to check his drawing.

Found numerous places where someone may dive to the ground to use the cover to return fire. Make notes in my notebook, that I'd taken from my inside jacket pocket, of any specific objects that will help identify its location and my best guess of distance from the sniper position. Identify several places before returning to the RV.

The other hasn't returned yet when I arrive, conceal myself under a pile of green ferns and wait. Simon comes back first, clutching a notebook. He will have done the same regarding distances and locations.

"Any problems, Simon?"

"No, found multiple locations and spotted the property in the distance."

"Yes, it's not far, will wait for George before we discuss our findings." Always best to examine conclusions while still on the ground, as people can relate better than several hours later, away from the target.

"Here comes George now." Simon points up the track.

"All good, mate."

"Yeah, no issues." Taking out his sketch of the area, George places it on an old tree stump. "You get a fantastic view of the location from up on the ridgeline. If we are planning an observation post, I would suggest this would make the perfect spot. Spotted you two stopped in several places. Take it this was potential firing locations? Marked them down on here." George put his index finger on the sketch.

"Yes, let's compare my notes to yours to find out if distances etc. match." Pointed to my map, "I make it around 74 metres from this spot. What do you have?"

"Make it 76."

"Close enough, but let us divide the difference and say 75."

Once all my locations are referenced with George, I carry out the same exercise on the sites Simon has identified.

"From your location on the hill, was it possible to see the trail to our right leading up the hillside?"

"No."

"Not an issue, George. For the mission or OP, I might place an IED across the track while I'm rigging the bridge to explode."

"You do know distances might not matter," Simon said, as he puts away his notebook.

"Why is that, smart arse?" George asks, packing up his equipment.

"Well, if after meeting Mark in Southampton we manage to borrow, on a permanent basis, the all-singing, dancing sniper rifle, well, it will make all the calculations for us."

"A fantastic point, Simon. Apart from two small issues, you and I will not have one. Besides, always best to plan for the worse scenario."

"True, I'll give you that one, Steve."

Take a glance at Mickey; the time is now 12:15. Journey through the woods had taken longer than planned, thanks to the detour down the middle.

I turn to the others, "time is getting on, gents; better make our way to the target."

Decide to take the trail leading off to the right rather than push our luck down the central pathway. Besides, I know the route is only a minor diversion and will be close to Dennis' place with the next 10 minutes, if not sooner.

Situated across the track from us, partially concealed by the trees and ferns that grow up the imposing red brick wall of one of the buildings, made up Dennis' property. To the left, a smaller building joined by a three-metre-high wall. From this, the wall continues for approximately 50 metres back into the woodlands. From our present location, it isn't possible to spot any other structures. Therefore, a complete reconnaissance of the whole outside side of the property will be required.

We have the advantage in this area because of the lack of windows on either building overlooking the woods. In the distance, just past the last structure, spot several trees not too far from the brick wall. This may be both a way in or a firing position for George, once he has finished at the bridge.

"Best you go that way, check if you can easily and quickly scale that big tree. May need this to operate from, if required, once we finalise plans. Simon and I will continue this way around, raising my right arm to confirm.

"Once we have located the entrance, we will conceal ourselves and witness any movement inside and out. A recce of the interior is required at some stage, but this can wait until we have the plan/drawing from Mark.

"Any questions, Gents?"

"Yes, why am I the one doing the climbing?" asked George.

"Simple, the laughter of seeing the Donkey Walloper scaling a tree would alert the people inside, George. Plus, I think the road comes from the right and need Simon's expertise in all things transport."

"True, I can't climb to save my life. Will use my transportation knowledge elsewhere. Happy climbing, fat boy."

"Fuck off, Simon, see around the other side," comes the reply from George, as he headed off into the treeline.

"Come on, Simon, better make a move.," I announce, leading off to my right.

With no visible places from which we might be seen, we keep adjacent to the building, following it to the right-hand corner. Stop short to listen for any sound of people or vehicles, Simon conceals himself close to a large tree and looks back the way we came. Spend a couple of minutes listening before laying flat on the ground, to perceive what could possibly be around the other side. No way I am I sticking my bonce around at head height. Fancy keeping it on my shoulders today.

My caution pays off. The gravel road is winding its way through the woods, about 40 metres away to my front, as I peek around the corner.

Tap Simon on the shoulder, "Let's go, mate."

The wall now directly on my left is comparable to the one situated at the far end, the one George is following. Which means the entrance to the property must be on the far side.

Gone only 20 metres when I spot a timber sheet leaning against the brick wall, concealed behind on a sparsely-leafed bush. Suppose in summer it would have been hidden from view. This doesn't look right compared to the rest, so it needs investigating.

"Take a peek behind that piece of wood, Simon. Check if you can gain access inside."

Carefully pulling back, first, the shrubs followed by the wooden board, a few inches, a small hole becomes visible. "Yeah, just big enough for me to fit through, but you wouldn't get your fat gut all the way through, though."

"Thanks. I think we may have found one possible way in for you, if a three-prong attack is required later during the mission."

Further along, and standing majestically about 10 metres into the treeline, an old oak tree which must have died several years back. Take a few moments to study the state of the tree's dead branches that protruded from the thick trunk. Hopefully, they will be strong enough to hold me. The advantage point would be a fantastic opportunity to discover what is on the other side of the wall, with any luck.

I Keep to the rear of the tree as much as possible. As I climb up, Simon keeps a lookout for any vehicles coming down the track.

To begin with, the first part is relatively straightforward, with branches in easy reach. Halfway up, need to stretch as far as I can to grab a dead branch, no other option with the rest well beyond my reach.

Balancing precariously on one foot, bounce to launch upwards. As I grab hold, the combination of my weight and the tree's age results in it snapping. Manage to throw my arms around the tree to prevent myself from falling.

"OK, up there? Would hate you to fall; you might hit me."

"You're all fucking heart, Simon."

I would have to stay where I am; not ideal, but at least I can view the property's layout. To my right, what appear to be a stable block consisting of two run-down stables facing the corner in a square formation. This is more than likely still in use, from the amount of horse shit piled up against the back wall. Beyond that, an old white Mercedes campervan parked, pointing towards the main gate.

Situated on either side of the entrance, two small buildings. Guess these are occupied by the armed guards Mark told us about. Confirmed a couple of minutes later, two men dressed the same as those we had encountered in the woods earlier walk across the gateway.

The stream we crossed previously ran down the centre of the property and was opened up to form a small lake. Along both edges, a line of bullrushes blowing in the slight breeze. The driveway ran from the gate across the middle via an old wooden bridge, broad enough to take one vehicle at a time.

This information will come in handy when we launch the attack. May be able to rig the bridge to explode on our reconnaissance mission, preventing any motorised backup. Any help would have to cross on foot; of course, I would have a surprise waiting for them...

On the far side, another smaller building, I couldn't perceive much detail due to the foliage blocking my view. Hopefully, George will have more luck from his side.

From the information given to us by Mark, the primary residence is where they work on the software, and their HQ. This ran parallel to the wall and not against it as I'd hoped. In fact, a small gap separated them, couldn't actually guess the distance from here.

About to climb down when I spot George in the tree on the other side, good news in one sense but bad in another because if I could spot him from here, then anyone on the property might have spotted him as well. Needn't have worried, as moments later a flailing of arms and he disappears.

I am now back on the ground next to Simon, concealed in the undergrowth.

"See anything interesting from up there?"

"Plenty to be going on with. I'll draw a map when we arrive home. Did spot something that will have you rolling around in laughter, George fell out of the tree."

"Hope the fat bastard didn't damage the ground."

"I've said it before, Simon — you're all heart."

"Learnt from the best mate — you."

Time is getting on, and we still need to meet with George across from the main gate. So lead off, heading towards the road as it curved back through the woods, to enter the property — no need for any communication here, as we'd done this too many times to count. With myself crossing first, Simon covers me, then vice versa.

The other side's area is dense with tightly-packed trees and dead brown ferns a metre and a half high, giving us sufficient cover as we make our way to a location near the gate, sufficiently back where no one could observe or be surprised by the armed guards earlier.

No sign of George when we arrive, so take up a position under the ferns facing the entrance, keeping away from the large tree as this would make an excellent firing reference point.

Busy observing the property for any movement, when Simon taps me on my right shoulder, "Someone is coming from that direction, Steve."

Shit! We both take up a crouched position, ready to pounce on anyone that stumbles on us. Moments later, a short break in the sound of foliage being trampled to the ground, the person must have stopped. Can feel my heart rate increase as the adrenaline starts to pump around my body. Glance over to Simon, giving him a raised thumb up to confirm he was ready.

Once more, a pause in the noise of movement, this time they are about 10 metres away from our location. We both spring to our feet and launchourselves in their direction. With one single action, Simon jumps on the figure and knocks them hard to the floor.

"Get the fuck off me, you lanky streak of piss. It's me, George."

"About time you showed up," Simon replies, not missing a beat, "Steve is behind me."

Once everyone manages to compose themselves, we make the snap decision to relocate in case some nosey bastard overheard the commotion. So find a spot deeper inside the woods, away from the view.

"We can't do much more today, gents. Might as well head back to my place; you both agree?" Simon and George nod.

Chapter Four – Newport

The following morning, I am up first, with a big mug of coffee and the aroma of freshly ground coffee beans filling the air. Slumped in front of the TV on my second cup, when Simon puts his head around the door.

"Kettle just boiled, mate."

"Thanks, Steve."

"You're welcome. Once George gets out of his pit, we need to go over our findings from yesterday."

At that moment, George appears, grabbing a fresh brew from the kitchen and joining us at the dining table.

"Morning, gents."

While the other two finish their brews, I snatch several white paper sheets from the printer and laid them out for us all to see. Make a rough drawing of the target property, well, the grounds at least. The inside can wait until Mark provides the graphics, plus, a more detailed plan of the potential ambush area, including the location we'd noted, complete with distances to targets.

I sketch the ambush/OP site on the first piece of paper, ensuring I pay particular attention to where George pointed out the best place for the sniper position. Then, using the details from all our notebooks, place an 'X' denoting possible firing locations. Take a ruler, drawing a line to each point, and then entering the likely target distance.

Once finished outlining the plan, hand it to George, "You happy with this?"

With his tea in one hand, George grabs the map with the other and studies the drawing for a few minutes. "Not too bad, one question... who is that figure by the tree?"

"Oh, that is Simon having a dump, don't shoot him," I reply, with a stupid grin spread across my face. Simon takes another sip of coffee, shaking his head.

Take a separate piece of paper and draw a big rectangle, with a break on the front edge to represent the target property's gateway. Fill in the lake's details down the middle with the driveway crossing from the gate. Sketch in the major buildings, including the stable block, before shoving the sketch in George's direction.

"Can you fill in the specifics of the small outbuilding in the top left corner? Couldn't see much from where I was."

"Sure, no problem," George replies, drawing a rectangular building with a smaller one between it and the perimeter wall.

"Before we move on to people, anything you would like to add, Simon or even you, George...? That is before you fell out of the tree."

"Fuck, you saw that then?"

"Yep, and as you said when I tripped near the boathouse in St Halb, we're going to hold this against you for the rest of your life."

"What about the farm complex, may be crucial if they are using the place for some reason?" Simon says, taking a new sheet of paper.

"Makes sense, bearing in mind we witnessed people moving between them yesterday. Make sure you include the pond in your sketch, Simon, we may need an OP on the farm, and the ground on the other side would be a great spot, as you have a perfect view of the forecourt. Your feelings on this, George?"

"Agree with you. We will need to check when people leave and return from both properties, probably indicating a change of people at Dennis' place.

Each of us take turns studying the drawings, trying to commit as much to memory as possible. It's never a good idea to take sketches on an operation, in case you lose it on the route. The last thing you want is the enemy discovering your plans and working out all your possible locations.

"We still have a lot that needs doing, gents, so once you've finished stuffing your faces and memorising the maps, I will lock them in my safe; the combination is oldest daughter's birthday, 2303.

"Priorities, Simon, can you make the call to call Katie and Cody while George and myself go and hire a car from the place down the road. Later today, we will have to drive to Newport to do some shopping for the mission. Made a list up earlier of what is required. To prevent any paper trail, we should split this up. Remember to use both cards and cash when you purchase them."

Car hire place is only a 20-minute walk down the bridleway we walked down yesterday. This time instead of turning left, we would keep going.

Leaving Simon to make his call, exit the lodge, again using an alternative route to reach the road. A car park survey uncovers the same black Audi as the day before, with the same person seated in the driver's seat. Decide the best course of action would be to keep an eye on him for several minutes, mainly because he is on the phone and pointing in my home's direction.

A couple of seconds pass before he finishes his call and disembarks from the car. Walks over to the footpath leading to my lodge, stopping short and standing behind the bushes which ran across the front of my place, only to return to his vehicle a few minutes later.

"Not too impressed with that. I think we need to have a word with him, George."

"Think you're right. You circumnavigate towards the back of the vehicle. I'll walk straight up to him, Steve."

"Wait till you spot me near our friend's Audi before making your move."

Knowing the resort very well, move another 50 metres down the road before crossing and heading among the static caravans situated to the rear. The good news here is the place is closed for winter. Therefore, most caravans are empty apart from one tucked away in the corner beneath the trees that ran along the park's back, meaning fewer people around to spot me.

The parking area sloped down towards the back, allowing me to stay in the dead ground below the ridgeline. Crawl up to the edge of the car park, ensured I would be in the mirror's blindspot. Stick my head above the parapet of the grass bank, just long enough for George to know I'm in position.

Moments later, he appears from behind the trees and heads for the Audi, ensuring he aims for the car's front to keep the person's attention focused on him.

Feeling threatened, the man opens the car door and clambers out, placing the door between him and the person heading straight at him. The split-second he does this, I launch myself from the ground, launching into him with my whole body weight, pinning him to the driver's door.

Arms flailing in every direction, he manages to land a forceful elbow into my stomach, knocking the wind out of me for a few seconds. Quickly place my right arm tightly around his neck and apply pressure while pulling him away from the vehicle and back down the slope, out of view.

Now screaming some incoherent words, he receives a well-placed punch to the gut from George. His whole body tries to double up in pain but can't, due to his head still being maintained firmly by my right arm.

With one swift movement I fling him to the floor, ensuring I still hold tight. Fearing for his life, he chooses this point for a fightback with legs kicking in all directions. Release my grip from his neck in an attempt to get him face down, to make it harder for him to lash out. Suddenly feel a sharp pain in my lower jaw as my head reels backwards. Bastard manages to get a punch of his own in.

"You will pay for that," I yell.

As I do, George gains control of his feet. We've now got him pinned to the deck at last. Just for good measure, I wallop him in the kidneys. Once again, he screams in agony.

"OK, dickhead, why are you spying on my friends and me?"

"I'm not," he protests.

"Don't fucking lie to us; we've seen you for the last two days observing us. You even followed us down the bridleway yesterday. Hit him again, George." Once more, he flinches in pain.

"No, I didn't. Have you ever sat in a car for an extended period? Needed to stretch my legs while the woman I'm watching went out," comes the stuttering reply.

"What fucking female…?" George asks.

The man takes a deep input of air, "The woman in the lodge at the end of the row. She is cheating on her husband; I've been hired to watch her place, to find out with whom."

"So, you have not been watching us then?" I say through my now aching jaw.

"No."

"Guess we attacked the wrong person," I look at George, "Better let him go."

With caution, we let go of our wrongly accused man. Then, standing back a few feet in case he wanted to have another go, we allowed him to stand.

"Suggest you climb in your vehicle and fuck off. If we find you anywhere in the park, you will receive more of the same, understand?" The man nods and returns to his car, and drives off.

Once the man had driven off into the distance, "Come on then, this car will not hire its self."

"On my way. Do you have any remorse for beating up an innocent man, Steve?" asks George

"Nope, one of the bonus points of my PTSD, don't do empathy, so couldn't give a shit about him, in fact, who are we talking about?"

"Come to think about it — you're a heartless bastard."

"Yep."

Twenty-two minutes later, we reach the car hire place on Osbourne Road. Between the office and the street, approximately 30 cars for sale, standing on a gravel forecourt. On one side, a burger van applying its trade to a couple of workmen. Something about the scent and sounds of frying burgers and onions that always made me feel hungry, might grab a burger one on the way out.

The rental office is situated in a white portacabin, stood on a concrete base at the rear. A few white plastic chairs occupy the space to the left, with the counter to the right as you enter. The smell of lavender fills the air in the vain attempt this would destress the hiring process.

Behind, a few desks furnish the room. A young lady dressed in a black skirt and a pink polo shirt with a blue jumper, occupies one desk towards the room's rear.

"Can I help you two gentlemen?" she enquires with a beautiful smile, joining us at the counter.

"Yeah, hi, I'm interested in hiring a car for two weeks, two named drivers."

"That shouldn't be a problem, sir. Which car group are you planning on? Here are the prices," she hands over a small colourful leaflet, fully opened to show all the makes of vehicles for rent.

"The Skoda Fabia will do nicely. How much does this cost?" Don't care less how much, but it might have looked strange if I didn't ask.

"With the additional driver and Collision Damage Liability Fee that would be £267.50. I will need your credit card for the deposit."

Turn around to George, "You happy with that?"

"Yes, mate."

The woman reaches behind the desk and produces a card machine, "If I could have your card, please?" she asks, with a smile.

Learned a long time ago to make sure you take photos of the hire car at the start and the end. One of the UK's major car rental companies once tried to rip me off when returning a vehicle.

Before we left, stopped to grab us all a burger from the van before driving off home.

Back at my place, Simon had packed everything away from breakfast and was ready to go. No point in hanging around, might as well leave now. Grab the list of stuff we need and head back to the car.

"Here you go," as I toss Simon the key, "you're our transport guy, so guess who's driving."

"Cheers, Steve, having never driven on the island, you will need to give me directions."

"Of course, and like every officer in the British Army, I will let you know which turning as we pass."

"Typical reconnaissance troop, not having a fucking clue where they're going," says George, tapping Simon on the shoulder.

"Do one, Grunt."

The drive to Newport would only take around 30 minutes. This being a small island, there should only be light traffic to deal with. As we pull into the car park next to the bus station, I take out the white folded pieces of paper from my jacket pocket. Wait for Simon to turn off the engine, want to ensure I had everyone's attention.

"Right, time to do some shopping, gents," handing to both George and Simon one list each, keeping one for myself.

"You have the easy task, Simon; you need to go to Morrisons, which is that large supermarket behind you and purchase eight of the five-litre beer barrels. They sell them here, as purchased one last week. Any questions?"

"Nope, will make sure I get the type I like, screw you two," says Simon, putting the list in his pocket.

"On your piece of paper, George, you will find cotton wool similar to what women use to remove their war paint/makeup. About 20 bags should be sufficient. Suggest several shops to stop any suspicion. Plus, see if you can buy a few syringes from the chemist. If not, we might be able to get them elsewhere."

"One question, Steve, we all know you like to make things go bang, but what the fuck you going to do with cotton wool?" says George, putting away the list.

"Will show you once we get back. As for me, I will be purchasing some pens, small nails, electrical wire, a few small metal rods and a fuel can.

"If nobody has any further questions, we can meet at the pub on St James Street. If you're there first, grab a table upstairs."

Now I have two choices, spend the next hour walking around like a moron trying to find a hardware store, or instead, take out my mobile and open the maps app. Soon locate one on Holywood Street, only a six-minute walk from here, they should have everything I want.

Depart ways with George, as he heads off toward the high street to locate a chemist to start on his list. Thankfully, the town centre isn't too busy. The last thing I want is for the bloody PTSD kicking in. I am tempted to pop into Mcdonald's on the road junction, but I will leave this to later when all the shopping is completed.

Turn left and continue passing various shops on my left-hand side and St James Square on my right. Well, they call this a square. The area is only a more comprehensive pavement with several concrete structures dividing the space from the main road.

Must have been about halfway between St James Street and Holywood, when I do what I usually do when in town. Stop to look in the shop window to check I'm not being followed by anyone. Spot a man I had seen earlier in the car park. Stopped looking in the window of a gift store. Decide this is the hypervigilant part of my PTSD being overactive again and choose to ignore it for now.

One hundred metres further down the street, the same person I spotted via the storefront window now knocks into me, forcing me sidewards as they pass. The chimp must be on holiday again. My instant reaction kicks in, and I slam him hard into the wall of the pharmacy, grabbing the lapel of his long black coat as I did.

"Look where you're fucking going, arsehole," yelling into the man's face.

"Sorry, nothing more than an accident; I don't want any trouble," comes the reply from the man, now staring directly at me.

Seconds later, George appears in the doorway, "Need any help, Steve?"

"No thanks, mate, I can manage. This idiot is just leaving," I reply, as I pat myself down to double-check the whole instance was not a pickpocket incident. "How are you doing with your list?"

"Nearly finished with the shopping, a few more shops for the cotton wool and I'm done." George lifts up some plastic carrier bags.

"I've not started yet, still on my way to the hardware establishment. It shouldn't be too long. Meet you in the boozer." By this time, the man had bolted, so I continue on my journey, arriving at the shop a couple of minutes later.

The store resembled one of the old-fashioned stores with tables outside either side of the doorway, complete with an assortment of plants, gardening equipment, and carpet rolls. Inside, running down the middle, rows of shelving, packed to the brim with everything you might want from this type of shop.

Isn't long before most of the items on my list were found. In normal circumstances, I would split the shopping up to prevent a paper trail. However, as I don't have that much and the boys would be buying stuff from a different location, I decide not to bother this time.

Stand off for a while, letting the two gentlemen in front of me go first before approaching. Behind the counter stands an older man, I would estimate in his sixties, dressed in a brown overcoat.

Reminds me of 'Open All Hours' with Ronnie Barker. Along the back wall behind the shopkeeper, packs of nails neatly arranged in different sizes, perfect the last of my items.

"Good morning, sir, just these and I'll have four boxes of two and four-inch nails." I do not need the four-inch, but anything to throw people off the track.

"Of course, no problem, would you be paying by card?"

I nod.

The man holds out the machine with one hand, "Enter your pin, please, sir."

Unlike most people, can't be bothered with shielding my pin as I enter the four numbers. I would like to see some idiot try and take my bank cards from me, it would definitely be the last thing they did before taking a trip to A&E. Once I had packed everything into the bag, headed off to meet with the others in the pub.

When I arrive, Simon is already sitting at a table tucked away in the corner of the first-floor landing, happily enjoying a beer. Forty or more people sitting at oak wooden tables, which surrounded the centre's large opening with views to the ground floor. One metre-high bannister ran around the edge to prevent any drunken bum from falling down to join the diners below. The brewery did its best to give the place a contemporary look, with exposed wooden ceiling joists stretching from the apex to the ground level.

"Been here long?" I ask Simon, now taking another sip of his drink.

"About 20 minutes, George is in the bog," comes the reply.

Right on cue, George appears, grasping two full glasses of beer. "Sorry, mate, didn't know you had arrived yet. Take mine. I'll get a new one from the bar."

"Typical, you two supping beer without me again — mind you, your wife says you always arrive first! I'll order from the app on the phone."

Park my arse on the seat next to Simon, with my back towards the wall. This gives me a perfect view of the other people enjoying their drinks and food. Reach in my jacket to retrieve my mobile to request my drink, when I feel something else. Place my telephone down in front of me. I dive in my pocket again, pulling out a minute, round black object no larger than one and a half centimetres in diameter, and place the item down on the beer mat.

"What you got there, Steve?"

"No idea, George, never seen it before."

Along the edge of the device runs a seam where two parts have been joined together. My right thumb's fingernail separate each piece, inside a small circuit board complete with a blinking red light.

Slowly lifting my head, place a finger to my lips, turning to the others. Take a pen and paper out of my coat and write down the words.

'Not sure what this is. To me, it is either a tracking or listening device, do not say anything for the next few minutes.'

I reassemble the two halves with care while scanning the room for a suitable location to dispose of the device. A few tables away, a blind woman sitting with her guide dog lying on the floor by her feet. Bingo, have the perfect place.

Still holding our little bug in my left hand, walk towards the woman and her pooch. "Hi, is it OK to stroke the dog?"

Turning to face the sound of my voice, "Yes, his name is Bravo."

Place my hand near its nose, not sure why but everyone does this when approaching dogs. The mutt takes one sniff and starts wagging its tail. Stroke the mutt's head with my right hand while securing the bug under its harness with my left hand.

"Thank you. Have a fantastic day," I continue to walk around the dining area before returning to Simon and George.

It's a good job I don't do empathy, would hate to be the young lady when whoever planted the device on me finds out they have been following a blind woman and her dog.

We all sit in silence for the next 10 minutes, sipping away at the beer until the blind woman gets up and left, confirming it was safe enough to talk.

"We have a problem, gents," I say, facing the others, "that was not in my pocket earlier, completely emptied them yesterday. The big question is, how did this object find its way to my jacket, and who put it there?"

"We've been with you most of the day, not seen you take off your coat since this morning. So, therefore, it must have been put in place sometime after leaving the car and you arriving here."

"You are right, Simon, but how did the bug get here and why?"

"Got it," proclaims George. "Remember the bloke you came close to punching outside the pharmacy earlier? So what happened before I showed up?"

"The bastard banged into me as I was walking down the road, then I slammed him into the wall, then you arrived."

"First, he must be our man; what can you recollect of him, dress, distinguishing marks etc.? Second, you nutter, go find the chimp!" says Simon as he shakes his head.

Think for a moment, "He was wearing a long black coat, blue jeans. As for his appearance, I would say neat, tidy brown hair, supporting a stubbly chin, and oh yes, there's a scar running down his left cheek."

"Anyone seen him before?" asks George. Both Simon and I shake our heads.

"No point in looking for him now. He will be long gone, so drink up, boys, let's head for home, and I'll show you what to do with all the stuff we've purchased."

The journey home is uneventful as the way to town. The situation has changed dramatically since this morning. Now we would have to make every move as if we were on operations. So far, we have had two incidents, one with the man in the Audi and the bloke in Newport. To err on the side of caution, not knowing if anybody was watching my place, parked to the rear of my lodge.

"If you stay with the car, Simon, then myself and George will go through the trees, approaching the lodge from the back before scouting the whole area, including the vehicle park. Wait 10 minutes; if you haven't heard from us, consider the area safe and join us."

The sparsely-spaced trees and bushes lead down a 20-metre muddy slope and don't give much cover. But, hopefully, we would have the surprise element, as more than likely, if anyone was staking out my property would be watching the front.

Walk down the road for about 30 metres and enter the treeline at the precise time George does. The plan is to check both sides simultaneously before stopping near the edge to observe the car park. Several minutes later, I arrive at the street. I don't spot any people in the area, or any evidence on the ground that people might suggest disturbance by individuals. Even our friend from earlier seems to have got the hint, or is now better at hiding.

Leave the door slightly open as I go inside as a message to George, the ground on my side is all clear. The kettle had just boiled when Simon arrived, taking up a seat at the table.

"Here you go, gents, one hot brew," placing the mugs down next to them.

"Thanks, Steve, could do with this," says George as he grabs the mug with his right hand and takes a sip.

As the others sort themselves out, I collect the materials I required to make detonators and the extra stuff I already had to make the homemade explosive. To be safe, I kept all these types of things in a 1 m wide, 2 m long, and 1.5 m deep metal storage container concealed in a hole in the grass beneath one of the bushes towards the lodge's front.

To make electrical detonators is a simple process. First, cut paper straws into 5 cm strips. Second, take a 12 cm piece of electric wire and bare the ends of both strands. The next step is the tricky bit, and I need to take this slowly — coil a length of Nichrome 80 resistance cable around one of the bare wires. Next, place two wooden matches, cut to a size of 2½ cm and a tiny slit for the wiring to sit in along the top of the match. Now wrap the Nichrome around the other stripped wire.

For the assembly, push assembled parts into the end of the straw and squirt glue in the back to secure the elements in place. Once dry, press a bit of tissue paper with care into the other end using a match until it comes in contact with the matchhead's top.

The explosive part fills the open end with gunpowder from a few fireworks left over from Bonfire Night. This I seal with another strip of tissue. Next, coat each in an isotope resin made from melting down ping-pong balls. This would keep them waterproof. Made another 30 to ensure we had enough.

"Excuse me, madman, sorry to interrupt your class in terrorism, but Mark is on the phone. Wants to know if we can meet him in Southampton tomorrow afternoon," asks Simon, holding his mobile to his ear.

"Fine with me, what about 14:00, if that fits in with yours and George's plans?"

"Make sure he brings the sniper rifle with him," George adds, now inspecting the detonators gingerly.

"All confirmed then, Mark will meet us at 14:15 with the rifle, at the pub at the end of the high street opposite the park."

"Cheers Simon, any news from Katie? It would be useful if we arranged both meetings for the same day."

"Will call her again now, Steve."

"Will need your help to make the explosive, gents. Outside is my old barbeque. Bang out the crap and fill the base with petrol; you'll find that in the metal shed."

"On it, bossman," says George, opening the front door.

While the drum is being sorted, grab a roll of plastic bags, cotton wool and the boxes of small nails, and went outside. Collect the sacks of 95% ammonium nitrate-based fertilisers purchased from specialist farming suppliers a while back.

As George fills the drum with the petrol, I add the fertiliser and stir until everything is dissolved. "Here, open these," tossing several packs of cotton wool to George.

While the cotton wool soaks up all the petrol, we pile the two-inch nails into groups of 10. A half-hour later, all the liquid had been absorbed, on to the next step.

"This is what we need to do. Take a hand full of the now volatile mixture and wrap it around one pile of nails. Lay one of the detonators on the bundle before placing everything into a plastic bag, any access space filled with the cotton wool and fertiliser mixture.

"That's all there is to it, George. Help me make another 19."

Finish placing our homemade bombs in the metal shed for safety when Simon appears with the barrels of beers. "Imagine you two might have a bad taste in your mouths, therefore appreciate a cold beer."

"Cheers, mate, anything from Katie regarding weapons?" I asked, pouring myself a beer.

"Yeah, good news. Katie came back quickly; she and Cody have a contact that can provide us with what we need in St Mary's in Southampton.

"We are to meet the connection at 11:00 tomorrow, at the market next to the Kingsland Tavern on St Mary's Street. One stall is selling electronic devices. We are to ask to speak to Shyam and ask if he knows Katie from Perth. If he answers 'no, but I know Katie from Headland', this is our man. He's got three old Army SLRs and four 9 mm browning pistols with ammo for sale, which will cost us £6,000."

"Thanks for that, Simon. How about we put away all this work shit and relax with far too many cold beers?"

"I'll drink to that," says George, helping himself to another beer.

Beer and conversation flows for a couple of hours, discussing our Army and missions experiences we had been on together since first meeting at Combat Stress. Including the fact George and I had got soaked in the Ops we carried out on our last mission on St Halb, while Simon stayed dry in his makeshift canopy on the Land Rover.

For some reason, our conversation turned to our fears in life. "Come on, Steve, we both know you're a cold-hearted bastard, but what is the one thing you fear most?"

"That is an easy one, Simon, apart from having to put up with you two for the next 20 years, dying alone. Not sure why, but I always had this one. Come on, George, what's your fear?"

"For me, it's being burned alive. Witnessed a colleague die this way once, not a pretty sight, the screams still haunt me."

"No need to tells us yours, Tanky, that's an easy one, you having to walk somewhere."

"That's true, Steve," George adds.

"You two arseholes might think that is funny, but you can fuck off. What I fear the most in life is surviving a battle and losing several limbs," Simon replied.

Time is getting on, and tomorrow will be an exciting day now we have a potential person following us, plus dealing with the unknown element — the contact in St Mary's.

"Better call it a night. Let us see what a new day brings."

Chapter Five — Weapons Collection

Today will be a long day, so essential we make an early start if we are to make both the meetings on time. When I say on time, it goes without saying we would arrive in plenty of time. Objective — give us time to stand off and survey the locations to ensure we are not walking into any trap.

"Grab the mirror on a stick on your way out, George. After yesterday, I'm taking no chances. Myself and Simon will complete a quick analysis of the area to make sure no nosey bastards are about."

No sign of anyone in the vicinity, so time to check the car for any evidence of tampering. While George checks underneath with the mirror, I go over the rest of the vehicle. Need to scan for signs of entry or anything that might look like someone tampered with it. At the same time, Simon walks along the other parked cars, glancing inside for anyone crouched down inside. You never know, our Audi man could have swapped vehicles.

Six minutes later, with all the checks complete, I shout to the others, "Come on, gents, better make a move if we are going catch the 09:00 ferry in East Cowes."

Several cars are queued up at the small grey ticket checking booth, at the entrance to the waiting area when we arrive at the ferry terminal. As Simon pulls up at the booth and opens his window to talk to the middle-aged woman sitting inside, I pass him my phone. I'd surfaced from my pit early this morning and purchased an open-ended return online. The plan is to come back later today, but if for any reason we couldn't, we wouldn't need to buy another boarding voucher.

"Thank you, sir, if you follow lane five to the end and hang this from the rearview mirror," said the bored-sounding woman inside.

From the number of vehicles parked up at the ferry, it is going to be busy. It's fantastic news as far as we are concerned as it's easy to hide in a crowd, but awful in another, as I had a problem with groups of people due to the PTSD. Let's hope no arsehole causes any trouble, or they may go for a trip over the side of the vessel.

With still 30 minutes until our ferry arrives, plenty of time to walk over to the terminal to get some drinks from the vending machine. "Give us a hand, George."

"Okey-dokey, you want tea or coffee, Simon?"

"Coffee, please, mate."

Amazed by the number of people waiting for the ferry boat, not many people are here, just a few milling about. On the way back to our car, George taps me on the shoulder and points to the other standing area across the road, running through the middle.

"Isn't that the same Audi as yesterday with our friend driving? Let us go and chat with him."

"No, wait until we are onboard, George. Then, he will have nowhere to run."

Once we rejoin Simon and inform him about the stupid personage who obviously did not learn from his previous mistake, it is time to leave and drive up the ramp to the ship.

Due to the time we turned up, we are now parked near the bow. Once embarked, we have a straight line of sight down the deck towards the aft. Audi man, our target, alights from his vehicle and observes his surroundings at the ship's stern.

Wait for most of the passengers to exit the deck, then approach our man. Seeing us, he tries to head for the gangway, but Simon anticipates this and now blocks his way.

"Don't tell me the woman you're watching happens to be on this boat, at the exact time as our good selves?" I ask, taking up a position in front of him.

"Yeah, she walked up the stairs a moment ago. Please don't hit me again."

"Listened to some shit in my time, mate. But that is the biggest load of bollocks I've heard in a while. So who are you really working for?"

"Sure I explained this to you fucking idiots yesterday. I'm not repeating myself."

With that and without any prior warning, George picks him up and throws him overboard. "Can't be bothered with his bullshit."

Both Simon and I shrugg our shoulders. Well, at least he will not bother us on the crossing. "What if he can't swim?" asks Simon, as he bends over to peer over the side.

"He better learn quickly; anyway, we are close to the shore."

Ship's two passenger lounges on the main deck are situated at each end, with a cafeteria and shop taking up the middle. Both areas are identical, rows of seats similar to an aircraft at the front looking out the expansive windows. Then tables and fixed seating using up the remainder of the area.

By the time we reach the passenger lounge, most tables had already been taken, apart from one near the back wall next to the window.

"Might as well splash out on a full English. If you save the seat, Simon, then, I'll get your rabbit food." By this time, George arrives at the counter's end and hands me a brown plastic tray.

"Thanks, time for a pigout."

Pile my own plate with two of everything available while taking one of each for Simon. It's the same price so he can leave it if he likes. Grab a coffee before paying and rejoining the others.

"Here you go, one kid-size breakfast, don't scoff it down all in one go."

"You're so kind, Steve, but I can't finish all that food."

Instantly George says, "If you don't eat up like a good boy, you're getting it for lunch as well."

"Second word is off," comes the almost instant reply from Simon.

"While you're stuffing your faces, here is the plan for when we disembark to meet Katie's contact, Shyam, in St Mary's. The first thing to remember is the area is prominently made up of Asians and Indians, so this is spot the white man country — we will stick out.

"Suggest we find a parking place on the far side of Hoglands park on Palmerston Road. Walk across the park towards the skate park before crossing the busy highway and entering St Mary's Street's bottom end. Then make our way along this street until we come to the junction of James Street. If you turn right, George, then the first left following the back lane to a point past the buildings." To ensure everyone is clear on what I said, I navigate to the Maps app's locations on my smartphone.

"Any questions so far?" Both George and Simon shake their heads. I continue, "Once George is in a suitable location and calls us to inform us he is in position, we will continue up the road till we reach the market and standoff for a short time. Once contact with Shyam is made, wait to observe if all goes to plan. If not, get your arse over here to assist us asap. For any reason we have been diverted away, follow at a safe distance. If we are about to be led off to a vehicle, we will stall them while you join us, George.

"If all goes wrong, split up and RV at the building in the centre of Hoglands Park. Once we are all together, head back for the car and retreat to Red Funnel to catch the next sailing back to the Isle of Wight."

Just wrapped up when the voice in the ceiling informs everyone they should return to their vehicles as we approach the Southampton terminal.

Before climbing into the car's passenger seat, I look back to where George's swimming partner had abandoned his car. That should get the deck crew scratching their heads for a while as people search the ship for him. Do not have to wait long before one of the staff wave us off.

"Once at the gate, Simon, turn right, then left at the traffic lights. Tell you more when we are past the lights. Hoglands Park is only a six-minute drive. The hard part will be finding a parking space."

"No problem," comes the reply from Simon as he turns right out of the entrance.

We are in luck. Plenty of spaces left, must be a quiet day in town. If we have to make a quick escape, we park up close to the gap in the grey metal railings that encircled the park.

"Anyone got change for the meter, would hate for you to receive a ticket, Simon."

"Couldn't give a flying fuck, George, the car's in Steve's name, the fine will be on him."

"Thanks a bunch, you bastards, here is a few pounds," throwing them at him, aiming for his face.

Follow the tarmac footpath through Hoglands, past the bandstand and building in the centre, beyond the skating area until we reach the central avenue running through Southampton.

After a snap observation, spot a set of traffic lights behind the back wall of Debenhams.

On the other side, between an old church and a residential block is St Mary's road. From here to where George leaves us, we would mingle with the other people walking along the route.

Five minutes later, we arrive at St James Street. "OK, George, this is where you leave us. Find your way around the back of those buildings." Point to the row of shops on the other side. "Will remain here until you give us a missed call."

Take the phone out of my pocket and wait. My mobile vibrates in my hand not long afterwards, turned off the ring tone for security reasons.

"Let's go."

In no time, the pedestrianised street is on our left immediately past the Buddist centre. Under the green and white gazebos that lined both sides of the street, various traders selling everything from fruit and veg to rugs and prayer mats.

Right outside of the Kingsland Tavern, I spot a stall peddling electronic devices such as radios and mobile phones, along with household items.

"That must be our stall, Simon. Better stand off for a while or until the customer's fucked off."

The coast looks clear, time to make our move. Approach with caution, we still didn't know if this is a trap of some kind. After taking a glance behind and down the road towards George's location, we move in.

Behind the stall stands an Indian man in his mid-forties, long brown hair wearing a blue kurta and green pyjamas. Over these, he wore a black puffer jacket. Hanging around his waist is an orange money belt.

Attract the man's attention, "Good morning, sir, looking for a man called Shyam, do you know him."

After a moment's silence as the trader spent time giving Simon and myself the once over, "Yes, that is me. How can I help?"

"Perfect, do you know Katie from Perth?" Simon asks.

"Sorry, no, but I do know Katie from Headlands," comes the reply from Shyam.

"Then we have the right man. Do you process what we need, and are they here?"

"Yes, I can produce what you required. They are not here... They're in my shop on Northern Road at Six-Dials. I'll take you. You got the money?"

"Yeah, fine with us," I reply.

Place my hand on my head to indicate to George. Needed him to rejoin us. Positive he would be watching everything that is happening and would detect my signal. Meantime, Shyam has been joined by another Indian man and are now conversing in Hindi.

"Catching any of that, Steve?"

"Not a fucking word, mate."

At that moment, George makes an appearance. "You can fill me in later on what's been said. Where we off to?"

"Not far —" interrupts Shyam.

"Come on, gents, my friend is looking after the stall, so we can go now."

Our Indian acquaintance leads us down the street to where a battered old white van is parked up. "Only three seats in the front, so afraid one of you will get an uncomfortable ride sitting in the back."

"Well volunteered, Simon, you're used to riding inside a metal box, i.e. a tank, you'll feel like you're back in the army." Before he has even a slight chance to complain, swing the door open and shove him in.

With that, the vehicle pulls away, heading along St Mary's Street, in the direction of the junction with Northern Road. Turn right at the end before turning down a small side street that ran parallel to the side of some grey rundown buildings. Towards the rear, tucked in under some trees, stood a dilapidated old 40-foot red shipping container.

"The weapons are in here," says Shyam, as he removes the three massive padlocks holding the door secure.

Open the rears doors of the van to let Simon out. "Can you stay outside while George and I go in the complete the transaction? Best not all go in, not sure if we can trust the man yet."

Rows of shelving filled both sides of the container, stacked with an assortment of boxed electrical goods. Underneath each row, the shape of larger objects under a green tarpaulin, against the back wall, a pile of wooden crates. In the corner are the unmistakable boxes of 7.62 mm SLR ammunition.

"Here you go, gents, three rifles, four 9 mm pistols. There is more if you need them?"

"Cheers, Shyam, the weapons and ammo will be fine for now, unless you've any plastic explosive?" I say, removing one of the SLR's from the box to examine the rifle's condition, paying attention to the firing pin. No way I'm spending this amount for several weapons, only to find out later they are replicas and didn't fire.

"Sorry, no explosives here, but I can place my mitts on some for you in a couple of weeks."

Take out the £6,000, which I took time to remove from my safe this morning, and hand to Shyam.

"Nice doing business with you, Mr Steve. Lucky for us all, Katie and Cody vouched for you and said you can be trusted. So my little store will remain a secret, yes?"

"No need to worry about us. We may need your services again at some point," I say, as I help George carry out the rifles hidden in some long black cases, along with 50 boxes of ammunition to Simon and the van.

"Would you like me to drop you back to the market?"

"We're fine, thanks Shyam." I would love for him to give us a lift but don't want him to find the location of our transport, nevermind the make and registration number, just in case.

"Stop moaning, both of you. I know Southampton very well, I was brought up here for many years, and the vehicle is not far. Besides, the walk will do us good; if nothing else, sweat out some of the alcohol from last night." So, divide up the ammunition, then carrying one of the cases, I lead off towards Hoglands Park.

Twenty — five minutes later, we arrive at the car, and I open the boot. "Put everything in here. Nowhere to park near the RV point with Mark, so best we stay parked here and walk. Someone feed the parking meter."

The time now, 13:30, which gives plenty of time to arrive and carry out a recce of the inside and try to spot any dodgy-looking people who may be working for Mark. Something learned from the meeting with Henry.

As we emerge from the park, the public house chosen for our rendezvous is now imminently in front. Occupying a substantial proportion of the pavement outside lay an enclosed space where several tables are occupied by people drinking and smoking. Upstairs, through the giant glass windows that ran the building's width, more people sitting at bench-type seating socialising.

Once inside, the place opens up with a huge bar running against the back wall, with four banks of beer taps along its length. To the left and right of the door, more tables; unlike outside, most are free of people. Spot a woman carrying trays of food exiting from a door at the rear, perfect. This would be the kitchen and offices. This would be our route out if things don't go to plan.

On the right, suspended from the ceiling, is a large projector, projecting live sports onto a screen hanging from the top of the wall. Close to this is the next level's staircase. Count 15 people seated upstairs, some in the window, others overlooking the bannister which ran around the open space to the ground floor. Lucky for us, one of the booths is free at the back of the room next to the window. From here, we would monitor what is occurring inside plus what's happening outside, towards the front of the boozer.

My observation of the place is disrupted by George, "Take it, you two want beers!"

"Please, Simon can drink water; he's driving."

"No, make mine a lemonade. Can't stand water that hasn't been flavoured with hops and yeast."

The problem with PTSD, you consider the vast majority of people as potential threats. Saying that, this also kept me safe. Identify three men scattered about the place that are more than likely here for non-legal reasons. The question is, are any of them connected with Dennis or Mark?

"Take a gander in the direction of the bar, Simon. That man keeps staring in our direction."

"Maybe you have pulled, you ugly bastard."

"You know what you can do. That's enough to put you off your beer. Is it me, or is the man dressed similar to the men we saw in the America Woods the other day?"

"You're basing this on the fact that they only sold this type of clothing to them and nobody else in the world."

"Maybe you're right, bloody hypervigilance, but I'm still keeping an eye on him."

Glance over to my right, the toilets are situated next to the fire exit. This must lead to ground level, another possible escape route. A glance down at my watch tells me it is now 14:00, only 15 minutes until Mark should be arriving. Lift my head in time to see George appear with the drinks.

"Last time I'm sending a guardsman to get the beers. What took you so long? Is it the speed your lot march at?"

"Go find yourself a big pack, and go hike in the fucking undergrowth, Steve," comes the instant reply from George.

"Now, now, children, play nice, besides looks like Mark's arrived early," says Simon, pointing towards the top of the stairs.

Left him to his own devices for a few mins, mainly to detect if anyone followed him into the boozer. Observe as he ambles in the direction of the bar, stopping near the man I pointed out earlier. From what I could see, they became engaged in a discussion before ordering from the barperson standing in front of them.

Better grab him, plus being a nosey git, I want to hear what he is saying to my person of interest.

"Hi Mark, glad you're here. We are sat over there by the window," tapping him on the shoulder. "Who's your friend?"

"Afternoon Steve, this is Eddie; he works for me, he's on a day off. Can I get you gents another round of drinks?"

"No thanks, come join us when you're ready."

Moments later, Mark comes over, slumps into the seat opposite me, places a briefcase down, removes a green folder, closes the case and puts it on the floor by his feet.

"Hope everything is going to plan," as he lay out the contents. "Which reminds me, Stuart informed me Dennis is over here and will be returning on the Isle of Wight by Red Jet tomorrow morning at 09:30."

"Interesting news, but if he doesn't work for him anymore, how does he know that?" says Simon, picking up one of the sketches.

"Do not believe he knows he is working for me again. From what I understand, his travel has always been arranged via Stuart. Guess he called him."

"Fair enough, useful to identify we have someone with knowledge of targets movements, may come in handy. Can you take us through this lot?" pointing at the paper on the wooden table.

"No problem, Steve," Mark pulls out the A3 sheet on which he has a plan of the entire property.

"Here is the principal residence. From what I know, the computer programme experts are working on changing the software on the sniper rifles and ammunition to allow them to be used by anyone from here. From Stuart's notes, two men work here during the day then spend the night at a farmhouse not far away, owned by Dennis' father..."

"That explains the men we saw travelling between the two," I interrupt.

Mark proceeds, "This smaller building here in the top left of the property is where Chad's men live, when not on guard or patrolling—"

"Who's Chad?" I intervene again.

"He is the US Navy SEAL we spoke about, managed to get his name from Stuart. Most of the time, you will not see them around as they use the tunnel to the house to get from one place to another.

But, if I remember, you will find an emergency hatch halfway along, hidden by the long wild grass that grows in that part of the garden. Any more questions before I continue to the layout of the inside?"

"Yes, when I climbed a tree a few days back to comprehend what is on the other side, the red brick wall which went around the perimeter, I noticed a stable block. Can you confirm indeed horses are present?"

"Yes, three of them, used by Dennis' grandkids when they visit."

Turn to my left to face Simon, "Forget that. The last thing we need when bullets start flying is seeing you prancing off into the distance parading on a fucking horse."

"Not going to dignify that with an answer. Ignore that idiot, Mark, and continue."

Unfolding the second piece of A3 white paper, "OK, let us move on to what I can remember about the layout of the inside. The house's principal entrance is via two old brown oak doors. They open up to a long corridor, leading to a spiral staircase to the first floor. To the right is the lounge, coming off that is a dining room. On the opposite side, a small library that doubles up as his office. Further along, you will find the kitchen and the door to the basement.

Upstairs are six bedrooms, all ensuite, with the master bedroom at the front having a generous size balcony overlooking the grounds."

"Thanks, Mark, seems your skills from your cavalry days haven't left you. From what you're saying so far, the vast amount of work and, therefore, the place we will encounter the most resistance is down in the cellar. Did you make a separate drawing of that?"

After taking a gulp of beer, Mark takes out the third sketch. "As already mentioned, two ways in, one from the door leading off the corridor, the other via the tunnel. Once down the black stone stairs, you enter a corridor. Off this are several more rooms. The largest of these opens up to one colossal space. Can't tell you which room is being used for what. The information supplied by Stuart only says where the work is being carried out there. Plus the whereabouts of the equipment before being shipped to Cowes."

"No problem on that, Mark. We will find out more when we carry out a recce on the interior later."

"You're welcome, Steve. Any questions?"

Putting down his empty glass, "I got one, hoping you might have brought one of the sniper rifles with you for me to become familiar with."

"It's in the car, George, with the ammunition. Far too heavy to carry here, plus it would be too risky to bring it in here. So we can go and collect it once we wrap up here. Any questions for me, Simon?"

"Only the one, what do you understand about the number of people, including innocent workers we might be dealing with?"

"Again, only going on what Stuart has said, maybe around 20."

"If everyone is ready, drink up and let's go. Where is your vehicle parked?"

"Around the corner, in a small car park behind The Marlands, Steve."

As we start to leave, my phone vibrates in my pocket. It is a message from Derek. He is in Southampton. Wants to know if we would like to catch up.

Read the text to George and Simon; both agree. To be on the safe side, I need to know if anyone comes downstairs after us, still not convinced of Mark's credentials. I suppose this is because of Henry's betrayal.

On reaching the staircase's bottom, I locate myself in front of the nearest fruit machine, insert money and begin to play. The other three plonk their arses down at a table out of view of the stairs, but they could still see anyone come down.

My suspicions paid off as the man Mark started the conversation with, Eddie, when he entered the premises, follows us down a minute later. Right, let's confirm he is following us.

Our tail stops in the bottom bar and scans the room, probably looking for us, before sitting at a circular table facing the door. For some reason, which at the time I'm not aware of, he either knew I hadn't left yet or decided to forget it.

Turn and nod at Simon and George. There is no need for words, done this too many times in the past. Collect my winnings from the machine and exit via the front door, followed by Mark and Simon. George would give our man five minutes to see if he made a move. If not, he would exit and meet with the rest of us round the corner.

Give the man his due; he is no amateur, giving us a two minute lead for leaving, to follow. Make sure he knew which way we went by stopping outside the window, just long enough for him to spot which direction we went. Also, being a professional, George gave it a few seconds before following out of the door.

Meanwhile, walking at a slow, steady pace, we turn left at the junction, past the row of shops until we come to the last one.

The plan is to turn in the service area around the back. Need to ensure our man witnesses us turning. By spinning 180 degrees and looking in the shop window on the other side of the road, I observe him come to a sudden halt and pretend he intended to cross the street.

"Time to move," I say, turning left. "Simon, take up a position behind the wheelie bins. Mark, remain close to me, but stay out of view."

Moments later, Eddie appears. Wait until he had no escape, then, with one fluid movement, swing my arm around his neck and wrestle him to the ground. Instinctively Simon rushes in to pin his legs to the floor, receiving a kick to his belly in the process.

"You little bastard," yells Simon through gritted teeth, absorbing the pain and landing a powerful punch straight into the man's gut. Eddie gives out a muffled scream, recoiling from the blow.

"If you would like to live, I suggest you answer my questions." Remove the dirty rag from his mouth, stuffed inside by me to stop any cries for help. "First, why are you following us from the public house, second how did you find out about our meeting?"

George plants his well-aimed boot with as much force as he could muster into his side, to confirm we meant business.

"Did not sign up for this shit," Eddie protests, gasping for air. "Received a call from Chad asking me to be in the pub for 14:00 and watch if Mark showed up and who he met with, then report back. Followed you to discover where you're heading."

"Must be your lucky day. Decided you are a moron who got caught up with something you shouldn't have done. Therefore we've chosen not to kill you. But, hope you understand I've now got a problem. If Chad finds out who the meeting is with and the fact we are on our way to the Bashp factory, it could be trouble for us."

Had no intention of going to the warehouse. This is, with any luck, leading them on a false trail. Still begs the question of how they knew about our meeting. No way it came from Geroge, Simon and me. So the leak must be with Mark.

"Tie this idiot up with whatever you can find and dump the body in the big dustbin. Someone will find him when they come to empty them." I turn to Eddie, "that's if you survive thill then."

Body disposed of, we continue in the direction of the multi-storey parking and Mark's vehicle, reaching there a few minutes later. On the fourth level, halfway down, nestled between several other cars, a cream Bentley.

"That's mine," said Mark, walking towards the car.

After what had just occurred, it would be best to stand off and watch for a while before approaching. But, once again, my fears are proven right. A body appears between the parked cars.

"Fuck, here we go again."

About to launch ourselves at the person, when Mark grabs my shoulder. "It's OK. That is my brother Paul. He's been protecting the expensive asset for me while I met with you."

Turn to glance at George, I could see the signs of relief and excitement on his face as he is about to get his mitts on the new sniper rifle.

After a quick introduction, Mark opens the vehicle's boot; inside is a long green case. Once the lid is peeled back, it reveals the sniper rifle. With care, George picks it up and examines it.

"Gents, this is the British military sniper, the L115A3. The rifle is a bolt-action weapon with a calibre of 8.59 mm and an effective range of 1.2 km. Used this as a basis for our brand new firing system," explains Mark.

"What you can see on top is our new optical sight, that button on the side, George is what sets all the settings in place. Take a look through the optics, and you will see a movable crosshair. This moves, depending on where the software predicts the best place to aim. The cross will move back to the target's centre for the shooter's comfort, once you've moved to point at the correct position and after the grey button has been pressed again. "

"How many rounds in the magazine?" asks George, placing the rifle back in the case.

"Five of these guided bullets." Mark opens a box of ammunition. "We need to programme the weapon to each of you via this control unit, or it will not fire."

As he is the group's sniper, George places his right hand's index finger on the controller unit's small, square plate until a red flashing light turns a steady green. In case our mission got fucked up, and we lost George, we all take it in turns to be programmed in.

"That's all there is to it. Nobody else can fire that rifle unless the individual is programmed into the system for that particular rifle. Here are 300 rounds for you." Mark hands over a metal box. "Will leave you now, as I've got a board meeting back in the office. If you have any questions or problems, call."

"Thanks, Mark, grab the kit, gents, time to go," I say, taking hold of the control unit.

Time is flying past and now getting late, plus the plan is to follow Dennis on the ferry in the morning. Suggest we stayed in the Premier Inn close to West Quay for the night. After picking up our own car from near Hoglands Park and on the way to the hotel, I contact Derek and ask him to join us for a few drinks later.

Chapter Six – Boatyard

As nights went, last night was best for a long time, with drinks and a delish meal, a nice change from my usual microwave cooking. Plus fantastic to catch up with Derek, plus great to find out about the aftermath of our adventure on St Halb. More surprising, the local police still didn't know who was implicated in the killings at Henry's place. Especially with the chief constable's connections to Hadley. Good to hear Abbie was recovering from her ordeal and is now back at her residence.

Sitting enjoying my morning coffee in the restaurant when the other three plonk their arses down at the table. "Good morning, gents."

"Morning, Steve, what's the plan for today?" says Simon, pouring a steaming hot brew from the flask the waiter kindly left.

"Once we've finished breakfast, we need to make a move back to the island. A ferry boat is leaving at 08:30. Simon and I will go via this route before driving around to Cowes using the chain ferry. Once we arrive in East Cowes, we will proceed to the RedJet terminal and park up. Mark told us that Dennis is returning on the 09:35 catamaran; this only takes 25 minutes.

"As Derek has offered to help, we have an advantage. No one knows what he looks like. So if he and George follow him on the passenger ferry, stay out of eyesight while Derek remains close to Dennis and take up a position relative to him as possible to overhear any conversations he might have."

Approximately 40 minutes later, the two are dropped off at the Town Quay terminal, yet again find ourselves parked in line waiting for the ferry. After the trip yesterday, we needed to make sure no idiot was following us. Not that I knew what the said idiot looked like.

Want a piss anyway from all the beverages consumed earlier, so I make my way towards the terminal building, taking a diversionary route up along the row of vehicles parked behind and on either side of us. Ensure I peeked into every car for any signs of dodgy people or surveillance equipment.

Meanwhile, Simon aimlessly strolls around the marshalling area, doing the identical thing as me. To be in position when the other three arrive in Cowes, this passage must go without any problems. There is only a short margin of error.

Thankfully everything goes with nothing out of the ordinary happening. Arrive at the chain ferry with still 30 minutes until the arrival of the others on the Red Jet. Selecting first gear, Simon drives gradually down the concrete ramp and boards the small boat. The vessel takes a maximum of 20 cars parked between a wall on one side, complete with expansive glass windows. On the other side, a small passenger enclosure situated the same side as the operator's cabin perched on top.

The crossing only takes a few minutes, but the floating bridge remains the only way to cross the River Medina between the towns, without a 10-mile trip via Newport.

Lucky for us, the ship lands on Medina Road, leading to the town centre, close to a multi-storey car park. So perfect. Make the snap decision to leave the vehicle here and make the rest of the short journey on foot. Besides, we would need to follow Dennis to the boatyard he used to ship out the weapons.

Arrive with only 10 minutes to spare, take a position in the nearby pub's beer garden. From here, it is possible to watch everyone leaving the terminal's central entrance and the spot where passengers come out after disembarking. Bang on time, Dennis, closely followed by Derek, emerges from the covered gangway with Geroge about 50 metres behind.

Feel relief flow through my body as Dennis walks past the taxis and out into the street. Shit, something I had fucked up in the planning, parking the car so far away. If he had taken a cab or been picked up, there was no way of tailing him.

Turn to Simon, "You tag along with George, and keeping a short distance from Derek and me. Even to the untrained eye, it would look suspicious four men following your every turn. Want to find out if Dennis made any calls during the crossing."

"No problem, as we know he is heading for a boatyard which has access to the water. This must be on our left. Once we can confirm there is only one way, we will try to make our way in front of him and come discreetly from the opposite direction."

"Great idea, Simon, RV near the point he enters the boatyard."

Head off to join Derek, who is now rounding the corner, still following his mark like a true professional. To ensure I don't startle him, I make sure I made contact from the side. By this time, Dennis turns left, making his way up the street going through the town centre.

"Anything to report, mate? Did he make any telephone calls on the ferry?"

"Yes, two, Steve. From what you said last night, one to Chad, the person running things when our man, " he points to Dennis, "is not on the island. The other to a woman called Nicole, to say he would arrive by 10:25; from the conversation, I would suggest she is perhaps in the target location."

Am about to say something when I have to dive into a premises' doorway. Dennis has stopped and turned to face in our direction before entering a Sainsbury's Local store. Wasn't a problem for Derek; he would blend in with everyone else mingling on the high street.

Fortunately used this shop on my last visit to Cowes and knew the place only had one exit. So all we need to do is wait for him to emerge.

Glance towards the other side of the street. See Simon and George making the most of this opportunity to make their way past, heading up Shooters Hill to get in front of our target. Logically this is the only way for Dennis to reach a boatyard, as the water is to the left of this road. By any chance, he made any sort of diversion for any reason, would only take a simple call to get everyone back on plan.

After emerging eight minutes later from the store, turn and head in the direction we predicted. Spot George sitting on a low wall with his head down in the distance, blending into the background, invisible to most people, unless you're trained in surveillance. Couldn't see Simon, but he would be around somewhere. They would stop here, as this was the first place since leaving the terminal, with all the elements we were on the lookout for.

Directly across the road behind a grey metal railing fence, a small, what seemed like a run-down boatyard. Proves to be the right decision as moments later, Dennis opens the gate and enters. Lose sight of him once he turns. Not an issue, as George would have seen where he went from his location.

Need to survey the area before we attempt to go in. The best place to do this would be across the street, in the spot selected by George. In case our man comes back out again, Derek remains on the same side and leans against a derelict stone house.

"Where did he go?"

"In the office-looking building," George points towards a one-storey brightly-coloured building, either side of the entrance, flags fluttering in the gentle breeze.

I notice several windows overlooked the yard and the massive aged wooden shed close to the water from my vantage point. Occupying the concrete area between it and the railing, numerous sailboats are mounted on trailers. A long, black wood storage box adjacent to the railings is slightly higher than the perimeter fence. This would be ideal for our entry to the property without being observed.

Start to form a plan in my head. Again using the advantage, nobody knew about Derek. So he could enter on the pretence of purchasing a leisure craft. In reality, he would be checking on the number of people and its layout, while the rest of us make our way inside. George and I climb over the fence while Simon hides in plain sight and walks in to check out the boats for sale.

Been sitting in the same spot for too long, so I head to the minor road to my left, signalling the others to follow.

"OK, gents, here is some sort of plan; first, this is purely an observation mission to find out what happens here. Therefore it goes without saying, but I'll say it anyway, try to avoid any contact if possible. Yes, I'm looking at you, George. We don't want anyone else taking up swimming lessons. The only person with any connection of any kind will be Derek, when he enters the office.

"Once he is inside, Simon, you walk through the gate, keeping your head down. Pretend you're interested in the sailing boats. Us two", pointing at George, "will enter via the side fence. The second objective is the old wooden shed, which I guess is where the weapons are stored when here. It's close to the river and away from the road. From what Stuart told Mark, we need to map the layout and position of any guards; there are at least two of them.

If the equipment is here, remember where and if precautions have been taken to secure them, like traps.

"When you spot George and me arrive at the building, proceed towards the water, Simon, check out the area from the shed to the end of the pontoons, see if any boats are capable of heading out to open water.

"Signal for the withdrawal is two rings from my mobile; make sure now your phones are on vibrate only. On the off chance everything gets fucked up for any reason, the emergency RV is in the multi-storey car park on level five, one above where our car is actually parked. When all goes to plan, I always like to be positive, meet back up at the car. Any questions?"

"I have one," says Derek, as he switches his mobile to vibrate, "if I'm brought outside by the staff, to be shown what's on offer and followed by Dennis, and he spots one of you reprobates, what do I do? Pretend I don't know you and carry on gathering information or make my excuse to leave?"

"Good question; if we didn't spot this, give the signal to withdrawal; same goes for anyone who feels things are not going as discussed, call endex."

"Thanks for clearing that up, Steve."

"Not a problem. If everyone is ready, let's get on with it. Give us five minutes to get in place, Derek, then proceed to the sales office."

Make my way with George back to the road, walk 50 metres back down towards the centre, before turning around and taking position close to the same brick building Simon used earlier to wait for everyone to be in their places.

Several minutes later, observe as Derek enters the courtyard, followed moments after by Simon. Pause for a short while before looking around the corner to make sure nobody is in the yard; I didn't expect to see anybody. George follows seconds later and climbs over the fence, taking a crouched position behind a large wooden box and the metal railings.

Open ground occupies the space separating the sailboats and the target building that we need to cross. Once I confirm again nobody is in the area, sprint across the gap to the far edge of the boat shed. Once in a suitable position, looking back across at the office and Simon wandering among the boats, I signal for George to sprint across to join me. About to make his move, when a smartly-dressed man in his mid-thirties leaves the main building, walking in our direction.

Now, only 20 metres from my location, shit, this is going to get fucked up before we start! With any luck, he won't peek behind the shed; if he does, I'm screwed — no place to hide down the long narrow space between the wall and building, definitely nowhere to go.

Simon thinks on his feet, observes the situation unfold, ignores the observation-only mission parameters, and calls the man over to him. A brief conversation follows before he is led off in the direction of the pontoons. Wait until they disappear before signalling George.

This was an old building, and the weather and sea had taken their toll. Some of the planks had shrunk, leaving a gap between them. Perfect, we could, at least, view the inside as the rear entry point is locked. Perhaps there is an entrance on the seaward side. This might be an issue.

Minutes earlier, Simon led the man from the office to the far side. A ray of light shone down from a Velux window, mounted on the rooftop to provide natural lighting. Installed many of these in my time as a roofer. Easy to break into if I could get up.

"Any ideas?" turning to face George.

"Maybe. The distance between the brick wall and the building is only small; you can spread eagle and shinny up, crawl along the roof, through the window, and let me in. Would go myself, but this is payback for making me climb the fucking tree the other day, so off you go, monkey boy."

Jump up, land with my left foot and hand on the wall. Simultaneously, the right foot and hand make contact with the shed's rear. My mountaineering training automatically kicks in. Ensure I had three points of touch at all times. Creep up the gap until I reach the hard part, traversing onto the flattish roof. Lucky for me, the weathering also took its toll up here. A hole had developed one metre to my front, exposing one of the timber battens used to secure the ply sheets.

With every muscle in my now aching body, now screaming in agony inch forward until I am in line with the hole. Only got one attempt at this; if I miss, I will fall the 10 metres, rejoining George on the ground. Take several deep breaths before launching towards the roof, grabbing the wooden baton with both hands. Thank fuck, it wasn't rotten. Pull my body up and take a short breather, for the body to recover.

I keep as flat as I can then crawl past the window until it is possible to see over the ridge. Through the windowpanes, I can see Derek sitting at a table in the centre of the sales office, drinking a brew with a young lady around a circular wooden table. Seated at a desk in a cordoned off room with glass windows towards the rear, I recognise the figure of Dennis talking on the phone.

Spot several people milling around the place, the problem being from this position can't see anyone in the yard. The problem is an extensive area of dead ground in front of the building, which I can not see.

Before I climb inside, might as well use the advantage height gives me, to monitor what is happening on the pontoons with Simon. With care, I steadily inch along the rooftop, trying not to make a noise. Still didn't know if anyone is within. Stop short of the far end and listen. The mellow tones of Simon can be heard a little way off, chatting with the salesperson, which means he is talking, therefore not looking up. Carefully inch ahead until I reach a position where I can peer beyond the edge.

A small ramp leads down to a floating pontoon, stretching out into the Medina River for about 20 metres. Another runs across the end, forming a T junction. Moored up in a flashy grey speedboat he man from the office steps off, followed by Simon, and both are now walking back in the yard's direction. Must be running out of things to say, and I haven't started our part of the task yet.

Stare straight down the side, can't see any type of incline coming from it to the water, which is good news, no fast getaway for Chad and his mates. To transport the weapons from the boatshed to the boat, they would have to be carried down the ramp, easily rigged to explode if required.

Better move my arse into gear before George does something stupid. Crawling back to the skylight, I gingerly peer inside below a tiny mezzanine floor about two metres square. As I scrutinise the interior in my mind, I am breaking this down into individual parts. First, open the roof window. Second, lower myself to the first level. Once I'm on the ground, let George in.

Remove the multi-tool I always carried and unscrew the top cover of the Velux skylight, placing this down silently on the roof.

Next, locate the small locking mechanism in the gap at the leading edge of the window. With the knife's blade, slide this to the right to unlock. The glass will now rotate in the frame. A stupid grin makes its way across my face. If I ever gave up the day job, at least I would make a living out of being a burglar.

Another cautionary glance down to confirm no nosey bastard is looking up, swing the windowpane open. Feet first, I lower myself down until I am hanging several feet from the floor's planks below. Then, quietly as a man could, dropping a short distance to old wooden boards, I let go and land instinctively, adopting a crouched position. Pause for a few moments, listening for evidence someone had overheard me entering. Couldn't detect any voices or movement, so on to step two.

Like the walls of this place, several gaps have appeared between the planks over time, giving me the perfect vantage point to scrutinise the ground floor immediately below. Assuming a prone position for a better look, beneath me, a cordoned off area secured by a heavy-duty metal mesh fence. Inside, sitting atop a battered-looking old bench, three green plastic boxes. I see the distinctive mark of the military upward-facing arrow. This has to be the control panels Mark told us about.

Shift to the other side of the mezzanine floor to find a way off. The interior walls consist of extensive crisscrossed beams, ideal for climbing down. About to start my descent, when I detect voices coming from the direction of the front door.

Better investigate. Inch my way back to the forward edge and glance down. Beneath, the shape of two armed men, half in and half out, making it hard to distinguish details because of the light. Due to the fact sound travels and echoes in partially-empty buildings, overhear their general chitchat. Sounds like Dennis is here to arrange the first shipment of weapons to France via Shanklin, Isle of Wight.

Lay observing until the guards left, must have been around five minutes. About time! I made for the back door. Scaling the wall takes no time; within seconds, I make my way to a position behind a pile of boating equipment close to the exit. Then, with the same caution I'd used so far, I ease the door open.

Greeted with the words from George, "Where the fuck have you been? About to assume something had gone wrong and call endex."

"Yeah, sorry mate, took advantage of the high point to examine the premises, plus two guards got in the way; think they have left now. Discovered three of what might be control panels inside. Need to try and fuck them up somehow. We can't take them yet. This would raise the alarm."

"Well, stop talking and let me in, Steve."

A search uncovers a lot of sailing crap, but nothing of interest to us apart from the items protected by the cage. Some idiot hadn't done their homework. Under a pile of tools on a wooden workbench in the corner, a crowbar and a length of rope used for tying up boats. Probably thought nobody will mess with armed guards.

"Chuck them over here, George. We can go back up and loosen a few boards and enter from the top." I could have simply broken the chain, but this will let people know we've been here.

"Makes sense, mate, show me the way up."

Once in the correct location, towards the rear of the caged area, insert the bar to prise the first board. The last thing we needed is too much shit falling on either the boxes or the bench. Once loose, hand it to George to stack to one side before moving on to a second.

"Your fat arse will never fit through that small gap, Steve. Take up another."

Remove the third, I can take a subtle hint. I drop inside, while George ties knots in the rope to help me climb back up again. Conceal myself from anyone who may enter, listen and wait for the two fuckheads to reappear.

Time is getting on. I can't afford to take much more time. Open the first crate, hinging the lid housing the screen backwards, then, with as much care as possible, quickly removing the four screws holding the bottom tray securely in the case. Underneath, a mass of wires and circuit boards. The question is now what to do, which wouldn't be too obvious.

A flashback from my computer repair course a long time ago helped identify a few places to break the circuits. Need to ensure they are hard to spot, even if you knew what you were looking for.

With the blade's point, scratch away part of the RAM card connection, also remove one end of an electrical diode on the underside. Put everything back, ensuring no evidence of tampering is visible before moving on to the next one, making sure I do not disconnect similar parts.

Once I've tampered with all three, "OK, George, chuck down the rope. Let's get the fuck out of here."

Once I replace the last board back in the precise position they were in before I took them out, "You go back down the way we came and out the door, I'll go the identical way I came in, through the window to make sure everything is back in place. Wait for me on the corner of the building."

"Roger that."

Back on the roof, close the Velux and secure all the components. This idiot hadn't considered how to climb off the rooftop to a position I was able to edge my way to the bottom. Only one thing for it, lay on my stomach and creep over the side until it is possible to connect with the brick wall and building.

First part goes well! Over the rim and stretch out my right leg until I make contact with the wall. With my left leg on the structure, I reach out with my right hand to place it on the same brick building. Well, that's the plan.

Nearly touch the other side as I fall like a rat down a drainpipe, bouncing off each side before coming to a painful abrupt stop on the hard ground.

With a knowing sound to his voice, George says, "You made a quick descent, you ready to move?"

I reply through gritted teeth, "Yep, you cross first," no way was I letting on the fall hurt like crazy.

As I run across the gap, I spot Derek and Simon wandering around the yard, looking at boats. Shit, what if Dennis recognises him. Fuck, all I can do now will find out on the debrief. Once I reach the storage box, I see George disappear over the railing into the road. Seconds later, I follow suit.

No point in me hanging around here. Everyone would now be heading towards the RV in the car park. Get composed and limp off to join the other three. By this time, my left ankle now giving me shit from the impact with the ground. Now do what the rest of them would have done before entering the multi-storey entrance. Stand off and observe for several minutes.

Need to ensure I'm not wandering into trouble. So, with nobody in sight, make my way to the staircase, walking up until I reach the level below which the vehicle is on.

The plan is to cross the parking deck to the up incline, stand off once more, and watch and listen. Deliberately got Simon to park close to the ramp for this reason. In the distance, I hear the others casually talking, so consider it safe to approach.

Welcomed with, "What kept you, fat boy?"

"Glad you all made it. Anyone checked the weapons are still here?"

"Yep, all here," says Simon, opening the boot of the car.

"OK, gents, nobody around, might as well have a quick debrief here while it's fresh in people's minds. So let start with you, Derek."

"Sure, no problem, Steve. After entering the office, Dennis disappeared into a glass-fronted room at the back while conversing with the young ladies at the counter. Overheard him say something about a collection in about two weeks. Guess he must have been talking about the weapon system. Not sure how long I was engrossed in chatting and drinking coffee when Dennis got up and left. That's about it, apart from meeting up with Simon in the yard, pretending to like boats."

"Thanks, your turn, Simon."

"While considering which boat to purchase, keeping my back to the office, just in case, spotted your position about to be compromised. Made the command decision to abort the observe-only part and engaged with the bloke. With the info required on the pontoon, got my new gullible friend to take me.

"Did find out the speedboat is what they use for trips to France, possibly what they utilise to transport all the components. Took the opportunity to survey the ramp and float connections, as I know you like blowing things up. It should go easy."

"Cheers, mate, as you know, George and I made our way in the boat shed. Found out it is protected by two armed men, also three of the control panels. I've made them inoperable. Removed any trace of anyone being there, even to me returning down the same way I went in to close everything up. Did I miss anything, George?"

"Only the best bit," pointing at me, "this twat fell off the roof."

With them all still laughing at my expense, "Come on, time for a few cold ones back at my place." Once all in the vehicle, "Have you tried the satnav, Simon? Does it work?"

"Yes, played with it yesterday. Why?

"Think about it. We are dealing with a couple of computer experts who can change complicated weapons programmes. Therefore it might be simple for them to tap into the system," point the screen in the centre of the dashboard, "think you better pull over so I can disable it."

"Fuck, you're right, Steve."

Once the car pulled into a small layby off the road, I exit only to re-enter moments later on my back, to obtain a more favourable view underneath. Find the central control cable and yank it from the rear of the unit.

"Should stop any nosey bastards keeping track of our movements. You can't be too careful. Drive on, chauffeur."

"Said it before, and I'll repeat it—the second word is off, guess the first."

Chapter Seven — Dennis' Place

Well, can't do much more here might as well head home, double-checking the desk drawer is fully locked.

After ensuring nothing of his plans are left out on display, grabs his mobile from a brown leather briefcase, "Hi, Chad, it's Dennis. Can you send someone to the boatyard to collect me?"

"Sure, no problem, what time?"

"Finished here, so now would be good."

Would take around 30 minutes for the car to arrive, so no need to rush. Better make time to catch up with the sales manager, Bob. A person with 25 years of experience in the sale of all things nautical. Been with the business for the last five years, and there is not much he doesn't know about the company, apart from the weapons shipments, of course.

Find him sitting with the young ladies in the breakroom. On spotting me, rises to his feet, "You off then, Dennis...?"

"No call to get up, Bob, popped in to say hi, while I'm waiting to be picked up, so how's everyone doing?"

A stunning young lady in her early thirties with long brown hair handed me a coffee from the percolator.

"Thank you, so how are you today?" I say.

"I'm fine, thank you, all going to plan today. Think I might have sold a boat to a man in here earlier, went by the name of Derek."

"Good stuff, Laura, keep up the good work. Can I have a private word, Bob, before I leave?"

"Sure, you want to go to my office or step out into the yard?"

"Outside is good. That way, I can keep an eye out for the driver."

Make my way into the front yard, stepping away from the door, "No doubt, you're probably wondering why I've employed two armed men to patrol the property."

"On my list to discuss with you, Dennis."

"It's nothing for you to be concerned about, stored a couple of expensive antique sculptures from home while we carry out some restoration work. Would hate for them to get stolen or broken. No need for you to worry."

"That explains that then."

"One last thing, I would leave the guards to do their own thing. Best you stay out of their way."

"Say no more, boss, will make sure the women in the office know."

That is what I like about Bob. He knows when not to push or ask silly questions, probably why I hired him. Minutes later, a grey Mercedes pulls into the boatyard, parking close to the building. A well-groomed man climbs out of the driving seat, "You ready, sir?"

"Yes, just coming. Catch you later, any issues, call me."

Clamber into the rear via the back door, held open by the chauffeur. "Take me straight back home, please."

On feeling the car's slow deceleration, raise my head from the pile of papers I've been reading, in time to monitor the driver's window effortlessly descend. Being engrossed in the paperwork, the journey went past in no time. Listen as the driver and the guard chat for a few moments, before the car once more accelerated towards the house.

"Can you drop me at the house, and then find Chad and ask him to meet me in..." look down at the gold-plated timepiece on my wrist, "30 minutes, in my office, please."

"Of course, sir."

Enter the house via the two generously-sized oak doors into the light-yellow painted corridor. Collected lots of fine art on my travels around the world, which now adorned both walls as you move into the house. Something my father always taught me, first impressions always count. I guess it still stuck with me.

Still have some paperwork to complete for the first shipment of weapons to a criminal organisation in Holland, so head off to the office. When I say office, it is a corner of the library, but it suits my needs.

On the green felt embedded into the extensive teak desk, a pile of letters neatly stacked in date order. I'll open them later. First need a coffee—a significant advantage in living in a big house, I am able to afford to employ a full-time chef. Pick up the phone and dial the kitchen, leave it to ring a couple of times before Nicole answers.

"Hi, Dennis, when did you arrive back home?

"Not long ago, could you fetch me a coffee, please? I'm in my office."

"No problem, give me a few minutes."

Place the receiver down and take out the paperwork from the briefcase, laying them out on the desk. These consisted of specifications for the sniper rifle, ammunition, optical scope and the control panel, and idiots guide on operating. Flick through the papers until I find the delivery details. The first shipment should go in the next two weeks, but this depends on the computer geeks breaking the code to allow anyone to use the equipment.

Deep in contemplation, I relax back in the chair to see the shapely figure of Nicole, my housekeeper come chef, a young lady in her thirties with long flowing blonde hair reaching halfway down her sumptuous body, appear in the doorway.

"Here you go, Dennis, a nice cuppa for you."

Most people I employed call me sir out of respect, but over time built up a friendly rapport over the eight years she'd worked for me, so we did away with formalities and moved on to first-name terms.

"Thanks, Nicole, sorry to be a pain, Chad will be joining me. Could you fetch another coffee?"

"OK, as it's you, I will let you off, just this once." Then, with a huge smile, she leaves the room, passing Chad on the way.

"Come in and take a seat," pointing to one of the red leather sofas facing each over in the centre of the room."

On the sofa opposite me is a slim, muscular built, five-foot-eight-inch tall frame with cropped brown hair. His demeanour gives off the air that this man wouldn't hurt anyone. Nevertheless, this person spent six years with the US Navy SEALs, carrying out black ops in hot spots worldwide. Now when it comes to injuring or killing anyone, there is a reason I've acquired his services. Chad wouldn't ask why. He would simply carry out the task. No questions asked.

"What's the latest on the programming and the three men Mark hired?" No point in small talk as my tame killer wasn't one for this.

After taking a sip from his coffee, handed to him by Nicole, "Let's start with our own manpower. Downstairs in the cellar is the four mainframe experts working on the coding, a 12-hour rotating shift. They are guarded by three of my men. No doubt you noticed the two armed guards on the front entrance when you came in.

"Another two are patrolling outside. Further, two are located at your dad's estate. The computer nerds stay there after their shift. Have implemented a two-hour shift rotation for the gate patrols and the two in the house with a six-hour rest period. The slack is being taken up by the extra 10 men, apart from the ones at the farm. The men are billeted in the building in the far corner of the grounds.

"For safety reasons, transitions to and from the property go via the tunnel to the outbuilding. Of course, this rule doesn't apply to you or any vehicle required to come up to the house. Measured to ensure any nosey bastards are unaware of movements such as times of shift changes."

"Any news on Steve, and his cohorts, Chad?"

"Not sure why anyone would call these three professionals. One of my men, Jackson, took some personal time in Newport when he spotted them parking near the bus station. Following protocol, he called this in, got him to follow Steve...

"By the way, Dennis, Stuart's fantastic idea to put in a code on Mark's phone that switched on the camera if anyone viewed my photo paid off. As a result, enlarged images of their three ugly mugs are now posted about the place.

"As I said, my man followed Steve through Newport, even managed to drop a tracking device in his pocket. Currently, Steve is at present in a country park near Ryde. Four men are standing by to break in and take him out of the picture."

"Earlier, at the boatyard, I saw a couple of your operatives. Are they changed as well?" Dennis interrupted.

"Yes, but only every 12 hours."

"Thanks for the update, Chad. Can we now check on the progress with the coding?"

Take the papers from the desk, place them in a transparent plastic folder and follow Chad down the long corridor to the end, towards the door to the cellar. On route, pass the kitchen, Nicole is standing behind a stainless steel worktop, preparing and chopping some type of vegetable.

"Dinner will be at 18:00, don't be late," Nicole shouts out, as we cross the doorway.

The white wooden door to the basement opens up to a black stone staircase, twisting clockwise before ending in a dimly-lit corridor. On both sides, open doorways leading into different rooms — the first, a small kitchenette; inside a man drinking some sort of brew. Instinct saw him reaching for his weapon as we pass until he catches sight of his boss, Chad accumpained by Dennis.

Next door on the left is a home cinema which consists of a giant screen mounted on the wall with four rows of three grey reclining chairs. At the back of the room, a well-stocked bar for use while watching films. Past this, another room used for general storage, plus the weapons system are being stored here. At the far end, the biggest of the spaces and where the weapon's operation is run from.

On one side, several banks of high-spec machines occupy an enclosed space fronted with glass. Above them, an air conditioning unit keeps the space at a constant cool temperature to stop the computers from overheating. Two men seated at two separate desks tap away on the keyboards while looking at several 32-inch monitors.

Off to the left of the room, another of Chad's men sits on an old sofa scanning the room, his weapon resting on his knees. Acknowledged Chad with a wave of his right hand before continuing to watch the area.

Muli-coloured lines of code scroll up the screens as the two experts try to break all the equipment systems' coding, including all individual components.

"How's it going? Are you close to breaking the programme?" I say, tapping Billy on the right shoulder.

"A lot harder than we imagined. Every time I think yes, I'm in, another firewall fucking shows up," comes the reply in an American accent. "Major problem here is when we hit a block, the system resets itself, the people at Bashp definitely know their stuff. But I'll break the bastards yet."

"Better make sure you do, or you may have to meet with a nasty accident," says Chad, in a joking manner but with an evil grin.

To give Billy some sort of reassurance, replied with, "Ignore this psycho. You're doing a grand job."

"Thank you, sir. I always disregard what the idiot says."

"What's happening in your area of expertise, Ricky?" I say, turning to the other man.

"Sure, Chad informed you that Jackson witnessed Steve and his crew disembark from a vehicle in Newport. Well, he wrote down the registration number FD08 XRP. Managed to tap into the car's satnav, we will observe the vehicle movements from this terminal.

"Me and Billy are staying at the farm. For precautionary measures, installed a motion-activated camera on the route about 20 metres before the bridge. Can monitor who crosses from this computer and react if required.

"Plus, Steve has a tracker planted on him. So again, I can track him from here."

"Thank you, gents, keep up the excellent work. You've only two more weeks to break and install the codes as the first shipment is due out then. Will give you both a £3,000 bonus if everything is completed by the end of this week."

"Will get it done, boss," as they resume entering lines of code.

"While we are down here, let's go and speak to the men in their living quarters, Chad."

The last door on the left leads to the 150 metre tunnel connecting the cellar with the outbuilding. The walls and ceiling had been painted white to maximise the electric lights' glow, evenly spaced along its length, with ample room for three people to walk together, three abreast, meaning the shaft can be traversed quickly by people and machinery.

Halfway down, an emergency exit leads to the grounds above, consisting of a painted metal ladder leading up to a heavy cast iron cover. For quick escape in a crisis situation, the hatch is deployed without a handle instead of relying on its weight to keep it closed.

Might as well check this still works while I'm here. Climb up the steps until I reach an illuminated small platform approximately two metres beneath the cover. Surprisingly, it opens without too much effort. The opening to the garden is concealed among a small hedgerow.

Rejoin Chad, making our way to the spiral staircase at the far end leading to the building above. The stairs exit into the middle of an open-plan room. Several bunk beds sufficient to occupy 10 men take the left of the quarters, leaving room for a makeshift kitchen at the other end. Sitting on long wooden benches on either side of a pine table, four men enjoy card games. A ray of sunlight shines through the skylight, reflecting off the cutlery in the centre of the tabletop. Another two relax on their bunks.

Leave the others talking and walk outside onto a modest patio, where a round iron table and three chairs stand with light flickering off the glass's surface from the two windows. Usually, the grandkids would use this place to camp out when they stay over, which reminds me they are coming over tonight for a couple of weeks.

Re-enter to find Chad briefing his men, while two more men kit themselves out to go on shift at the front entrance. I know better than to grab him to attract his attention and don't fancy a broken arm or worse. So instead, call out from the doorway, "We need to make a move from here, to visit the gate and catch the people patrolling in the next half-hour. Want to be ready for when the children show up."

One-armed man relieves the boredom of guard duty between short periods of excitement by walking continuously across the gate's opening — another inside the tiny shed used as a gatehouse.

Spotting two people approach in their direction, the duo stop what they are doing, with hands-on triggers they face towards us.

"Morning gents, seen anything interesting to report," Chad says as he approaches.

"All peaceful here, nothing of interest happening on our watch," comes the reply from the man at the gatehouse.

"Fantastic — where are the men patrolling?"

A voice from about 10 metres away speaks out, "Right behind you. And we have nothing to tell, all fucking quiet."

Leave them to it and head down the driveway, towards the wooden bridge which ran over the river crossing the garden. "You know this could be a problem if this is taken out of action. You prepared any continuity plans?"

"All in hand, Dennis."

"In that case, I'll catch up later. Need to get ready for when the grandkids arrive."

"Before you go, Dennis, what do you want me to do about Steve? Four of my armed men are standing by to grab him or kill him. The choice is yours."

"Best bring him here. He might possess important info."

"You're the boss," Chad takes out the mobile phone from his pocket and dials his operative. "OK, you have a go."

In Ryde, the four-man unit is divided into two groups to approach the lodge where intel indicated the target is located.

With the synchronisation of watches, the assault would go in five minutes. Smack on time, the front attack pair charge, and burst through the central door of the wooden lodge, crashing into the living room; meanwhile, the team at the back make their way via a rear door.

Moments later, the sound of a ferocious dog can be heard coming from another room. Rear assault team are first on the scene. One man takes hold of the round doorknob and swings the door open as the second man rush inside.

The voice of a young woman cries out, "Who's there, and where are you?" The labrador launches at the attackers to defend its owner.

One person holds his pistol out at arms reach, ready to put a bullet in the dog's head and dispatch the annoying hound when one of the others cracks the door open and kicks it outside, closing the door behind it.

"What you do that for? Could have shot the fucking thing."

"Could have, but I, for one, don't shoot blind people's guide dogs. Look the woman can't see a bloody thing."

The assault team leader is about to start questioning her on Steve's whereabouts when he spots the small tracking equipment near the dog's harness.

"Come on, let's get out of here. Appears the bastard Steve gave us all the runaround and planted this..." holding up the device, "planting the tracker on her dog."

The moment the door opens, the mutt barges its way past and ran to its owner, now shaking uncontrollably, tears flooding down her face; "What happened? Why are you attacking me?"

Back at Dennis', the mobile's vibration in Chad's pocket interrupts the snack he is making in the kitchen while chatting to Nicole.

"Have you got the arsehole?"

"Sorry, Chad, it would appear our man is a lot cleverer than we give him credit for. He attached our tracker to an innocent blind woman who has no idea who the fuck Steve is."

"Shit, get your backsides back here ASAP."

Nicole enters the living room, where Dennis is slumped on one of the green leather sofas reading the book he'd picked up in Southampton called 'Danger in Paradise'.

"Made you a few sandwiches, shall I place on the coffee table in front of the television, or would you like them with you?"

"Thanks, Nicole, here would be good, engrossed in this novel. Can you ensure the kids' rooms are ready? They should be here soon."

"Yes, almighty one, right on it, master."

"Come on, you know I don't mean it like that."

Half an hour later, three kids come rushing in, throwing their bags on the long teak dining table, shouting, "Hi, Grandad, we are here."

The youngsters now hugging their grandad are his daughter's three children; Aimee-Leigh, a 13-year-old young woman who already possesses grandeurs of being 18, complete with the attitude to go with it. She should make a perfect young lady, being near five feet tall and a slim figure and plenty of intellect.

The younger of the two girls is Lola-Mae. With her ninth birthday coming up soon, she has the 'I can do anything, try and stop me' mindset. She is the reason I have several horses in the stable, as she loves horse riding.

Joshua, the only boy, who has now relocated himself in front of the TV, is seven and suffers from autism, but he doesn't let anything hold him back. Amazes me how he can already speak a lot of words in different languages.

"Come on, you rabble, you know the rules, bags up to your rooms before you do anything else, plus while you're here, there are some men here working in the cellar, so for this visit only, can you stay out of there, please?"

"OK, whatever," comes the reply from Aimee-Leigh.

At that moment, a figure passes the door, "Chad, can you come and see me? We need to discuss the shipment of the weapons to the boatyard, once the coding is finished."

"Sure will be with you in five."

Chapter Eight — Observation Post Planning

Another shit night with not much kip, sees me up before the sparrows even thought about farting. Might as well make most of the time while the other lazy fuckers continue with their beauty sleep. By God, the ugly gits needed it. For the mission, I plan on making a few things go bang by remote control.

For this, I require several cheap mobiles. The two superstores close by should be open soon. For security reasons, I will purchase five phones from each superstore and PAYG sim cards that require no registration and are therefore untraceable.

Apart from me, not many people in the store doing early morning shopping. The staff are too busy restocking shelves to give a flying shit on what is happening around them. Been here lots of times, so know where to find what I came here for. Task now is to locate the cheapest ones available. Let's face facts here, they only have to ring once; saying that, I need phones with long battery life. The last thing we want is an explosion to fail to go off when required because the power source goes flat.

What I like about supermarkets are the self-service tills. Not a single person to interact with, which means nobody can recognise you when the police come asking stupid questions if everything gets fucked up. Several swipes across the glass plate as the machine reads the barcode, and I purchase the first five sets of phones. Now on to the next store to collect the remaining mobiles.

Back at my place, grab my soldering iron, wire, electrical voltmeter and other bits from the shed, placing it along with the rest of the equipment on the dining table.

The others at long last emerged from their pits by the sounds of the noise coming from the bathrooms and bedrooms. Get the home automaton system 'Alexa' to turn on the coffee machine and make myself a freshly ground beverage. Plonk my arse down at the table, grab up the first phone and remove the back cover and inside until I expose the circuit board.

The plan here is to make them with a failsafe built-in. First, I take out the asymmetrical wheel. This is what makes the telephone vibrate when someone calls the number. Now carefully solder two electrical cables to the electronics, ensuring I mark the positive end. Find the speaker and again join two more to the circuitry for the failsafe. Twist the two positive wires together, the same with the negative ones. Pick up the small hobby craft drill and insert two holes into the casing.

That's the first one nearly finished. All I need to do now is rejoin the two halves of the case, ensuring none of the cables become trapped while poking through the tiny opening I just made. To check everything is working, place one sim card in the mobile and connect the wires to the voltmeter.

When I call the phone, the meter should show a current. The needle shoots rapidly across the dial, indicating all is in operating order. The protruding cables would be attached to the homemade detonators we made the other day. Erring on the side of caution, remove the sim. This will only be put in again once the IED is in position, in case some idiot dialled the wrong number, blowing us to tiny bits of flesh.

About to start the second one when George sits opposite me at the table, "What you doing?"

"The next part of our plan to make things go bang. This is what we will use to remotely set off the bombs if and when required." Hand him the complet mobile.

"Thank God you're on our side, Steve. That's all I can say."

I grin and give him a phone, "You can assist, if you like?"

"Sure, show me what to do."

Moments later, both Simon and Derek appear. "Glad you two lazy bastards are able to join us. Help yourselves to a brew, thought we might go to the café for breakfast once we are finished with this stuff."

"Makes sense to me, Steve, as your cooking skills need a lot of imagination," said Simon, pouring out two brews.

"True, but I do make a fine Polo Donkey casserole."

"See you're making remote detonators," says Derek, examining one of the completed articles.

"Yup, and when you two are ready, I need you to make some vehicle IEDs."

"Not a problem, as long as you tell us how. Both George and Simon said you are an expert in this type of thing."

While brews are being sipped, I spend the next 35 minutes showing and explaining how to make the car bombs out of beer cans acquired the other day.

"Here you go, gents, your lesson plan in making a vehicle IED. Like being back in the Army."

Take hold of one of the beer barrels Simon purchased the other day. "The first and most important step is ensuring we save the life-giving nectar inside," I pour the contents into a white plastic container and secure the lid to prevent our beer from going flat.

"Pass me the angle grinder from in the shed, please, Derek."

Proceed to cut the barrel along its length creating two halves, but ensuring I left the back still connected, this would form the IED top once it is flattened. Next, turn the container on its now lid, then with a small lump hammer pound until flattish.

"Right, gents, now the fun bit."

Take a 7 cm long plastic tube, wrap this heavy-duty wire around the middle. On one side, I make a hole with the point of a screwdriver. Thread the cables through the opening. Wrap the ends around a piece of a metal rod, securing the assembly to the inside.

"As you can see, gents, this is free to move," pivoted it about a few times, "you will see why this is important in the next step."

Grab a 10 cm solid plastic shaft and bang a drawing pin halfway in. Take a length of electrical wire, bare one end and twist this around the pin before hammering it the rest of the way.

"Now, you will see why it is essential the other part can move freely." I pass all cables and the rod through the tube. Squirt a substantial amount of super glue to the top, close the lid.

"Whilst we give the adhesive time to set, do any of you have any questions so far?"

Both give a resounding, "Not yet."

"In that case, let's proceed to the bit which goes bang and fucks up someone's day."

Take one of the nine-volt batteries purchased earlier and glue this to the bottom, inside the barrel. From this, I attach the cable from the shaft. On the other battery terminal, connect another but leave this unattached for now. Under the plunger, I install a tiny square metal plate to which I attach another wire.

"Pass me one of the bags of explosives, please, Simon." Place this inside. "Look closely. This is how everything works, minus the bang," demonstrating as I speak. "Now, when a vehicle runs over the device, this will close, forcing the plunger down. This strikes the plate and completes the electrical circuit to the detonators, and bye-bye vehicle.

"Both of you have done this too many times for me to have to explain that the detonator's wires are only connected once in the ground. For a secondary safety device, to make sure you don't push the lid down too much, I suggest using something like a carrot, hard enough for you to feel the resistance but still easily cut by a car driving over.

"As for the remainder of the cans, slice off the top just below the rim. Inside, place one bag of explosives with one of the mobiles George is finishing off. Don't connect the leads yet. We will do this once they are in place in your OP. For now, mix some extra two-inch nails with the clay you will find in the shed.

"Once you're on location, this will be packed in hard against the explosive mixture. Then if some idiot comes too close to your position, they will not only receive the full force of the blast, but also a body full of flying metal.

"There ends your terrorist lesson for today, questions?"

"Nope, just goes to prove yet again—you're fucking mad, Steve!" says Simon, examining the device.

"True. You need to make another three which, if required, can be laid side-by-side.

The remaining ones we can make into homemade claymores, using the phones as detonators. Before any of you clowns mention the length of time it takes to enter the number, ensure it is pre-programmed into your phone and on fast dial. If you do not have any questions, I suggest you move your lazy backsides and get to work."

"Straight on it, bossman."

Two hours later, with all tasks complete and explosives back in the underground metal storage shed, "OK, who's for some brekkie? George said he is paying."

"Don't mind buying, would hate to see any more moths die when you open your wallet."

"Where did you put the car keys, Steve?"

"Don't need them, Simon. The café is only a few minutes walk from here."

Standing on the corner not far from the rail station, with its extensive windowpanes on two walls projecting out towards the street, an old-fashioned eating establishment. Several weather-stained picnic-style benches with long seats attached on both sides occupy the space under the windows on the outside close to the road.

The window's blue-painted theme continues inside, with the counter and walls painted a light blue. Around 10 plastic-covered tables, each with an array of condiments, fill the interior, one of which is taken by a group of six people. By the way, their uniforms appeared to be identical. So they are part of the same company, probably still claiming they're hard at work somewhere.

Sit at the table for a couple of minutes reading the cafe's menu when an oldish woman in her mid-fifties comes over, complete with a green and white striped apron.

"What can I get you four fine gentlemen, today?" with her pen hovering over a small white notepad.

"I'll have the all-day breakfast and a white coffee, with two extra sausages as well, please?"

"And for you three?"

"I will have the same as the fat boy, minus the extras, but with tea," says George, putting down the menu.

In unison, both Simon and Derek say in a firm, polite manner, "Same."

"So that is four breakfasts, and three coffees and one tea. I'll bring the drinks straight over."

Isn't long before plates filled high land in front of us all. "Tuck in, boys," the waitress says with a pleasant smile.

Wait until the other group leave and the woman enters the kitchen, where she couldn't overhear our conversation. "Thank you for all your assistance so far, Derek. One question we haven't asked... are you into the completion of our mission? If so, we can make it worth your while, plus your expertise will come in very handy."

"Might as well help you boys out. Sounds like fun, and my flight back to St Bethanie isn't for a few more weeks."

"Excellent news, welcome aboard," I mumble while shoving a sausage into my mouth."

Finish stuffing my face for a moment, "In that case, here is the plan for the next stage of the mission. First, before the assault on the properties to retake the equipment, we need to gather more intel on troop movements. For this, I suggest four separate observation posts.

"One needs to go in near the farm complex to monitor people coming and going. Can you take this one, Derek? There is a perfect spot opposite the gate, on the far side of a small pond.?"

"Of course, is it possible for me to carry out a short recce beforehand?"

"Yes, mate. Now on to Dennis' property entrance, think you'll be best suited for this, Simon, because of the transport movements. Once on location, find a suitable spot to place the vehicle IEDS you made. Due to the fact we've already recced the sniper position earlier, no point in explaining where you are going. You already know, George.

"As for me, I will take the boatyard in Cowes. Plan on kayaking up the River Medina, using the cover of darkness and plant explosives on the pier and speedboat to stop any getaway once we assault Dennis' place."

"Sound like a strategy to me. Getting a fresh brew, anyone else fancy one?" says Simon, rising from his chair.

"Better fetch drinks all round."

"I've got an issue of no equipment with me, didn't know about the mission until I arrived and spoke to you lot. Do any of you process a spare Bergen and camo kit?"

"Plenty of extra stuff back at the lodge, Derek, so no need to worry."

"That's sorted then."

Decide it is best, even though the place is still void of people, not to go into more details until we return to my home. So stay for a further 20 minutes or so before finishing up and heading back.

Just as we emerge from the bridleway, which led from Lidl to the park, in the distance, I spot a familiar-looking vehicle speeding away from the direction of my place. "Isn't that George's swimming partner's car?"

"Possible, maybe the idiot still hasn't got the message, will give him high marks for his persistence though," replies Simon, watching him disappear up the road.

Once inside the lodge, "Help yourselves to a cold one if you want, while I find Derek my extra Bergen, waterproofs and other stuff he may need. My trousers might be a bit big for you —"

"Yep, you're a fat bastard, alright," interrupts George.

"Before you opened your trap, I was about to say, Simon, do you have any spare ones that will fit him?"

"Think so, but they are a little crumpled."

"Give them to the ugly Guardsman. The numpty loves nothing more than pressing and cleaning kit."

"If he's lucky, I can shine his boots as well," says George sarcastically.

Moments later, I enter the room with my spare Bergen, "Here you go, even found some other stuff that might come in handy for your OP."

"Cheers, Steve."

"Not a problem, chuck over one of the beers."

Whilst everyone starts to sort out their personal equipment, they would take on their individual OPs. I couldn't get the man and the car out of my head. What if someone is observing the lodge? This would compromise the next stage of the mission if someone watched us leave and, in the worst-case scenario, followed one of us into position—only one thing for it.

Wait for everyone to finish what they were doing before interrupting. "Can not put the notion of some idiot watching this place to the back of my mind. This leaves us with only one course of action to keep the OPs covert. We will need to depart from an alternative location. Are you ready for the best bit? You might want to sit, Tanky... Would hate for you to fall over in shock.

"About three miles from here, over the downs, is an isolated copse. Best we tab there tonight just before last light. Establish a base in which to leave from unseen to our relative positions." Pull out a map from my pack, "We are here," point to our present location. "The woods are here," I draw a line across the map with my finger. "Both of you would be able to take this shorter route to the main entrance, Simon, and be on location before first light.

"The same goes for George. Sorry, Derek, you and I will have to take the long journey, but we are Green Jackets and not afraid of a little tabbing. For safety, and to stop any nosey bastards watching me leave, best I secure the kayak to the car's roof, park in a different location in the resort, and come back to collect the car later.

"Gents, we are under full operation conditions from this moment on, so better take your weapons with you. There is a spare SLR for you, Derek, with 100 7.62 rounds.

"No need to take the vehicle IEDs with us on the OP. Just the three claymores, one each for you three, pointless me taking one. Once in position at the copse, we can go over the finer details. And don't forget to take the Ex-military PRC 350 radios I managed to acquire. These should give us enough range to reach from America Woods to Cowes."

"I spent years as the CO radio operator. If you like, I can try and boost the signal strength for you. One issue is the PRC 350 only has an operating distance of up to 4 km; therefore, it will be no good for you in Cowes, Steve."

"Cheers, Derek, that would be useful. Might have to use text messages to contact me."

Take a glance down at Mickey, who tells me the time is now 13:00 and last light isn't until 19:30, giving us plenty of time to ensure all our kit is packed away correctly with no annoying rattles.

Everyone here is a professional, with the three of us knowing how each other worked. This is gained over time, plus the many missions completed together since we met at Combat Stress. The only variable now is Derek. He operated the boat, which helped us depart from St Halb in a hurry, and even joined the gunfight on St Bethanie's pier. Have no doubts in my mind that he will pick things up quickly.

Each takes turns putting on all their kit and running backwards and forwards before diving to the ground, then repeating while the others listen for any unwanted sounds. I go last, running forward, leapt to the floor. As I get up, detect the deafening noise of metal on metal. To most people, this would hardly be audible, but at night sound travels further. Detectable to anyone listening. Worse of all, I fucked up, and those three arseholes are going to take the proverbial piss out of me.

"Thought we are only taking professionals on this operation," comes from Simon, sitting down and laughing to himself.

"Do one, Donkey Walloper," rearranging the ammo magazines in the pouch on my webbing belt.

Each of us spend the next couple of hours preparing the mission equipment. The range of the radios are being increased by Derek, while I double check all the explosives. Meanwhile, George sets up the control panel for the sniper rifle on the dining table, confirming he still possesses a link enabling him to fire the weapon.

We wouldn't be taking the box with us, so after he confirms he is entered into the system, called us all over individually to check our details and fingerprints. Not being with us when Mark programmed us all in, Derek needs to be fully integrated with the primary system.

With all the tactical stuff sorted and packed, attention turns to rations we would need for the OPs. First, of course, we will not be able to cook due to the risk of a naked flame being seen. Fortunately, I anticipated this and stocked up the fridge with a selection of cooked meats, cheese and other stuff. In addition, in the cupboard several packets of oatmeal biscuits and bread.

With our OPs being silent, I remove the contents from any wrappers that would rustle or make any sound when opening.

Luckily on my many flights in British Airways business class, I managed to build up a napkins collection that I borrowed on a permanent basis.

Wrap up several sandwiches I make in these. For any reason we had to extend the observation phase of our mission, pack enough rations for two days. So while the boys follow my example and prepare their own rations, I grab a fresh brew and slump back on the sofa running the plan through my head numerous times.

This part of the mission, and come to think about the whole task in hand, should go without any significant problems as now Derek has joined us, we now have the perfect four-man team; consisting of an explosive expert in myself, Simon, a specialist in reconnaissance, George, a skilled sniper, and Derek, our communication professional.

But as he is an unknown, the boys will keep an eye on him during the OP stage.

Soon joined by the rest, who'd also finished with what they were doing. "Best to leave in about half an hour to reach the night RV with still some daylight left. Even though walking in a line 50 metres apart makes perfect tactical sense, it would look stupid to the civies.

"For that reason, Derek and I will lead off first, with you two following 20 minutes later. As per SOPs on operations, I will leave the usual markers at each change in direction, so keep an eye out. Pass me a sheet of paper, I will draw a sketch map to give you a basic idea of the route. Take it there are no questions, then give me time to go and park the car somewhere, and we can depart."

Great, our nosey friend is nowhere to be seen. Out of habit, give the vehicle a once over to confirm nothing has been tampered with, securing the kayak to the roof with webbing straps and a locking cable- would be fucked if I returned later to find some arsehole pinched the bloody thing.

Find the perfect spot in among other parked cars down a gravel road that some of the owners had dubbed Dibble Lane, to the rear of my lodge.

When I return, the rest are waiting for the off with their kit on and weapons concealed in black bags out of view of any person we encounter on route. Sling on my own Bergen, pick up the SLR, which the boys placed in a bag for me, and turned to Derek, "You ready, mate?"

"Ready as I will ever be, let's make a move."

Like I say, there is no need to spread out at this stage, so we walk together, chatting away. To any onlookers, we would give the impression of two men going for a hike.

After walking through the park for around 10 minutes, we approach a bend in the road. There is no point in leaving a marker here, as I explain and shown Simon and George the route while walking through the park previously. Shortly after, reach the start of a small dirt path no more than five metres across. A quick observation indicates nobody is watching us. Bend down on one knee on the right of the trail, break off a stem of a green bush. With this, I form a 10 cm arrow facing up the track.

The first part of the route contains the most turns. It isn't long before we encounter the next one. This time, turning left off the footpath we are on and leading to the Red Squirrel Way. A more prominent marker would be needed here. Bend a thin, growing sapling in the direction of travel.

While I do this, Derek scrapes another arrow in the mud at the tarmacked trail's edge, indicating a turn right is required. Of course, anyone with half a brain would think this is blatantly obvious to any idiot, but you would be surprised what people don't see even if something looked wrong and staring them in the face.

The following change in direction isn't for another kilometre or so. Both of us knew better than to discuss any mission while walking. Anyone might overhear the conversation, so covering the ground to the next turning is carried out in silence.

Once we reach there, I turn to Derek, "Can you make a mark here? I'm going up to the top of this track, where it turns right over the bridge we just went under."

"No problem, will join you in a moment."

This muddy path ends about 40 metres from turning off the Red Squirrel trail. At the end of the track, you can go either left or right. We would turn right across the brick bridge. The parapet on both sides stood about one and a half metres from the trail.

The majority of people who come the way I did would only stare aimlessly directly at the wall immediately to their front, the one on the left and be oblivious to the wall's start on their right. Thus, reach down, grab a medium-sized stone, placing it at the beginning of the right-hand parapet.

"From here, the route is all narrow tracks separated from the wild green grass-covered fields on either side by barbed-wire fencing. The majority of the way being uphill, this should make Simon groan. Talking of which, they should have left by now," I say as Derek rejoins me at the overpass.

With me leading, we start up the steady incline towards the treeline in the distance. The only sound audible is the wind blowing steadily over the open ground, interrupted by the occasional mooing of cattle far off in some other part of the downs.

Ahead, emerging from the opening in the copse to our front, I could see the outline of two figures heading down the track. Turn around, "We have company. Try to conceal the SLR, best you can."

Hold onto the pistol grip and lay the rifle vertically along the side of my body, shield with my right arm. Derek is doing the same as me, and his weapon is now out of view.

With what seems like ages, the now visible older couple dressed in bright red waterproofs come within passing distance. Half out of courtesy and the other half to ensure they bypassed on the opposite side to my hopefully concealed weapon, I step up the verge.

As they go past, "Hi, a great day for hiking."

"Sure is," comes the reply.

Once the couple walked to a point they couldn't overhear us, "Derek, contact George on the radio to warn them that two people are approaching." Worked with them a long time and knew they would take cover, giving the impression that only one group of men travelled this way.

The area for the RV is in the woods we just entered. I've walked this way many times and noticed a suitable location away from prying eyes, just off the trail by about 100 metres on the reverse edge of the extensive woods.

Due to the heavy rain a few nights back, plus the cover from the trees stretching overhead across the trail preventing the wet ground from drying out, this resulted in the soil underfoot becoming soft and muddy, making it hard going. One slender area ran up the right, which looks solid and broad enough to walk on. This gave the only relief from the mud. I'm taking that route, I think to myself.

Finally reach the point on the other side, where the route is blocked by a metal fence spanning the gap between two wooden posts. However, a separate trail now led off along the back of the woods. This is the one we need to take. While I indicate the way we are heading, Derek kept a watch back down the way we had just come.

At last, we reach the location of the RV. To be safe, conceal ourselves a short distance away and stand off for a while to ensure nobody else is in the area. After 15 minutes, make the command decision the site is void of anyone.

The place I'd chosen is ideal for our requirements. Trees are packed together but far enough apart to allow sufficient light to enter through the canopy, to enable dense patches of ferns to grow and blanket the ground beneath. Towards the edges, vast areas of brambles not only provided cover but would act as a natural barrier. If any person walked accidentally into that during the night, they are going to make a noise.

Find myself a nice patch of undergrowth and burrow underneath before taking the poncho from the Bergen. With the help of two short poles, erect an inverted V-shaped tent. Make sure that the cape is not visible from the outside by covering it with extra ferns. Turn to look at Derek, to watch him doing the same. The other two should be here soon. Half an hour later, George appears, entering the RV.

"Glad you could join us. Where's Simon?"

"Behind me, he is changing the direction of your markers to face the way we came, in case we need them for the way back, it will be dark then."

"Sounds good to me. Find a spot somewhere over by the trees."

"Why you grunts enjoy walking miles carrying heavy kit is beyond me, you're all fucking idiots if you ask me."

Crawling out from the ferns, "You made it then, Simon! Steve and George said you're not one for tabbing. So, to make you feel comfortable, I scouted the area. Found an old cattle water trough complete with a hole in the bottom. You can turn it the wrong way up..."

"Come on, then let's hear it," says Simon, dropping his Bergen next to a massive tree.

"Was going to say, climb underneath and stick your head out and pretend you're a Tank Commander."

"Well, that didn't take you long, Derek, to join the other two arseholes. What regiment were you in again, oh yes, a Green Howard or as some would say 'falling plates'."

"Actually, a Rifleman in the Royal Green Jackets..."

Once I compose myself and stop laughing, "Leave it there, Derek, the Donkey Walloper knows what regiment you were in."

Leave the others to settle in while I clear a section of the ground, using twigs, rocks, and other stuff around, construct a rough layout of Dennis' place and the boatyard.

Chapter Nine – RV

Reach into my Bergen and pull out one of the explosive packs. However tempting this might be, the people who might stumble across us are more likely to be innocent civvies and not one of the professional men from Chad's group. Now when it comes to killing someone, I don't have an issue if they deserve it. Take the people at Dennis' place, for example. When they took up arms, they accepted the risk of being killed, a bit like us. The fear of dying is what keeps me from making stupid mistakes.

Instead, I better use the radio and receivers from the last mission, a far safer option. So I dig deeper into my pack until I find the package containing a high-breaking strength fishing line, batteries, clothes peg, and receiver.

First light tomorrow isn't until 06:35, which means we will not be departing here until 04:30. Therefore a protective perimeter is required around the RV. Probably need a couple, one on the route we entered and another one across the gate, which divided the track and the open ground of the downs.

On the way to position the first tripwire, pass Simon crawling from his hide. "Off to set up our defences, fancy knocking up one of your famous Army chuckins?"

"Sure, no problem, Steve, will get straight on to it."

Stand off from the iron gate inside the treeline, listening for any sound of movements coming from either direction. Wait five minutes to ensure nobody goes into the area. This will be a gamble. Didn't expect any hikers to pass through this late in the evening, but experience tells me not to take chances. Could have unwelcome visitors during the night.

Some think I learned from last time. Rather than having several individual components, they are installed neatly inside a shallow plastic container, with an opening on one edge and a hole on the adjoining side. This would allow the insulator to be placed between the two halves of the clothes peg, which is fastened close to the side of the box and near to the slot. All makes the setting up a much quicker affair.

I take a paracord length from my jacket pocket and secure the package to the bottom of the wooden post, close to the opening part. Then, unwind a small amount of the line, attaching this to the metal upright; the other end, I fasten a short twig I found laying close by.

Press the point from my multi-tool through the hole in the container, prising open the jaws of the peg. Into this, I place the twig. The piece of wood is now acting as a circuit breaker. Once the gate is opened, the wire will be pulled out, re-establishing the connection, setting off the alarm in my earpiece.

Return after inserting the second of the security measures, to find the rest sitting near a fire pit a few feet deep, which Simon constructed to conceal the flames as he made dinner.

"Here you go, get that down you," George hands me a plate of Army chuckn.

"Cheers, mate, is there a brew on the go?"

"One beverage coming up," says Derek, pouring boiling water from the vessel on the fire into a black plastic mug.

"Thanks, Derek. As we don't have much daylight left, I think it's best to eat the scran around my target zones model I prepared earlier."

"Makes sense, plus the SLRs still requires a check zero," replies Simon, between shovelling food into his mouth.

Once everyone is sitting where they could scrutinise the whole map, I take out a car aerial I always used as a pointer. "Here is Dennis' place. The twigs represent the boundary wall, with this stone indicating primary residence. The front entrance is on this edge," I point at the plan. "Conceal yourself in this area, Simon."

"Think the place we used the other day will be my best location. It is not visible from the idiots operating the gate and provides me with plenty of cover from view. One question, do you know of a back way here, or will I need to go the same way as last time?"

"Yes, Simon, as mentioned earlier, there is a short way. I will brief you separately with the map at the end."

"Cheers, mate."

"Ok, let us move on to the next OP, which is your one, George." Again, with the aid of my pointer, point to the ambush site's location we marked up on our visit to America Woods. "As you are familiar with the area and the firing position, suggest you enter from the rear, by following the treeline along from the point we cross the road. Questions?"

"Not at the moment," says George, sipping away at his brew.

"Sorry, mate, things are a bit trickier for you, Derek, as you haven't seen the location of your potential OP yet. Shame you didn't have time to visit the scene as you wanted." Once again, indicating to the ground, "You need to conceal yourself around here at the back of the pond, in a position you can see the farm complex."

"One question, is it better to go through the woods or via the lodge?" asks Derek, while making notes.

"Best you take the same route as Simon and George, to a point where George leaves you, then follow the track to the farm. I will draw a map later for you. An alternative route is via my place. You will find a road that leads away around a bend from the farmhouse. Follow that. You can then double back into location."

"Thanks, Steve."

"Before we move onto my own OP, you three will be keeping track of people's movements between locations. It is essential to know who is where and when once we carry out the mission's attack on Dennis' place and the boatyard. To do this, I suggest that besides the notes and logs you all will make, we use the radios.

"For example, if Derek witnesses two persons leave the farm, he broadcasts 'DR out two'. Let's presume they will take the same trail between the properties. Your task here, George, to confirm that when they pass you. Any suggestions on how?"

"An easy one, if they cross George's location after I made my call, he can say 'GD, F two', to indicate they came from the direction of the farm. If they come after Simon, he can say, 'GD, D two'. The same applies to checking them into the new location, i.e. 'DR, in, two'.

"Perfect, Derek, that's why I'm glad we now have a communications expert on board. Now, if one of you signals people leaving your perspective locations and are called in without George's confirmation, we can assume they are varying their routes. The primary objective, gents, is to find out as much as possible how many people are in each location overnight. Any more questions before I continue to the Cowes boatyard, OP?" All three shake their heads as they continue to eat.

"My plan is to go back to the campsite to collect the car before driving to Newport, keeping on the East Cowes' side of the river. Then, if all goes without any problems, I will launch the kayak from a point close to the Beefeater restaurant and proceed downstream until I reach the sailing craft moored up in the harbour.

"From here, while it is hopefully still dark, climb under one of the tarpaulins of one of the boats and set up my observation post overlooking the pontoon and yard on the opposite bank.

As Derek said, I will have my own radio but will be out of range most of the time. So my phone will be on vibrate only if you need me."

Before continuing, I grab a fresh brew from the pot George left on the fire's embers. "Almost there, gents, need to cover the continuity plans, then we are done. Let us start with me. If something goes wrong with my task, I will head for Simon's position, stopping on the route when I have a signal to transmit the following, 'boat out'. Then, when I'm approaching Simon once again, I will send a message, 'location plus five'; don't fancy a bullet up the jacksy from Simon."

"What I understood from that is when Steve fucks up, turn my radio off and shoot any fucker who gets too close."

"Wouldn't expect anything less from a Donkey Walloper, Simon."

"Back to you three idiots. If any position is compromised, send the message, 'bugging out', preceded with your own call sign. Remember, if only one shot comes in your direction, don't be a wimp and stay put. Could be somebody taking a hoping gunshot?"

"What the fuck is a hoping gunshot?" asks Derek, looking puzzled.

"When someone fires wildly at a location in the hope someone is lurking in the bushes and returns fire," Simon intervens.

"Emergency RV will be at the bridge we crossed to make our way to this position. Avoid my place, more than likely a nasty surprise waiting for us if we go return back to the lodge.

"If all goes to plan, we will rendezvous back here at 18:30 the day after tomorrow. Any more questions, gents?"

"Not from me," says George, tapping his head gently with the index finger of his right hand.

"In that case, apart from George, the weapons still need to be zeroed. To keep the noise to a minimum, only use three rounds each. The sniper will spot for you, as he's nothing else to do as his rifle does everything for him."

"Easy life, hey Steve."

Chose this place because there is a natural dip in the ground running down the middle, acting as a sound barrier and slightly muffling the distinctive crack and thump as the 7.62 round left the rifle barrel and hit the target.

While the others mill around, I need to find a spot with a simple dirt bank to stop the bullets from travelling into the distance. Maybe hitting some living or dead thing. Besides the healthy kick, the weapon processes, if not held correctly, this is something every recruit found out during basic training the hard way. Remembered nursing a bruised shoulder for a week. The SLR has an effective range of about 800 metres.

After a short search, I locat an ideal spot about 100 metres away from our location. Here, the earth, for some unknown reason, had piled up over time. Not having any figure 12 targets at hand, would have to do with a white piece of card. On this, I draw a circle in the centre. Place this approximately one metre high, on a tree that conveniently stood immediately in front of the bank. With the aid of a walking app on my phone, mark out a distance of 25 metres from the cardboard target. This would be the firing position.

"Saw you over here. Want me to spot for you?" comes the voice from behind me.

Turn around to discover George making his way towards me. "Yes, please."

With rifle in my left hand, lay on the floor facing the target. Grab the pistol grip, pull the SLR tightly into my right shoulder. I don't want to get kicked by the bloody thing. Remembering my training, ensure the left arm's elbow is tucked in and the right leg bent, to form a stable shooting position.

Close the left eye and look through the rear aperture along the weapon's top, to the front sight at the tip of the stock. With the end of the horizontal bar placed in the circle's centre, take a deep breath. Let this out, breathed in again, exhaling halfway before holding my breath. Take up the first pressure, pause for a split-second before squeezing the trigger the whole way.

The recoil forces the SLR hard into my shoulder, as the 7.62 mm round exits the rifle at 823 metres per second, making me flinch, as it did, been a long time since I sensed the force of this fantastic weapon.

"Not too bad, but low, right," said George, looking through his binos.

Make the necessary changes to the rear sights before taking aim once more. Carry out the same routine as the first shot, squeeze the trigger until the bullet strikes home.

"Better, mate, will make a sniper out of you yet. Fire your last shot to confirm and you're all set to kill some bad guys."

"Cheers, George."

The third and final round hits the middle of the target, "That will do me! If you stay here, I will go back and send one of the others over to you."

Back at the RV, I find Simon covering the earlier fire with dirt to ensure they didn't glow in the darkness. "You will find George down that way, on the makeshift firing range, where you can zero your rifle."

"On my way, boss man."

The light is starting to fade as Derek and George return from the range. "All sorted, gents?" Both give the thumbs-up signal and head to their hides.

Not wanting to shout out, proceed to each of them in turn, "Meet me at the firepit in five minutes." Meanwhile, I walk over to my own hide and pull a one-litre container from the Bergen.

Once everyone joins me, "Just a couple of points before our mission enters the next stage. First, and most importantly, who wants a drink?" I hold out the bottle of Southern Comfort.

"Thought you would never ask," says Simon, handing me a black plastic mug.

"Fancy one, Derek?"

"Yes, please, I know I'm the new boy around here, but is this normal before a mission?

"Yep, our motto, always take time to relax before any operation. Never know, it could be your last." Pour him and George a generously sized drink.

"A toast to our new task and hope to see all you ugly bastards at the end."

"I'll drink to that," Simon said, raising his mug.

The next hour is spent laughing at the fuckups each of us made while in the British Army, and other operations worldwide. Of course, the arsehole reminds me of when I fell flat on my face in St Halb.

"Better call it time — an early start in the morning for us all. Zulu time will be 04:30, giving us over seven hours from now. Which means approximately two-hour stags each.

"If Simon takes the first one, I'll take the second watch, then Derek, followed by George."

"Well, you can do one. Did the last shit stag on our previous mission."

"Don't worry, George, I'm new to the group, so I'll take the last one. Anywhere in particular for the guard post?" Derek enquires as he picks up his rifle.

After a short discussion, it is agreed that we might as well patrol around every 20 mins, using our current spot as the sentry post.

Feel like I've only been in my pit for five minutes when I sense the sensation of someone shaking my foot. Then, through my half-opened eyes, I see the figure of Simon holding his index finger to his lips.

Once up and crouching next to him, "What's the problem?"

"Sounds like," he points to his earpiece, "someone's tripped one of your alarms."

Silently as we can in the pitch darkness, delicately make our way to the track, running across the position's back edge. Take up a firing stance behind a patch of foliage, close to the edge of the copse, and look both ways. Just about to move to head in the direction of the gate when Simon grabs me from behind.

"Look to your left about 50 metres. Someone is coming this way."

"Fuck, you're right," I glance down at the illuminated dial of my watch. "Far too late for hikers. Here is what we will do, you go along the trail a few metres to our right, I'll stay here. Once they pass me, I will pounce on them from the rear. You come at him from the front."

As the man passes, I leap up, running hard towards the person walking cautiously down the path. Jump off the ground, hitting them with my full force, knocking him to the floor, temporarily thumping the wind out of him. As the man starts to lash out, Simon joins the affray, receiving a punch to the face as he does. Having none of this, Simon strikes him several times in the head with well-placed blows of his own.

"Grab the fucker's hands, Steve."

Manage to hold them still enough for Simon to get a heavy-duty cable tie around his wrists. Then, to muffle the shouts now echoing from between his lips, shove a snotty handkerchief from my jacket pocket into his mouth as he receives a massive kick to the gut from Simon.

"Let's take the idiot back to the RV to find out if he is an innocent passerby or someone else, Simon." What he says will determine what the next course of action is likely to be.

"OK," Simon produces a thick black pouch. "Put this over the man's head, as he hasn't seen the other two and our location."

With one arm interlocked through our now protesting individual appendage, with Simon doing the same on the other side, I force his head towards the ground while keeping his arms high, making the captive easy to move.

Back in the RV, Derek and George overhear the commotion. Both have adopted a kneeling position with rifles raised, ready to fire and pointing in our direction.

"Who is your friend?" George asks, lowering his weapon.

"Not sure yet. Need to interrogate the man a little first." Selecting my words carefully, if this person happens to be just the incorrect place at the wrong time, then expressions such as 'interrogate' would have him shitting himself.

To reinforce the fear factor, take away all his clothing, apart from his boxers. Remove the cable tie from his wrists, snatch both arms to the front, fastening a length of paracord before lashing this to a nearby tree. Make sure it is high enough to make our new friend stretch, pull his legs back to make him have to stand on the balls of his feet.

"Right, I'm going to ask you a few questions. Then, depending on your answers, I will decide if you leave here alive or not. Nod if you understand." The man nod.

Take the rag from his mouth. "Now then, who are you and what the fuck are you doing walking around woods at night. Think before you answer. Your life does rely on me believing you."

With a voice of defiance, he answers, "My name is Martin. Couldn't sleep, so I went for a walk across the downs, when I overheard what I believed to be high-velocity weapons being shot. Being ex-military, decided to investigate."

"Nope, don't believe you," I land a punch to the man's side, "try harder," he doubles up in silent pain. "Let us give that one more go."

"It's the fucking truth. Let me fucking go."

About to land another well-placed blow when George pulls me to one side.

"Been going through our friend's kit, found his mobile, need his fingerprint to open."

"No problem, give it here." Took the mobile and head back to our man, who is now starting to shiver uncontrollably.

"Require a finger to unlock your phone," I reach behind the tree, take his index digit, bending it that far backwards, nearly breaking it in the process. He yells out in pain. Place the sensor on the finger, the telephone unlocks, showing a fascinating screensaver.

Throw the mobile at Derek, "Go through his contact list, check if there are any names or numbers you recognise."

Within a few minutes, Derek pulls me to one side, beyond the hearing range of the prisoner. If he is an innocent person, no point in him being able to identify all our voices.

"Seems like the man has signed his own death certificate. Look here," Derek scrolls through the list, stopping on Chad, "We have more. Here are Dennis' and Stuart's numbers. This could be coincidental!"

"Only one way to find out," I remove the hood from our friend's head, while shoving the phone directly in front of his face. "Any reason you have these numbers in your mobile?"

"Easy, I work for Chad. Wait, I meant to say, Dennis," as the words tumble and trip from his mouth.

"Take it that is not you, in this group of 16 men behind the board saying 'Seal Team Six' in this photo, with everyone dressed in pretty US Navy SEAL uniforms then?"

Our friend grins, as he knew the game now is up, "Yeah, that's me, what you fuckwits going to do about it?"

"Nothing much, but you now know where we are, and no doubt that you being as highly trained as I believe you are, you've been taking notes on any noises you heard to work out how many of us might be here. Plus, from the sounds of cocking rifles, you know what weapons we are armed with. As you can see, I'm now faced with a problem—"

"Go fuck yourself," he interrupts.

Then without saying another word, reach inside my jacket pocket and take out the trusty multitool, unfolding the razor-sharp blade.

"Well, Navy SEAL, seal this," as I draw the knife slowly across his throat, cutting deep into his neck, feeling the slight resistance of the windpipe as the blade slices through its thick texture. Dark red blood oozes, gradually at first before turning into a torrent from the wound as he thrashes about, gurgling as life drifts away, leaving a limp body hanging from the tree.

Not flinching for the slightest moment, Simon, George and Derek cut him down and dispose of the body in the undergrowth, concealing the blood at the base with fresh earth.

"You sliced a man's throat, doesn't it bother you, Steve?" asks Derek, staring into my face, probably looking for some kind of empathy for the poor man.

"Of course it does. Despite what people say, I am human. Now I need to wipe the arsehole's blood from my knife. Pass me the man's jacket."

"Stop looking for answers, Derek. You won't find any. That man doesn't have any feelings," says George, pulling him away.

The RV is compromised, so there is no point in staying here, "Grab your kit, gents, let's bug out. We will head for the emergency RV."

With me leading and the others following at 20 metres intervals, head with caution through the night down the track. Through the pitch-black darkness of the night, the bridge appears to my front. Stretch out my right arm and slowly lower it to the floor several times.

This is the signal to the boys behind to take to the ground. Each person covering a separate arc, with Simon at the rear of the line, facing the way we came, while George and Derek take alternate sides, while I covered the front, stood off for 10 minutes to confirm nobody else was in the area.

Once positive in my mind, everything is clear. After a quick check over my shoulder, walk across the small bridge and through the metal gate on the other side towards the secondary RV; the rest follow in silence. This location doesn't have identical protection as the last RV, only a deep hedgerow running along the path heading downhill, but it didn't need to be. Time is now getting on, and we would be leaving soon for our individual Ops, so this place will have to do.

"Find a spot—make yourselves comfortable for the next four hours gents. Might as well continue with the same stag rota, George, you are up next.

"One last thing, we can't go back to the previous location, in case they are waiting for us. This is now the primary FRV, and the emergency RV is now at the edge of the resort, where we entered the first dirt track from the campsite." I didn't ask for any questions as I knew they understood what I've just said.

Chapter Ten – Steve's OP

Lay awake, staring into the blackness of the night, listening to an owl hooting in the distance. All the while, the procedure for reaching the observation post in Cowes acts out in my mind, each time, ensuring every eventuality and every turn is planned out in my head. If I leave at the purposed time, there would be no way I could reach my OP before sunrise. For this, I would need to go now.

Crawl down inside my maggot, closing the top to prevent any light from escaping. I remove my notebook, pen and torch, draw a quick sketch of the route to the farmhouse. And the position of Derek's observation post. To get to my own location on time, Derek would have to travel with the others.

Note finished, all kit packed away, I make my way to where Derek is concealed in the undergrowth. A gentle shake of the bottom of his sleeping bag sees him bolting up, looking in my direction.

"Change of plan, mate. I have to go now, so you will have to make your own way. Suggest you leave with Simon and George until they turn off the track to go to their own OPs. From there, I've drawn you a new map to your OP," I pass him the drawing.

"Not a problem, Steve. See you once the OPs are over."

"One last thing before I depart. Every three hours, at 18 minutes past each hour, starting at 08:18, will transmit you the following message via text, 'S3 OK'. Then, once you've received the radio check from the other two again at 17 minutes past the hour, at the same hourly intervals, send me a message saying no more than 'all OK' if everything is going to plan. Any questions?"

"Nope, now fuck off so I can get some sleep."

Pick up the Bergen, along with the SLR and head off into the night, following the identical route we used to the RV. Not long before I reach the resort. Need to make my way across the park without being seen by security staff or any other idiot taking an early morning stroll. Not wishing to draw attention to myself if seen, conceal the weapon out of view.

So far, everything is going as expected. The car is still where I left it. More importantly, no thieving bastards helped themselves to my kayak. Not leaving anything to chance, stand off for a couple of minutes to check the surrounding area for anybody who might be watching the vehicle.

About to move when a light appears in a window of one of the caravans close by. Through the gap in the curtains, see the figure of a woman, still half asleep from the way she walks. Now stood in front of the sink, drinking from a glass. After a few minutes, the place is in darkness again; time to make my move.

I open the rear driver's side door and throw my Bergen and rifle on the seat, before closing it as quietly as possible so as not to wake any nosey people. Drive off with only a slight pressure on the accelerator, not wanting the engine to rev up too much, causing unwanted noise. Once I am 110 metres away from the accommodation, turn on the headlights and depart for East Cowes.

My original plan was to launch my kayak near the Beefeater restaurant, just on the edge of Newport. Then paddle downstream, to one of the small sailing boats which are moored opposite the boatyard. Because this idiot fucked up the timings, and I am the group's planner, this is now not possible. An alternative launching site is now required. Lucky for me, I know the ideal spot much closer. The new plan, park up in the East Cowes Esplanade long-stay car park, a small area situated between rows of residential houses and close to the ocean.

Would launch from the tiny stony beach no more than a couple of metres deep on the backside of the Sharpe Breakwater. A barrier a few feet wide stretches out to sea for about 300 metres, protecting the boats moored in the harbour. Even when the tide was entirely in, it appeared several feet above the waterline.

Perfect, it is still dark when I arrive. A short drive along the road, which ran parallel to the seafront, confirms no sign of anyone in the area. Make a u-turn at the end. Switch off the lights and drive to towards a space near the parking area's rear.

Wait for a few minutes to confirm nobody follows me. Then, clamber out of the vehicle and walk over to the ticket machine. When returning after the OP, the last thing I would need is to find some arsehole with a tow truck had kindly removed my car to the pound.

With the ticket displayed in a prominent position on the dash, the car is checked several times to ensure it is locked. Now time to prepare the yellow and green kayak. To the front, attach a night vision camera that fits in the palm of my hand. This is something that came with the purchase of my new Blackview BV9700 mobile phone.

Clip the cable into the lines that extended the whole length. Once I am in the cockpit ready to depart, I will connect the other end to the telephone and use the camera to have a clear view of where I'm going.

From the boot of the car, pull out my dry suit; I might as well stay dry and warm, just in case I happen to roll over. With all the equipment stored in the kayak's storage compartments, it is time to get the observation post underway.

After a final check for people, I pick-up the kayak, resting it on my right shoulder and cross the road to the seafront. Step over the small wall to the pebbled beach, keeping the Sharpe Breakwater to my left. Once in the water, I place the spraydeck in position and started to paddle around to the moored boats.

Because the tide isn't in fully, the structure stood four feet above sea level, providing plenty of cover from anyone on the other side. Across the Solent, the unmistakable shape of the early morning car ferry emerges close to the coast guard tower on Calshot Beach.

From this point, the ship would take 30 minutes to reach Cowes, giving me sufficient time to round the sea defence and hide behind the barrier out of the view of the crew, never mind the half-asleep passengers.

With the paddle resting on the top, I hold on to the breakwater as the ferry glides effortlessly past. I observe the captain out on the ship's wing through my night vision camera, ready to dock his ship in East Cowes. Immediately the vessel passes, I push myself off in the direction of the sailing boats bobbing up and down, caused by the wake of the passing ferry.

Start to recognise the shapes of buildings on the opposite side. A good indication first light isn't far away, and I still need to get to a position opposite the boatyard. Found the perfect boat at the end of the row. A canvas sheet had been spread over the boom and tied down on each side of the sailboat, forming a tent-like structure. Due to the mast rising from the cabin, this left a tiny gap at the leading edge. I would use this as the OP.

After securing the kayak, I lift the rear flap and pull myself in. Fortunately, the craft is generous in size. Towards the bow, a door leads into a modest cabin. Inside, a table fills the centre space, the galley is off to the right, a seating area to the left. In fact, the area under the cover is sufficient for me to sit up and watch out without causing any indentation in the fabric's shape.

Might even use the kitchen at some point, but first, I want to bring my equipment on board. This includes the kayak. Leaving it tied up on the outside is not an option, as it may indicate someone is snooping around. Right, everything inside, time to set up the observation post for the next 36 hours or so.

Place my Bergen to my right and reach in, pulling out the binoculars, which I arrange on the bulkhead, along with my mobile phone. Also take out the solar-powered battery bank, slipping this out of the front of the canvas to catch the daylight once it appeared over the horizon. Bearing in mind the radio in my pack is out of the others' range, I need to make sure the telephone doesn't go flat. The rest of my kit would remain packed away, ready for a quick withdrawal if required.

Made it, I'm in a position with everything ready before the first rays of light reflect off the surface of the sea. Plus, there is still one hour before I am required to transmit my first message to Derek. Time for a brew before settling back to observe the movements going on the boatyard's pier.

The approach to the main harbour looked calm and tranquil in the early morning light. A few people are milling about near the water's edge, close to the Royal Yacht Club; besides, Cowes appears void of life. For the moment, the target is quiet apart from the occasional appearance of one of the armed guards parading down on the pier.

What didn't register the first time I looked over through the binos earlier, the speedboat. The same one Simon climbed on the other day is not tied up at the pontoon. Wonder where the fuck that is? While taking a sip of my coffee, I turn to the entrance of the harbour. Well, at least the question of the missing boat is about to be answered, as it entered the Medina River heading for the boatyard.

Within minutes, the vessel is secured in position, the continuous humming noise from the engines becoming silent. An assortment of people gather at the stern. Need a better gander at this, so focus on the group. Men, women and children dressed in bright red lifejackets are escorted from the boat along and up the ramp. From what I could see into the building, looks like our friend Dennis is into more than straightforward arms dealing. From what I just witnessed, the man's got a sideline in people smuggling as well.

Always wondered how the illegal immigrants arrived on the Isle of Wight. Spotted them many times, crossing from the island to the mainland on the Red Funnel ferry. You can always tell them apart from other passengers, as they are the ones carrying empty suitcases trying to look like holidaymakers.

Glanc down at my watch. Time is coming up to 18 minutes past eight, time to send the first text to Derek. To save time, I preprogramme the information yesterday. Message sent 'S3, OK'; still staring at the mobile, waiting and hoping everything is going to plan and the others are safely in their individual OPs. I don't have to wait long before it starts to vibrate in my hand. The message read, 'All, OK'. I exhale as my shoulders drop in satisfaction, all in place; the mission is underway.

Can't see anything happening over at the boatyard. Might as well utilise the time to check and assemble the remote detonated IEDs I'm planning to use, to separate the pontoon ramp and the shore. Remove each in turn from the dry bags. Now is the time to double-check the detonator is still inserted into the explosive. The trailing wires are exposed from the phone being used as the remote.

Delicately open the back to confirm the power pack isn't in situ. Positive in my mind, it is still in my Bergen, but you can never be too careful. Plus, I don't fancy getting blown to fucking bits if some numpty dials the wrong number. The battery will go in once I'm under the pier later tonight.

Once I connect the wires from the mobile and IED, return them back to the sacks. Ensured the wire used to extend the aerial and therefore, the range is sticking out of the top of the mobile.

Place them on one side, ready to go until the niggling voice in my head reminds me that everything gets put away when not in use, in case I need to bug out. Like a conforming soldier packed them away. Better see what's happening back at Dennis' place. No sooner I pick up the binos, right on time, the Red Funnel ferry crosses in front of me.

On the other side, two figures appear, standing on the quayside behind the boathouse, one of them looking in my direction through binoculars. After what seems like ages and feeling like the mission is compromised, the tall figure slowly lowers the binoculars. This is the man who knocked into me while in town. According to his profile, he goes by the name Jackson and is Chad's second in command. Standing next to him, another man I don't recognise. Not a problem. After the episode in Newport, I got Mark to send us all the known players' photographs, which are now stored on my phone's memory card.

A quick flick through the pictures has me stopping on Stuart. That's interesting as, according to Mark, he finished working for Dennis a while back. So it would seem our man is playing on both sides. Note all this down on my notebook as not to forget anything on the OP debrief.

Minutes later, they are joined by a third man, dragging another body harshly by their jacket. The fourth person tries their best to struggle free, but in vain. Soon they are standing in front of Jackson. The dragged figure is an older man in his sixties, dressed in baggy brown trousers and a tattered old blue coat. I could hear people shouting from my location, but I am too far away to comprehend what is being said.

After more yelling, I witness Jackson raising his right arm, stopping momentarily at shoulder height before it recoils sharply upwards as the bullet silently leaves the chamber. Would guess he is using a silencer. A split-second later, the old man falls backwards, his arms still hanging down by his side. The limp body bounces a few times before resting motionless on the ground. The bastard killed this man. The question is, why?

If I still needed proof that we are dealing with a trained team, the dead body is picked up and taken down to the speedboat. Would take a guess it would be dumped in the ocean at some point. A non-professional would have just rolled the body into the sea. The problem with that is bodies float, and it wouldn't take a person with half a brain to work out where it came from.

Showing no remorse or even considering what just occurred, Jackson and Stuart continue to stare out towards the entrance to the river. Even though I can see that he is acting similar to myself, it still feels different to see someone else performing in the same manner. Grab the SLR, placing the forward sight on Jackson's head, and dry fired just for the hell of it. Shame I needed the mission to be covert, or I could have shot the arsehole and save problems later.

Time is thankfully going fast, nothing worse than sitting in an OP with nothing much happening, making it seem like time itself is on a go-slow to piss you off. Open the protective case on the phone. The time now is 17 minutes past 11, time to send Derek a text to say all going as planned here.

'S3, OK'.

Dead on 18 minutes, the telephone vibrates from the return message, 'All, OK'. Well, at least everything is going to plan at both locations so far.

With lack of activity over in the boatyard, make most of the time; reaching into my Bergen, pull out one of the bundles of sandwiches and the flask of coffee. My old MTO Roy Stanger says that you should be eating if you're not sleeping or working, as you never know when you will get the chance again. Plus, I can scrutinise and eat.

The scene in front stays the same for the next three hours, with not a lot happening, apart from the occasional glimpse of the guards as they walk behind the boatshed for a cheeky cigarette. The river traffic continues as it always does, both the Red Jet and the car ferry coming and going out of Cowes. Several small craft come, then disappear up the Medina towards Newport. Other sailing boats use their engines to enter the many small jetties along the riverbank close to Cowes' town centre.

The three-hour mark comes, time once more for the check-in. 'S3, OK', wait for the response. One minute passes, followed by a second. Finally, a third comes and goes. Fuck, what's happening at Dennis' place? That is the problem when you're out of radio range. You have no sense of what's transpiring.

Whatever it is, I have complete faith in the other three to handle anything that might go their way. Seconds later, a message appears on the screen. 'All, OK'. Phew, what a relief. Will find out what happened when we meet up. For now, there is some movement across the water.

An articulated vehicle is reversing down the yard in the direction of the shed. Once level with the barn, the truck comes to a complete stop. The driver climbs out of the cab, making his way around to the rear. The metal doors of a 20-foot container are swung open. Within minutes the people seen this morning are being loaded into the back. Why would someone take more risk in moving immigrants throughout the country? Typically once on UK soil, they're left to defend themselves.

Like a hard slap around the back of the head with a sledgehammer, it comes to me. The bastards aren't smuggling people into the UK. They are trafficking them into slavery.

The old man they killed mustn't have reached the buyer's requirements. Can't wait to take this gang out of action.

Even with my lack of feelings, and I don't have any for the people, modern slavery is wrong. Begs the question, how come none of the office staff have seen what is happening? Maybe they're turning a blind eye as it isn't their problem? Makes my job of blowing the pier with them on it an easier one.

No sooner than the truck left, our guards start to carry huge bundles down the jetty. Need a closer look at this. The packages are wrapped in green plastic, tied securely with blue nylon rope. The good news is, these aren't the control cases for the sniper rifles George and myself altered the other day.

The last thing we need is the shipment of weapons being brought forward. But, on the other hand, the attack part of the mission may need to move forward just to be safe.

Quite an entrepreneur is our Dennis. Looks like we can add people trafficking and drug smuggling to his arms-dealing CV. I count about four of the green bundles being loaded on the speedboat. Now I need to plan how I would attach an IED to the vessel. Needed a place where it will not be seen or fall off and blow the arseholes to bits along with the drugs at sea.

Study the boat down its entire length. The obvious answer is to stuff the device into the white plastic fenders dangling down. Lucky for me, they are identical to the ones hanging from the sailing craft I'm on. A stupid grin crossed my face, thinking about the idiots taking care to place the fender onboard when they depart, not knowing they are handling explosives that are about to fuck up their day.

With nothing much happening across the river, I stretch out, listening to the gentle tapping of raindrops as they strike the canvas cover. With any luck, it will not rain too hard, not that I cared.

I've got shelter, thinking more of the boys out in the woods with little protection.

Grab one of the fenders hanging down on the outside and pull it inside. Insert a small hole in the side near the top, just big enough to slide in the explosive and mobile phone. To disguise the hole from inquisitive eyes, cut a piece from an additional fender, glueing it over the slit. To a casual glance, it would look no more than a standard repair.

Still, nowt going on, so settle down with one eye on the opposite bank to wait for the 17:18 check-in. One of the best skills in any observation post, or an ambush, for that matter, is keeping the mind active during the long periods where nothing happens. As someone once said, an OP is 23 hours of boredom followed by 60 minutes of excitement.

After sending the next message, there are only two hours until last light. Everything I need for the trip over to the boatyard must be packed in the waterproof bag attached to the top of the kayak. To ensure this idiot didn't end up tumbling about, while looking for stuff and turning head first in the cold water, made sure all the kit is placed inside in reverse order. The last part will be securing the IED to the speedboat; this goes into the pack first.

One hour after the light faded, I lower the kayak slowly into the sea from the rear and glide gingerly into the cockpit. A quick check confirms the canvas is back in place to conceal any movement before I push off. Would use the night vision camera to get a better view — however, there might be a reflection from my mobile screen, so I decide against this.

Take slow, deliberate strokes of the paddle, ensuring they enter the water at the right angle to prevent any splash or noise that might give me away to anyone looking across the river.

With hardly any wind and the tide entirely in, the water's surface lay flat with occasional ripples from boats passing in the distance. All looks quiet in the stillness of the night. Over in the remoteness, Cowes' quay's lights break through as people walk along the front. Luckily there is no movement or sight of anybody as I approach the pier.

Gently coming in contact with the wall below the ramp leading to the pontoon, I steady myself, clinging to a metal ring that protruded out. Take time to sit motionless, as I listen for any noises that may indicate the guards' presence. Hopefully, I managed to time the crossing for when they are elsewhere.

Give it five minutes for any sounds. There isn't any. Reach in the pack and pull out the first of the two explosive packs and the roll of tape and plastic ties. Identify the attachment points, secur the first package to this, ensuring the wire used to extend the aerial is still hanging down the outside, along with two cables that will be joined to the other device to ensure they exploded together.

With one hand in the water, I paddle forward to a location beneath the second joint. Take out one more package, remove the phone, connect the wires to the connection points and secure it firmly. Right, on to the next job, the boat. Once more use the paddles to make my way to the vessel's seaward side to be out of view. Shit, they only attached fenders to the side in contact with the dock.

All of them are trapped. After several attempts of trying in vain to separate them while sitting inside the cockpit, I give up. Only one thing for it, I'm going to have to get on the pier. I lay flat along the top, which gives me sufficient room to pass underneath. Again stop and listen for any sound of our friends. Once I confirm nobody is around, I pull myself up and take the altered fender from the forward hatch.

Now faced with two options. Take this slow while keeping as close to the boards as possible, or move quickly, taking less time. They say the best place to hide is where everyone can see you, but don't; I choose the latter. The slack in the docklines makes removing the tension on the fenders a breeze. Soon have enough space to remove the last one from the rope dangling from the cleat on deck. Ensure the replacement is hanging at the same height as the rest before slipping back in the waiting kayak.

The instant I do, the sound of someone coming in my direction can be heard through the otherwise silence — no time to paddle off into the darkness. I will have to conceal myself under the pontoon, hoping the guards are not switched on enough to glance down at the deck. Not moving a single muscle and taking shallow breaths, wait as the man stood above me.

Feel like every nerve ending in my body is now tingling, as hairs rises on end as he kneels down. I held my breath. Moments later, he rises to his feet and walks back towards the ramp and the yard.

Fuck, that was close. Will give it another few minutes before heading back. Halfway, the front of the boat springs into the air as it hits the bow wave of the Red Funnel ferry, which just passed. Due to this taking me by surprise, it takes all my experience to keep upright. Back at the small boat, paddle the whole way around, double-checking nobody's taken up residence before entering the rear.

As soon as everything is back on board, I glance back across the Medina, take a glance at my phone. Shit, one message which read 'All OK'. Taken too long making my way back and missed the 20:17 check-in by five minutes. Sent my text 'S3, OK'.

The hard part, the night OP is now underway, with nothing to do but stare into the darkness, trying every trick in the book to stay awake. However, the fresh breeze from my little outing has me alert for the moment, so no need to resort to the usual routine of reciting different rhymes and badly singing bits of songs and carols. Plus, the hot coffee I just poured myself is also helping.

The time now is 22:00. Through the night vision attachment on the phone, spot two men heading down the ramp to the speedboat. As they climb on, the distinctive outline of Stuart comes into my view on the screen. Confirm seconds later, via the light in the cockpit.

After about six minutes, the sound of the two big, mighty engines roaring into life, breaks the still silence of the night. Note the time down on the notepad. Once away from the pier, the boat heads out of the river's mouth, turning right, heading in the direction of Fishbourne, losing sight of them moments later.

From what I witnessed earlier, I guess they are off on a delivery — the question is, will they be making a collection as well?

The caring side of me — yes, I have one, despite what the other idiots think — hopes they do not pick up any more people for their trafficking activities. If they do, the first person to get their fucking brains separated from their skulls will be Stuart, as he is doing the collecting.

The next check-in isn't due until 23:17, with nothing of importance occurring across the river. So I sit back and listen to the pitter-patter of water hitting the canvas, as it has begun to rain again. Took the time to tuck into some of the food prepared earlier.

Not long before, the stupid brain began to ask the same questions it always did at times like this. Mainly, why I'm concealed in an OP watching some numpty doing a myriad of illegal stuff.

Well, it's getting the stock answer. First, I enjoy the thrill of a mission. Second, the money always comes in handy and something new for this particular job which is nothing to do with the rush or gelt.

Personally, I may not have any empathy for the individual people being trafficked. The whole idea of people being sold as slaves or prostitution really winds me up. Once this task is over, there will be an anonymous phone call to the local constabulary. Can't do it before as the police might surround the place, and we need the control boxes back.

Once the stupid voices in my head finally shut the fuck up, peer through the night vision camera towards the target. Nothing is happening of interest, just the car ferry travelling backwards and forwards. A glance down at Mickey told me it's time for the 23:17 check-in with Derek. Notice the phone battery is also getting low. Reach out to the forward deck and grab the solar-powered charger I placed there earlier today. Time to send my message, 'S3, OK'. This time there is an instant reply from Derek, 'all, OK'.

The following two check-ins at 02:17 and 05:17 came and went with nothing out of the ordinary to report. After making sure everything used during the night is packed away in my Bergen, pick up the binos and looked across to the boatyard.

Observe two of our friends walking to the end of the pier. One takes out a powerful torch, which shines a bright white light across the surface of the sea, eventually landing on the speedboat approaching from my right. Within minutes, it is being lashed to the pontoon. As the engines go silent, Stuart, followed by a second person, steps off.

At least this time, they didn't bring some unlucky people with them to be sold to the highest bidder. About to turn away when Stuart returns, he climbs back on board, only to appear minutes later with a group of around 10 people dressed similar to the ones yesterday. The bastards are at it again. Like the people from yesterday, they are escorted away to the boatshed under armed guard. Like the others, there is nothing I can do to help for now.

Wait for a while to see if any packages are unloaded. They didn't disappoint, with three substantial plastic-wrapped bundles being carried ashore. Then, continue to watch as a man drags a sizeable black hose down the ramp to the boat. From the angle he is standing, I assume they are refuelling the vessel for tonight's activities.

With all the movement on the far side, time flew past. Once more, it's time to message Derek, 'S3, OK'. Almost instantaneously, at 08:17, a message read, 'All, OK'. All that is left is to observe if the idiots had set up a pattern of movements, or are indeed professionals at what they do, and staggered things. Didn't have long to wait for the answer.

About the same time as yesterday, a container lorry is reversed down towards the shed, completing the same procedure as before; the rear doors are opened, the people are loaded inside before being sealed shut.

Run everything that occurred over the previous 24 hours through my mind, and ensure everything is entered in my notebook, along with times. Depending on the next few hours going the way yesterday went, I will leave the OP after sending the check-in at 11:17. Like a good boy, everything I used and then finished with is instantly packed away, leaving very little to load into the Bergen later.

I take a final look across the harbour. Glad I did, as Dennis is standing with Chad on the pier, talking between themselves. As there is nobody around them, I will take an educated guess; this is a private discussion. About 10 minutes later, conversation over, they depart, heading back to shore. Right, time to leave once I sent the last message, 'S3, OK'.

After checking for any persons out at sea near the OP's rear, none were visible, so I lower the kayak into the water before slipping into the cockpit. Take one final glance to confirm Derek's message has been received; it was. As I'm leaving in daylight, I paddle over directly to the nearest sailing boat from the one I just departed from in a straight line. Undoubtedly, the plan will convince any nosey bastard looking my way that I left from a different location.

One bit of good news, the car hadn't been towed, plus no indication of it sprouting large yellow boots. A quick check all around, including the underneath, confirms there isn't any sign of tampering. So open the rear passenger door, throw my stuff inside, fasten the kayak to the roof and make my way to Parkdean Resorts.

I still don't know if my home is being watched by Chad's men. To err on the side of caution, park the car outside some other poor sod's lodge. But, of course, if someone spots the vehicle looking for me, they would beat the shit out of someone else, and don't care who, as long as it isn't me getting the fucking kicking.

Sling the Bergen on my back, pick up the SLR and head for the RV. Carry out the usual NOPs (Normal Operating Procedure) when I come close to the rendezvous point, stopping in a hedgerow approximately 100 metres short. Stand off for 10 minutes to ensure our RV isn't compromised. Once clear, approach with the weapon at the ready, just in case. Once on location, I conceal myself in the same place I used the other night, to wait for the other three to return.

Chapter Eleven – Simon's OP

Half asleep, I feel a kick to my back. "Come on, sleeping beauty, time to make a move." George says.

With my eyes now open, I notice George standing above me.

"OK, give me five."

Over near the centre of the RV, the other two are crouching down and all ready to go. "Glad you could join us," says Derek, removing a piece of white paper from his jacket pocket.

"Before we leave, Steve left me this sketch of our route—suggest we go over this before heading for our OPs."

"Makes sense to me," says Simon, now taking a position on the ground next to the others.

"We are here," Derek points to the sheet of paper stretched out on the floor and illuminated via a dimly-lit red torch. "The first leg is to the turning off the Red Squirrel Trail. According to the map, we make a left when we hit the concrete track. Proceed for roughly 2,000 paces or about 10 minutes until we come to some houses, a concrete road, and a metal gate. We turn left here. Within 50 metres, we will encounter the principal highway into Shanklin. America Woods is on the other side.

"Once in the woodlands, we are to proceed along the dirt track to a point in the trail where Simon leaves us. As it is dark, Steve has marked a few landmarks to confirm we are still on course. The first is a long wooden bridge, which should be reached in around six minutes or 580 paces.

"After another four mins, we will find a junction in the track. This is indicated by a slim silver birch on one side and a tree stump about a metre high on the other. This is the point you leave us, Simon. Any questions so far?"

"Not from me, anyway Simon is the recce expert, so I'll be following him up to this point."

"Cheers, George, what's the matter, afraid of getting lost?"

"Nope, merely want to see you find your way without the use of navigation equipment of your little tin tank."

"From where tanky departs," Derek continues. "We need to stay on this track for another 2,000 paces or eight minutes. Then, according to Steve, we should locate a metal gate. You should recognise this area, as you came here the other day. This is where I will continue to the farmhouse while you go to your own OP, George."

"We have about one and a half hours before first light, so we better make a move. Over to you, Simon."

"No problem, George, if you take the rear. Derek, slot yourself between us."

Pick up my Bergen and head off into the night, soon arriving at the road running along the edge of America Woods. Stop on the verge to scrutinise the area for a few minutes. Because of the proximity of the houses, both Derek and George join me. About to sprint across when out of the pitch blackness of the night, two headlights appear to my left, approaching at some speed. Moments later, they disappear towards Shanklin.

Once all-clear, make my dash for the cover of the woods. Find a suitable spot on the other side and signal for Derek to join me. Once all three of us are across, check the time on Mickey and head down the track, counting my paces as I go. Because Steve is a short arse, will allow some wiggle room on the number of steps.

Remember to shut one eye when the vehicle goes past on the main road, therefore retaining my night vision, making the trail easy to recognise as it twisted and turned, meandering its way through the trees. Still counting 570 in my head, the bridge is now in front of me, as indicated on the drawing.

Turn to spot George and Derek are about 20 metres behind, closing in on me. Right, to the next landmark where I would leave them. A recheck of the time, set off again, this time counting 300 paces.

Not bad, Steve. As you said, I'm now at the junction in the trail. Will make a mental note to myself to ask Steve why in the hell does he know this information.

Crouch down at the side of the track and place my hand on my head, the signal for the other two to close up on me. "This is where I depart. See you both tomorrow at the RV. Stay safe."

"And you, mate," says George, leading Derek deeper into the woods.

The new trail heads uphill through some sparsely-spaced trees and bushes. At the top, the rear wall of Dennis' place comes into view. To my right, a track leads off, following the edge of the property. Still being dark, and with the movements of the people protecting the place still not understood, I stay off to one side. Make my way around to the opposite side and the principal entrance.

The road leading up to the main entrance is now in front of me. I stop a few metres short, take up position under some brown ferns covering an open ditch, and observe. Perfect, nothing coming either down the track or from the house. Using the brackens as cover, I continue to a spot directly opposite the entrance, which would be my OP.

A place close to where Steve and myself used the other day, would be the ideal spot. This is now only 40 metres to my front. As usual, stand off to ensure the whole area isn't compromised by some idiot.

Once I confirm this, I approach with caution. Let's face it, we are not dealing with amateurs here. Soon find a location up a slight incline, which allows me to stare straight through the gate across the grounds towards the house, plus the small building identified by George on our last visit. The area below the canopy of the thick trees is covered in bushes, plus clumps of dead vegetation, proving excellent cover to establish the observation post.

My first task is to set up the position. Burrow my way under a clump of bracken to the forward edge. Ensuring enough remains upright on the leading-edge to protect me from view but still enables me to keep eyes on the target. Place the Bergen to my right, taking out a notebook, pen, binos, and the mobile phone. The rest will remain packed until I need them, such as the claymore, which I will place to my rear once I'm comfortable the OP is safe.

The mind flicks to the last mission on St Halb, where it pissed it down, so above me stretch out my poncho, held up in all four corners by short sticks, giving me enough space to crawl in and out without disturbing it.

Finish setting up as the first rays of first light start to break through the canopy. Two men with rifles slung over their shoulders stand between the brick structures on either side of the entrance to my front. Further, in the grouds, some more armed people walk in the direction of the building off to the right.

A check of the time confirms the first check-in is only a couple of minutes away. The C350 is packed in my Bergen with the aerial poking out of the top skywards. The cable with the mic dangles down the outside.

Not long before, the words, "DR, OK," broke radio silence.

This is followed by, "GD, OK."

With one hand, take hold of the radio transmitter, and press the transmit button, "ST, OK," we are all in place. The responsibility for keeping in contact with Steve in Cowes is down to Derek. Hopefully, all is going well at his end.

Sip on the warm coffee poured from my flask, once again, the radio crackles into life.

"DR, Out, Two."

This means two people are leaving the farmhouse and are heading in my direction. If they take the route, we anticipate they should appear at my location within 20 minutes.

Confirmed a short time after with George, sending the following, "GD, F Two."

Another 11 minutes pass before two men in their early twenties, dressed in black jeans and jackets, emerge, strolling along like they didn't give a flying fuck about anything.

The instant they stop at the front entrance to chat with their colleagues, I get the transmitter and send, "ST, In Two."

A half-hour later, a man and a young woman whose attire is comparable to the other two exit the gate, turn right, and head down the track. The moment they do, I transmit, "ST, Two Out." My head is now telling me we may have some sort of handover between them, but this will need confirmation.

These two must be off duty; after 10 minutes, with no confirmation from George, they had passed him. They might have diverted to an unknown location? Another five mins by before the message, "GD, D Two," comes over the airwaves.

Now either the lazy bastards are sauntering, or the last two walked fast, will compare with other movements. Similar to what the others would be doing, make notes of all timings in my notebook. They must have smelt breakfast or got their fingers out of their arses, as it isn't long before Derek reports them entering the farm.

"DR, In Two."

Through my binoculars, two men appear around the corner of the outbuilding, heading in the gate's direction. Within a few minutes, both are standing, talking to the two people protecting the entrance. Soon after, the man and woman who previously carried out this role ambles off into the grounds. Make a note of the time, 09:30.

In the distance close to the residence, a couple of men walk to meet them. All stopping on the wooden bridge which ran across the stream-come-lake, making its way through the property's grounds. Once again, a short conversation, followed by the two patrolling the grounds, head off to the barrack block.

If I didn't know better, this shows all the signs of a changeover of personnel. A smart one at that, bearing in mind the other people entered and left half an hour earlier. Watched these people's movements for a while, ensuring all incidents, routes, and timing are noted down.

Still, time before the next radio check, giving me time to set my rear protection. Decide against the claymore as this is a public woods, didn't fancy blowing some innocent person taking their mutt for a walk into tiny fragments. Well, not today anyway. Instead, reach into the Bergen and take out the tripwire connected to the radio receiver. As a replacement for likely being hit by flying body bits, resulting in me getting covered in some idiots blood, instead, I will hear them approach.

The vision of body parts lying about had me frozen with a numb, tingling sensation creeping its way through my entire body. For a moment, I am taken back to Baghdad in Iraq and the Gulf War.

Found the ideal location about 50 metres to the rear of my position, where a small dirt track passes between several silver birch trees. Attach one end to a tree, about 12 inches from the floor. Stumbling backwards, unwind the fishing line until I reach a bush at the bottom of another about six metres away.

Place the plastic container with the receiver, battery, and trip device behind the foliage and secure the box firmly to the tree's base. Open the clothes peg through the hole in the side, insert the small piece of wood attached to the line that acted as a circuit breaker in the jaws.

With the trap set, returned to the OP in time for the radio call at 11:17

"GD, OK."

Grab the transmitter, "ST, OK."

Next is Derek with, "DR, OK."

There are now different people on the gate — I must have missed the changeover while setting the rear defence. Will make a note and observe the target area for anything out of the ordinary. Not much happens for the next hour, apart from the guards continuing to man the entrance and patrol the grounds.

Use this time for a quick snack, as now peckish. Unwrap one of the sandwiches from the Bergen and tuck in. Typical, halfway through eating the sarnie, four men exit the property via the main gate, turn right and head in George's direction. Better call this in, "ST, Four Out."

Twenty minutes pass, still no confirmation from George. They might have taken a different route. If they did, Derek would have called this in by now. Only two possible answers: one, they could be heading to the farm and gone off somewhere else, or second, they are up to something in the woods.

Another 10 minutes pass before George's voice came over the airwaves, "GD, D Four."

At last, the questions now running through my mind are: what have they been doing, clearing the area or perhaps setting their own explosive charges? This information needs questioning on our debrief. Note the timings and enter them in the notebook.

Whilst waiting for Derek to confirm all four are at the farmhouse, they reappear at the entrance 15 minutes after George checked them in. Appears they have extended their patrolling to the whole area surrounding Dennis' place.

The distinctive rumbling and rattling of a vehicle approaching down the uneven road and heading in my direction, grabs my attention. A grey Mercedes car pulls up, stopped by one of the guards. The driver lowers the their window. After a short conversation, heads off in the direction of the house, following the driveway across the wooden bridge.

On reaching the house, a smartly-dressed man climbs out from the rear of the car, making his way up the front doorsteps leading to the house. Through my binos, it is easy to identify this person as being Dennis. Before entering, he turns around to face the chauffeur and says something. The vehicle is parked, ambling slowly across towards the outbuilding; the driver makes his way across the grounds.

A few hours after the first change of people on the entrance, the cycle repeats itself. Two men from the building, which I'm guessing is the barrack block, replace the people at the main entrance. They, in turn, take over from the ones patrolling. So now, if the same happens in another two hours, we have our shift pattern.

14:17 — time for the next radio check. I initiate the call with, "ST, OK."

This is succeeded by, "DR, OK."

Half expecting the instant reply from George, put down the mic. But something is wrong—one minute passes, followed by a second and a third and no response. So then, with a rescue plan starting to form in my mind, finally across the airways comes, "GD, OK."

Thank fuck for that—I didn't fancy rescuing his fat arse. Place the binos down on the ground, after trying in vain to peer through the skylights on the back wall of the outbuilding. This was passing the time as not much is happening, when a cream-coloured taxi pulls up at the gate. Our friendly guard makes a half-hearted walk around the car, looking in all windows before finally waving the vehicle through.

Three young children, I would estimate no more than 11-years-old, climb out at the house. One of the three is a young boy wearing a grey jumper and blue jeans. When it comes to the others, the tallest girl is wearing a white dress coated with flowers, covered with a pink cardigan. Which leaves middle girl, who appears to be, from here, slightly smaller than the other young lady. She is dressed in black trousers with a red jumper.

After collecting several bags from the vehicle's boot, they charge towards the front door, flinging the wooden door open and rush inside. Better stay focused on this area until the cab drives back out, which is does without stopping to speak to anyone.

The 17:17 radio check goes past, with everyone checking in without any issues. Last light will be in two hours, time to prepare the observation post for the night, ensuring everything I didn't anticipate using is packed away neatly in my Bergen. Confirm the poncho is still secured, in case the heavens decide to piss it down tonight.

Barely finished this when the distinctive sound of crumpling foliage came from behind me as someone walks in the woods.

Without making the slightest noise, turn around and crawl out, staying close to the floor. I quietly creep forward to an evergreen bush, taking up a concealed location nearby. The noise is now getting closer, and expecting this to be one of Chad's mates, raise the rifle up into the fire position.

Still, the sound gets louder, but I can't yet see anybody. A long couple of minutes pass as I crouch silently, ready to pounce on anyone or thing coming my way. A few more seconds go by before, at last, they are in striking distance.

Took a deep breath, with one mighty movement, spring to my feet and dive at the person on the other side. Scatter the ferns as I land, pushing them aside to grab hold of whoever is lurking in the undergrowth. As I did, a loud rustling sound comes from underneath as a dog darts out. The little shit scared the fucking life out of me.

Over in the distance, I now spot a man clasping both hands around his mouth, shouting, "Colonel, here, boy."

Back in the OP, a message came over the airways, "DR Out Two."

Check my wristwatch, the time is 18:00. Approximately 10 minutes later, George verifies they pass him.

"GD F Two."

Soon after, two men appear, strolling along the trail. Pick up the mic and call the event, "ST, Two In."

If this is a changeover, two people should emerge from the barrack block and head towards the gate in 30 minutes. Confirm, a woman and a man leave via the entrance and disappear down the track.

I grab the radio transmitter, "ST Two Out." The same procedure as before, with both Derek and George calling in their respective parts.

The last light of the day fades away from all areas around the grounds. Small dim lights raised off the ground on short wooden posts, partially illuminating Dennis' place, burst into life. Over at the house, expansive windows at the front are highlighted by the glow of internal lighting shining through the glass.

Thanks to the illumination, Dennis can be seen through the window, slouched on a green sofa through the patio doors on the building's facade. While the thought of blowing his head across the room flashes into my mind, he's joined by the young lad I saw entering earlier. With any luck, the kids will be gone by the time we make an assault on the property in a few days.

The important 20:17 radio check is due. This is the first one of the night, vital because this signals everyone is OK, plus we are all settled in for the night.

"GD, OK," now pierced the silence.

Send my own call sign, "ST, OK."

Last to check-in is Derek with "DR, OK."

With nothing to do now but stare into the night and follow the movements of Chad's men as they go about the task of protecting the place, at least there is something for me to scrutinise, unlike poor George, who would be staring at the woods while trying to keep himself awake. One of the reasons Steve insists on the regular radio checks is to assure we are still conscious. The farmhouse should be busy with people coming and going, so Derek will have plenty of activity to keep him alert.

Might as well pour another brew before the coffee goes too cold. Like always, when I have fuck all else to do, the mind asks the same stupid question, mainly why am I here? After every mission, I tell myself it will be the last. The only answers that constantly play in my head are the fact I enjoy the thrill of the mission, the banter with the other two, and the money.

Thankfully my self-reflection is interrupted by the light coming from the door to the house, which is now open. Standing on the doorstep is Chad with three other people, one of whom is held in a kneeling position by the other two. An interchange of loud shouting takes place between them, followed by even more yelling between all parties. Then, like watching a movie in slow motion, Chad walks over to the person on their knees and rests the barrel of a pistol on the man's head.

Go on, shoot the bastard, one less for us to deal with, I thought to myself. A second later, the weapon is raised only to be brought down with incredible speed, striking the side of the person's head. He sank to the floor as the others let go. Continue to watch as Chad and the two men go back indoors, leaving the victim to pick himself up. Made a note of the time it is 21:00. All I can say is, I'm glad he is not on our side if this is how he treats his own men.

The following five hours go without anything significant happening, just the routine of the two-hour swap of guards and the 23:17 and 02:17 radio check. Not until 02:30, when what resembles an old British Army long-wheelbase Land Rover turns up at the front, did things change.

A man dressed in green overalls climbs out of the driver's seat, walks around to meet the man exiting the gatehouse. All indications would suggest they are more than likely friends, as they give each other a hug before climbing back into the Land Rover and driving off in the stables' direction.

The stables are off to my left to the house's right, illuminated by a light fixed to the wall between two stable doors. It is hard to recognise what they are unloading from the rear, from the angle I'm looking at and the nightlight's dimness. But, from what I can see, they are huge bundles wrapped in plastic that require both of them to carry inside. Counted four in total. Within 20 minutes, the whole operation is complete, and the vehicle drives out of the gate.

Three hours later, my favourite time of day, first light started to break through the canopy. Not only have I managed to witness the morning sunlight, but so did the others. Let's hope everything went well with Steve. Knowing that psychopath, the only people in danger are the ones who strayed too close.

Time for a brew before the 08:17 radio check, so pour what is now stewed coffee from the flask. At least the stuff is wet, I think to myself. The moment Mickey's second hand hits the 12, I grip the mic and transmitted, "TS, OK."

This is followed by George, "GD, OK."

Twenty seconds later, Derek sends his call sign, "DR, OK."

Over at Dennis' place, there is a hive of motion with shift changes. The kids I witnessed arrive yesterday are messing about on the bridge in the cold morning air. Observe them for a while — kids playing innocently, oblivious to what is happening around them always makes me smile.

Brought back to the here and now by the words, "DR Two Out."

I wait for George to confirm, "GD F Two."

Before focusing my attention on the track running alongside the house, not long before the two people I witnessed leaving last night from the farmhouse's direction now appear ambling along the trail towards the entrance. I call them in, "TS, In Two."

After conversing with their mates at the gate, they continue to the barrack block. From what I've seen since being here, not one of Chad's group of men, apart from Chad, walk to the house. Now, if I remember rightly, I think Mark said something about a tunnel. They must be using this to transverse from one building to the other.

Shortly after, the same people who arrived yesterday head back to the farm. Seen lots of evidence of how professional Chad's men have been, but sticking to a routine like this is amateurish at best and lets them down. Not that I'm complaining, as patterns are easy to take down.

With everything else quiet and the kids back indoors, take advantage of the fact and opened a wrapped sarnie from the Bergen. There is a debate if you should be eating in a two day OP. I'm in the yes camp; if something happens, you need to keep up your strength to overcome any issue that might arise.

Meanwhile, back at the house, the grey Mercedes pulls up in front of the main door's steps. Five minutes later, Dennis can be seen climbing into the rear seat, clutching a black briefcase. Moments later, Chad is also seen getting in the back of the vehicle. Soon after, the car drives straight out without stopping. Scribbled some notes in the notebook, including the time, 09:30.

Spend the next few minutes flicking through my entries, to ensure I noted everything down that occurred so far. On its own, my data is essential, but they don't start forming an accurate assessment of what's happening until they are combined with everyone else's. This is where Steve's expertise comes in.

The time is 11:16, about to transmit my OK message when three figures, two men and a woman, exit the gate. Rather than send multiple messages, I alter mine to read, "TS, OK, Three Out."

"DR, OK," comes from Derek.

The last to send is George with, "GD, OK."

There should be a confirmation as they pass George in a few minutes, so I keep the mic close. Similar to yesterday, a delay in reporting. Maybe they are patrolling the woods again. Forty minutes pass before the radio crackled into life.

"DR, Three In."

Appears our trio had taken an alternative route to the farmhouse. Out of all the movements so far, this is the first to deviate from the rest. Make a note, but with an asterisk, one change doesn't alter the routine but suggest they are capable of random switches, something we may need to consider.

No sooner than the 14:17 check is completed when a 20-foot container lorry enters the grounds. Drives towards the stables before stopping on the concrete area between blocks; the truck driver, a short man with a massive trucker's belly. At least we know who eats all the pies. Climbs out of the cab and walks into the stable. Learnt a long time ago during many recces with the calvary not to put two halves together, no matter how many times my sums make sense. Can't stop my mind thinking he is here to collect the packages brought in early this morning.

I am correct not to assume, as moments later Chad is seen heading for the lorry, meeting the driver as he emerges out of the door. Pick up the binos in time to notice Chad hand him a generously-sized envelope with a blue stripe running down the middle. The vehicle engine revs into life, before leaving via the gate and disappearing up the road.

With only the 17:15 check in to do, turn my attention to preparing the observation post for departure. The first task is to retrieve the rear protection. Turn around and crawl out before making my way to where the transmitter and tripwire are set up. Pull the piece of wood and line from the clothes peg trigger.

Now screaming its head off in the OP, is the receiver. It would have been hardly audible to most people. To me, the loud noise sound like some rock band decided to play very loudly. This fucking idiot forgot to disconnect the battery first, a rookie mistake. Good job the others are not here to witness my fuck up, or I would never live it down.

Pull down my makeshift cover and stuff the poncho with everything else back into my Bergen, and wait for the radio check. Once sent, I will leave.

The first to call is Derek with, "DR, Out."

This is followed by, "GD, Out."

Held the mic in one hand, "ST, Out,", put all the equipment away and leave the OP.

I will take the same route we all came down yesterday, making sure my rifle is as much as possible out of view as there is still daylight. Don't want to scare the civvies. Not long before I reach the road into Shanklin. Unlike last time, I don't stop, this would seem odd if seen, so dart across. Once on the other side, head up the Red Squirrel Trail and the RV.

The rendezvous point is now 50 metres to my front. Take cover on the side of the track, where I stand off for a while to listen, hoping the place hasn't been compromised. Stay for 10 minutes before approaching cautiously, trying not to make a sound. Then, as I enter, a voice bellows out from under a bush.

"About time you got your sorry arse back here."

"Good evening to you as well, Steve, trust all went well?"

"Yes thanks, mate."

Chapter Twelve – George's OP

Thankfully my stag is over. Due to bugging out from our previous location, I ended up on the last guard duty, yet again. Right, time to get the lazy fuckers out of their cosy slumber. First is Derek, who lay under some bracken off to my right. By the sound of deafening snoring going on, his subconscious mind forgot to tell him this is a covert op. Gave his feet a gentle tap, then wait to ensure he's utterly awake before heading in Simon's direction.

Ahhh, Simon looks all cosy and warm wrapped up in his maggot, soon put a stop to that. One kick to his back should sort him out.

"Come on, sleeping beauty, time to make a move."

"OK, give me five."

Once again wait until he is alert with eyes open before making my way back to my own location to collect my kit.

Sling my Bergen over one shoulder, walk over to the centre of the RV and wait for the others to join me. While waiting, plonk my arse down on top of the pack on the deck. Use the time to double-check the sniper rifle. Let's face some facts, mainly this weapon hasn't been fired in anger.

Finished checking the equipment when I'm joined by Derek, with Simon joining us a few minutes later. Before leaving, Steve gives Derek a sheet of paper with all the route details. This could have been handed to Simon, as he's the one leading us to the area of the observation posts. But there is an excellent reason why he didn't.

Yes, Derek helped us on St Halb, but apart from that, we know very little about him, like his tactical skills and how he operates on a task.

Plus, until Derek proves himself, we don't have total trust in him. Let's face facts, he shows up in England when we are about to start a mission. This might simply be a coincidence, or maybe planned. Then, of course, we still don't know how Chad's men know about movements in Newport, Southampton, and the last RV.

Both mine and Simon's task is to scrutinise how he handles himself throughout this phase and take the appropriate action if required, including dispatching him if the need should arise.

So far, all is going to plan as Derek takes out the sheet of paper and suggests we go through the sketch before leaving. If he didn't, I would have prompted him. Not knowing what is written down, listen attentively, making mental notes in my mind. With the briefing over, Simon takes command of the patrol to our OPs, indicating Derek to slot himself between myself and him. Again this is planned so I can see his every move.

After one final check of the RV to ensure nothing is left that would indicate anyone's been here, such as accidentally dropped rubbish, follow Derek out of the location down to Red Squirrel way. There is no need to count the steps to the first landmark, as I remember the gate from the trip to our original rendezvous point.

Due to the short distance between turning off the trail and the street, plus the houses, again no point in spreading out like we always do in this situation.

Join the other two at the grass verge. No sight of any vehicles approaching in either direction—Simon is about to dart to the other side of the highway when suddenly, from our left a set of headlights appear, coming this way, heading for Shanklin.

A few moments pass before Simon leaps to his feet and sprints across the road, taking cover in the edge of the woods. After double-checking no other vehicles are heading this way, tap Derek on the back for him to cross over. Once they are both across, I make my move, joining them on the verge opposite.

With Simon on point, followed by Derek and myself at the rear, we start to walk cautiously down the path. To the left, about 10 metres further along the treeline, two wooden fence posts about two metres apart marked the start of the dirt track that led into America Woods. I begin to calculate the 580 paces to our next checkpoint, the timber bridge from the bottom of the wooden steps, in case the idiot at the front forgot how to fucking count, he is a tanky, after all.

In my head, I count the required amount of paces when we come to a stop. Due to the absence of artificial lights in the wood, I now have my complete night vision, making things a lot easier to see, including the edge of the track. In the distance, I could see Simon pause at the bridge and looking back, as to say we've now arrived at the second landmark.

The next waypoint where Simon leaves us should be only a short 300 paces from here. As Steve indicated on the map, we come to the junction where a track leads uphill between a silver birch tree and stump within a couple of minutes.

From this point, I will lead as I've got some idea of where I am going from our last visit here a few days back. So after getting rid of Simon, follow the route as it meanders through the dense trees and over a small timber-clad bridge, no more than three metres in length that span a slow running stream passing underneath. Eventually, we reach a split in the path. One headed back up the steep hill, the other leading to the metal gate separating the woods to the open meadows.

"This where I leave you, Derek. The gate on Steve's map is beyond the trees," I point to my right. "Stay safe—I will see you back at the RV at 18:30 tomorrow."

"Thanks, George—see you later, and try to come back minus any small holes."

Wait for Derek to depart, hopefully to an observation post and not meeting up with his possible mates at the farmhouse. I continue along to the top of the hill. The last time we came here, I counted the number of steps to the wooden bridge crossing the stream close to my OP area, 60 paces from here on the right of the track. I marked a thick oak tree easily recognisable to let me know where to head off up the embankment to approach the OP from the rear.

OK, there is the mark, time to leave the track. Climb up the grass bank and through the tightly-packed trees until I'm in a position just below the skyline. Locate a suitable place out of view with plenty of natural cover, while I change into my ghillie suit.

Will use the same spot as on our previous visit to this area, which is now only 20 metres or so further down the slope from my present location. There is no point in coming back up here later, might as well find an appropriate place for my rear defences while I'm here. Reach into the Bergen and pull out the homemade claymore and the plastic container holding trip circuitry of the device, laying them on the green grass-covered ground.

First, find a tree about 10 metres down the bank away from the ridgeline, secure the package to the bottom and cover the box with piles of green foliage from the surrounding area. Next, pick up the claymore but decide against this. Might be civvies around who didn't deserve being scraped up off the deck. Reach back in the pack for the transmitter instead. Fasten this to another tree 15 metres from the other one.

Now for the OP itself. First, place the pack on the ground in front of me. Then get as near to the floor as possible, crawl forward, stopping short of the location. The next few minutes are spent watching and listening for any movement. Once I confirm the whole area is safe, I scramble under some dense brown bracken and a green bush on the slope's leading edge that ran down to the bridge.

From my Bergen's side pocket, take out a strip of camouflage netting approximately one and a half metres square and place this behind the row of ferns I leave along the front edge to help with concealment. Behind the net, make a small mound of dirt move back several inches, lowering the rifle's legs and resting them on the ground. The wind gauge still needs to go out to my front, will do this after checking in. That's the firing location sorted, time to make some cover in case it pisses it down.

Take out the groundsheet, raising the sheet up on sticks on each corner, giving me just enough to move, but not too high where someone might see it. With the sniper position all set, glance down to see the time. It is close to the first check-in. Once more reach in the Bergen and pull out the mic, the rest of the radio would stay packed apart from the aerial, which now protruded skywards.

Smack on 08:17, "DR, OK," comes over the airwaves.

I squeeze the transmit button, "GD, OK.”

Seconds later, Simon replies with, "ST, OK."

Still need to place the wind indicator out towards the front of the OP. This requires a place where the equipment would be exposed to any change of airflow. Crawling backwards, exit the position and creep forward, stopping every few feet. Take a few moments to listen for any sounds of movement of people.

Find a perfect spot on a dead tree lying horizontally on the ground, complete with some small, slender branches reaching for the sky, excellent camouflage. The device is no thicker than my index finger, with several vertical slots around the top and painted green and black. Blends beautifully with its surroundings.

With everything set and nothing left to do but scrutinise the woods in front, this will be a wiry OP for me as, unlike the rest, there isn't an actual target area to watch, only the possible coming and going of people from the farm to Dennis' place and vice versa.

Reminds me of one sniper operation in Iraq, where I laid in wait for six days for the target to appear. Then one shot, a dead terrorist and a bug out. One of the ways I found to keep alert is chewing on gum and sucking boiled sweets. I came prepared. Back at Steve's place, take time to liberate a packet worth from their individual wrapper along with two packs of gum. These are now wrapped in serviettes, to stop any rustling of wrappings that might give my location away.

Not long before the first signs of activity are transmitted across the airwaves, "DR, Out Two."

If all goes the way we expect, they should pass me in about 10 minutes. Do not have to wait long, for two men dressed in black jeans and jackets come ambling down the track forward of my position, heading towards Dennis'.

Grab the mic and transmit, "GD, F Two."

This is confirmed soon after, when Simon sends, "ST, In Two."

Don't expect a rush of movements straight away. So I will make most of the time by pouring a brew from the flask, taken from the side pouch of my Bergen, as feeling a little parched. Almost finished, when a message on the radio from Simon interrupts me.

"ST, Out Two."

Sorry, but not wasting a good brew, so place the black mug to one side and observe the dirt track for people heading in the direction of the farmhouse. Wait 10 more minutes, and they've still not appeared near me. Maybe they've gone via the other route and fucked up our plans? Stay focused, in case our friends are lazy bastards and strolling.

Another five mins go by before two people, one man and a woman, emerge wandering along the trail, chattering away like they didn't have anything to worry about. If they only knew three men are watching their every move.

Better call this in, "GD, D Two."

Listen to Derek moments later reply with, "DR, In Two," while I finish the rest of my tea.

Take the now laminated paper with all the potential firing positions out of my inside jacket pocket. Set the sheet on the ground near the sniper rifle. One point at a time, aligne up each mark on the range card to the relevant places in the killing zone. Even if they don't return fire from the exact location, I will have a good idea of the distance to the target.

A glimpse of Mickey tells me there are a few minutes before the 11:17 radio check. Want to get back to what I'm doing, so I initiate the check-in. "GD, OK."

Next comes Simon, "ST, OK."

The last to call in is Derek, "DR, OK."

Right, now we are all still OK, back to the task at hand. Pick up the weapon with my right hand on the pistol grip, with the other resting on the butt and peer through the optical sights to a treetrunk approximately 150 metres away. With crosshairs on the middle of the selected target, I press the grey button on the optics side.

Observe as a small flashing arrow appears below the crosshairs pointing to the right. Move the rifle slowly right until the indicator stops blinking. The sight has me slightly off to one side. My sniper training tells me I should be aiming here, due to the slight breeze blowing across the whole area. This must be the wind-indicating gismo picking up the moving air.

Impressed with this thing and will definitely be adding this to my permanent kit, especially as it keeps itself charged via a tiny turbine housed inside the opening on each edge.

With playtime over, time for an early lunch. Unwrap one of the sandwiches I made back at Steve's place and tuck in.

The moment I do, Simon broadcasts, "ST, Four Out."

Sure that man is in the procession of a camera that is trained on me, just waiting for me to start eating or drinking. Revenge will be sweet. Still, 10 more mins until they reach my location, hence finish what I started before paying attention to the woods to my front.

Another 20 minutes pass before four men stretched out in a straight line appear, making their way through the dense undergrowth. While one man walk down the track, the others space themselves out, about 50 metres apart. Each seems to be checking the area for something, stopping several times for a more extensive examination of a particular location. Then, finally, on reaching the bridge, the person who had been travelling along the trail stops, bends down on both knees and peers underneath.

Appears we have almost professional people on our hands, saying 'almost' as it seemed his actions are half-hearted. If that is any of us, we would have checked the other side as well. Any explosives that madman Steve's got in mind needs to go on the other far side, closest to the farmhouse.

I was about to pick up the mic to confirm they reached me, when one of the idiots began climbing the bank through the undergrowth to my front. Then, with slow, careful movements, place the rifle into firing position, taking aim in the centre of the man's face.

As he comes within 20 metres of me, I start to control my breathing. One deep breath, exhale, another breath, then breathe half out before holding my breath. I take up the first pressure, ready to fire. As I begin to pull back on the hairline trigger, the man trips, falling headfirst into the ground — I release the trigger.

After a lot of loud shouting of words that would make his mother blush, he gets to his feet and walks back down to join the others, heading back towards Simon. If only he knew how close he'd been to having the contents of his skull spattered across the place, decorating the ferns a crimson red.

Better call this in, "GD, D Four."

Must have been 10 minutes before Simon signals they are re-entering Dennis' place.

Stare at my surroundings for the next hour, with nothing occurring apart from the growing ache in my stomach. I desperately need a shit. What you did in a normal OP situation, you would have a dump where you lay using a plastic bag held tight against your arse. As nothing is happening and the presence of a generously-sized bush conveniently to my rear, decide this would make a better option.

With time getting close to the 14:17 check-in, will I make it back in time? If I don't go now, I will end up shitting myself. Besides, got plenty of time. After a quick scan, crawl out of the location and hastily make my way to said bush. One of the OP rules is, don't leave anything behind that might indicate someone's been in the area. Grab several leaves to pick up the waste, placing the steaming brown logs in the cellophane bag.

The operation, relieve my bowels, takes longer than planned and arrive back in my OP three minutes late for the radio check. So to prevent any panic or rescue mission send, "GD, OK."

Not a lot happens for the rest of the afternoon, and the 17:17 check goes without a hitch. The last lights of the day will start fading soon, leaving the place in darkness, time to prepare the OP for the night. This includes ensuring everything that isn't required for the night to be packed. The only equipment left out is the binos, rifle and the mic dangling from the Bergen. However, due to me memorising all the information from the range card, I also put this away.

Out of the dim light, penetrating the tree canopy about 200 metres away on the leading edge of the bank off to my right, I spot a deer trampling its way through the bracken. That will be an easy kill if Bambi shows up again tomorrow, perfect for the barbeque along with more than a few cold ones.

Take time to look through my notes to perceive any patterns forming in Chad's men's movements, when Derek breaks the evening silence.

"DR, Out Two."

If the identical people witnessed going to the farmhouse this morning, come wandering down the track towards Dennis' place, this might indicate a pattern. But this also raises the question of what's unique about these four people. Sure, either Mark said, or we worked it out of our previous recce, the men stayed in the building on the grounds away from the house.

Well, that's confirmed as the two figures now walking past my location are the same two men.

Send by confirmation over the radio, "GD, F Two."

This is followed soon after by Simon, "ST, In Two."

Jot down the two times, the call from Derek, 18:00 and the time they passed me. The time is now 18:10. Also make a comment at possible shift change, sure the others will realise this as well. Can't think of anything more unprofessional than not making a note, thinking someone else would write this information down, and they don't.

If we needed even more proof at 18:30, Simon confirms two people left the primary residence, "ST, Two Out."

A long 12 minutes pass before the same people, a man and woman I saw go to Dennis' gaff earlier today now appear, walking in my direction. Once they all cross the front of my location, I call it in, "GD, D Two."

As expected, a short while later, Derek counts them into the farmhouse, "DR, In Two."

With last light, comes the darkness and eerie silence of the forest at night. In fact, the only sounds audible are that of nocturnal wildlife burrowing through the dense undergrowth. The only problem at night is stopping the brain from playing stupid tricks, convincing you every sound is a person creeping up on you. Not all bad news, being away from any artificial lights, I soon regain my night vision, enabling me to locate the firing position from the range card.

Time to settle in for a hard OP. From everything seen so far, not much is coming my way tonight. One of my roles is, if things do kick off at either the farm or Dennis' place, people will come sprinting this way to meet their final resting place, as I put a bullet in their heads, splattering blood and bits of skulls everywhere.

Tuck into the last meals of the day, consisting of a sarnie and a surprisingly still hot brew before getting comfortable for the night. The 20:17 radio check comes and goes without any issues.

If I'm honest, pleased everyone stayed safe during the day and now in their night routines. Looks like Derek is shaping up well, and our fears are unfounded; saying that, he might be transmitting his messages from the comfort of a nice warm farmhouse kitchen.

Not long after the 23:17 radio check-in, about midnight, I start making like a nodding donkey, time to unwrap the boiled sweets and a little more tea to keep me awake. Half-wished for something to occur, to concentrate the mind away from sleep and constant questions of what I'm bloody doing laid under a bush in some strange woods at night.

This time the answer is an easy one — It's the thrill of this kind of work. Unlike our last mission, there is no moral dilemma to deal with, no drugs or even innocent people getting hurt. Suppose the other reason is the money is good.

Of course, we are constantly facing the chance of being injured or killed. But this is something people in my type of business always put to the back of their minds, and secretly believe this will not happen to me. Did get shot on one mission. It fucking hurt, so not doing that again.

My self-contemplation is interrupted by a rustling of foliage from the rear of my position. Will need to investigate this, if for nothing more than my own peace of mind. Turn in the OP, pause to listen for any more sounds. The noise is still coming from my rear — my brain convincing me the sound is that of someone walking towards me. Crawl out and head for the base of a tree before stopping again.

A couple of seconds later, the white and black shape of a badger sprints across my front. Take several deep breaths to calm myself down and get a grip on the situation. But what spooked the fucking thing, is the question. Something that I'm now frantically trying to find the answer to.

With no more noise, I start to head back to OP when I spot the figure of a person strolling along the skyline in the corner of my eye. Now confronted with two options. Launch at whoever is wandering through the forest during the night, ask questions later, or stay concealed and hope they continue walking.

I choose the latter, mainly because I might be faced with more people than I can handle on my lonesome. Besides, nobody is coming in my direction at the moment. So stay where I am under the bush and watch. I make the right choice as moments later, two more men pass within metres of me.

These are definitely Chad's people from how they are dressed, but what are they doing patrolling at night. Did they know someone could be somewhere hiding in the woods? If so, who told them? My mind, for some reason, went to Derek, but thinking carefully, they are heading his way; if it is him, they would be approaching from the opposite direction.

Arrive back in the observation post in time for the 02:17 radio check. Reach for the mic and send my message. "GD, OK."

"DR, OK," comes the reply from Derek.

Last to check-in is Simon, "ST, OK."

Well, at least with that excitement, I'm alert again and no more nodding for England. The rest of the night goes without a hitch. The signs of first light start to break through the treetops. As far as I'm concerned, there is no better time of the day, plus I'm still alive, and fighting fit at dawn. Which reminds me, brekkie time.

Through the rifle's scope, spot some early morning type of person ambling among rows of scattered trees in the distance, accompanied by a couple of big Alsatian dogs. Reminded me of my days as an Army Dog Handler. Study the area for a while to confirm this isn't one of Chad's men, before turning my attention to ensuring the OP is clean of any mess. Just finished cleaning the place when Simon checks in.

"ST, OK."

Shit, forgotten about the 08:17 radio check, not a problem, pick up the mic and send, "GD, OK."

It would seem I'm not the only one, as Derek replies with, "DR, OK," a minute late.

The big question now is, will we witness similar activity as yesterday, forming some sort of pattern? Really hope so as it makes our jobs easier. Don't have to wait to find out.

"DR, Out Two," comes clearly across the airwaves.

After positioning myself behind the L115A3 rifle, I glance down at Mickey on my wrist. The time is 09:00. Our friends should be passing me in 10 minutes or thereabouts. Ambling towards me are two men chatting away as they walk towards Dennis' gaff. Not long after, Simon confirms they reached their destination.

"ST, In Two."

Several groups of people now come into my view, both among the trees to my front. Would appear that America Woods is a trendy expanse for walking the mutt, possibly on the other trail that circumnavigated the forest. Little things like this confirm we are dealing with a professional outfit.

At first glance, it may sound stupid to use your own place for the type of activity Dennis is carrying out. But when you think about it, this location is chosen for many reasons, part of which is now strolling through the woods; yep, civvies. Why? Because the killing ground will have to be contained within the perimeter, these people need to be considered to reduce civilian casualties. Plus, the place is isolated at night.

The sound of Simon's voice breaks my line of thought.

"ST, OK, Three Out."

That's one way of keeping the radio chatter down. Appears three people coming my way, time for some aiming practice. With my new toy in the aim, pointing down the track, peer through the sights, ready to carry out some dry firing.

Fifteen minutes pass with no sign of them. Where the fuck have they gone. Wonder if they are patrolling like yesterday? Better remain alert and looking down the barrel for a further 20 mins, still no sign of them.

Shit, what if they are coming along the ridgeline behind me? Similar to the ones last night, turn in the OP to face the rear. Can't see or hear anyone approaching that way. As I turn back to face the front, Derek spots them entering the farmhouse and calls it in.

"DR In Three."

All this excitement, I've now got a mouth like a camel's flip flop, so I might as well finish whatever is left in the flask. Pour what remains into my mug, take one sip, spitting the contents out a split-second later, yuck, stewed tea. Oh well, doesn't matter, will be back at Steve's place tonight for a few cold ones.

Not much happens for the rest of the day when it comes to Chad's men. In fact, the 14:17 check goes without a hitch. The only thing happening is more people taking their daily exercise. I use the time to ensure everything is noted down in my notebook, ready for the debrief later at the lodge.

I will be leaving here to head back to the RV in one hour to collect the tripwire. Confirm there is still no movements of interest before heading up to where I laid my rear defence. Like a good little squaddie, stop short and stand off for a while. Check through my binos for a close look for any signs some idiot has been tampering with the device.

The foliage at the base of the tree in which I hid the control box has been disturbed. This is not the time to jump to any conclusions. Better play safe. Keeping flat to the ground, inch forward, clearing the land as I go. Finally reach a spot where I can glance along the tripwire — it is still tight. My attention now focused on the plastic container strapped to the trunk. With one hand, I brush aside the grass one blade at a time. Fortunately, the box is still as I left it.

Collect all the bits, then head back to my OP to remove the poncho, packing it away with everything else apart from my mic and the breeze direction indicator. Decide I would pack these away as I bug out after the 17:15 radio check.

Use the short time before the call to confirm I'm leaving the observation post in the exact same state as when I went in. If Steve's master plan involves using this location during the mission's attack phase, the last thing I need is one of Chad's men to find the site. Several moments later, Derek's voice comes over the radio with the 17:15 and final check-in.

"DR, Out," the signal he was leaving his OP at the farmhouse.

I pick up the mic. "GD, Out."

Thirty seconds after, Simon checks out, "ST, Out."

Perfect, we are all heading back to the RV. A final scan confirms nothing is left. Collect the wind finder before heading up the slope away from the OP. My plan is to return the same way I came in, following the track to the main road between Shanklin and Newport.

Been tabbing for several minutes when I spot a family heading in my direction. My first reaction is to ensure that the rifle is out of the line of sight. To be safe, I conceal myself to the left of the track. Wait until the man and woman with two small children passes me by.

Give it a short time before continuing towards the road. Not long before I come to the long wooden bridge, I stop and look behind to see if Derek is coming up behind me. He isn't. Pause for a few minutes before proceeding.

No cars were approaching when I come to the tarmac highway, so I sprint straight across to the other side. The route up the Red Squirrel Trail is uneventful and soon reach the turning to the right, which leads to the RV.

With the rendezvous point just ahead, I go to ground. One of our standard operating procedures is to always standoff before entering any location.

Observe and listen for any sounds or movements for about 11 mins, before making my silent approach. As I stand to move, smack my head on a low-hanging branch, my own fault for not looking. With any luck, the rest will not be here yet and have not witnessed that. If they did, the bastards would take the proverbial piss.

As I start to think I am the first back, Simon's voice comes from under a pile of bushes off to my right. "Come on in, fat boy, and don't bang your head."

"So you saw that then!"

"Sure did, George, and I'm not going to let this go for some time."

"Thanks, Simon, you twat. Where is Steve?"

" Over here, mate, and yes, I saw it as well, idiot," comes Steve's voice to my left.

Chapter Thirteen – Derek's OP

Seems like I have only been asleep for a few seconds since Steve handed me the sketch, when I sense a gentle kick to my feet. Open my eyes and stare up, to be confronted with George's fat, ugly face staring down at me. OK, I'm awake—give me five.

With only the maggot to be packed away, I am ready to go in no time. Grab my gear and join George, who is sitting on his Bergen in the centre of the location.

"Good morning, George," I say, taking up a spot next to him.

"A pleasant morning to you, Derek, just waiting for sleeping beauty over there."

Not long before Simon is perched on his pack on the ground next to us. "Before we leave, Steve left me this sketch of our route—suggest we go over this before heading for our OPs."

"Makes sense to me," says Simon.

I stretch out the sheet of paper on the floor with both hands, illuminating it with the dim red glow of my torch, which I held in my hand. Now need a pointer, so I reach out with my right hand to snap off a small twig from the bush close by. Use this point to the landmarks on the map.

Halfway through, I pause, partly to ensure everyone understands what I've said so far. Plus, it's been a long time since I did anything like this. Want to make sure I'm on the right track when it comes to giving a tactical briefing. There are no questions—that is a relief, apart from George taking the piss out of Simon for being a recce expert. So I continue.

Once the briefing is over, I pick up the sketch and hand it over to Simon. "We have about one and a half hours before first light, so we better make a move over to you."

"No problem, George, if you take the rear, Derek, slot yourself between us."

Wait for Simon to get 20 metres down the track before I tuck in behind him, walking down the narrow path to join the Red Squirrel Trail. Before turning left onto the trail's hard surface, I glance back; George is 10 metres behind me. Shortly after, we arrive at the houses close to the street.

Not sure how the other two typically played this situation, something I'm going to need to learn, so I meet Simon at the side of the tarmac road. Seconds later, George joins us.

The highway seems deserted, with no indications of approaching vehicles from either direction. A minute before Simon goes to sprint across, when to our left, two unmistakable shapes of vehicle headlights come hurtling towards us. Once more, we wait until the place is in darkness, then Simon legs it across the road.

That's the first one across. With my head sticking out of the long grass, I look both ways for any signs of movement. Once I feel George's hand on my shoulder, I know it is time to go. One complete action, spring to my feet and run as fast as I can to the other side. Conceal myself on the forward edge of the treeline a couple of metres away from Simon. Once George crosses, Simon heads for the start of the dirt trail into the woods, indicated by two wooden posts.

The first landmark should be 580 paces from here. The instance I begin walking, I start to count in case, for some reason, Simon loses count. The forest is in complete darkness, apart from the small amount of light from the night sky penetrating the treetops. This is good for me as I soon acquire my night vision, making the trail faintly visible.

One trick I learned while looking through the opening of the commanding officer's FV432 command vehicle while on radio stag, is to look up at the tops of the trees. Tracks are easier to follow this way.

Up in front, Simon stops, looking back in the direction of George and me. Guess from the pace count, he's reached our landmark, the bridge. As we continue, within a short distance I am standing on the bridge's wooden planks. From here, there are only 300 paces to the place where Simon departs for his own OP.

Within a few mins, Simon can be seen crouched down at a junction with his hand placed firmly on his head. This is the signal to close in, a message relayed to George by placing my right hand on my own head. Once we are all close together, Simon says, "This is where I depart. See you both tomorrow at the rendezvous. Stay safe."

"And you mate," I say.

From here, to where George and myself go our separate ways, George takes the lead as he's been in this area before and knows where he is going.

The dirt track continues to meander through the densely-packed trees, passing over what I would loosely class as a bridge. The old wobbly thing consists of old wooden boards stretched across two beams. There are no handrails of any type in place. But, as Steve indicated in his sketch, we soon arrive at the point where the trail divides.

Up ahead, George has come to a standstill. Once I close in on his location, George says, "This is where I leave you, Derek. The gate on Steve's map is beyond the trees," he points to his right. "Keep safe — I will meet you back at the RV at 18:30 tomorrow."

"Thanks, George — see you later, and try to come back minus any small holes."

I follow the track for about two minutes before I come to the metal gate. Right, from here is where I stay on this track. Then I will be in sight of the extensive farmhouse complex in 300 paces. At this point, I need to get across the grass meadow to the woods directly opposite. This route is challenging, compared to the one I've been following. This must be due to it being used not only by people, but also by looking at the shape of some footprints — cattle.

To mitigate any chance of a twisted ankle on the uneven ground, make the decision to cross earlier than planned. Once past the small muddy lake beneath a clump of trees, down a slight grassy slope on my left I turn 90 degrees and start across the field.

Fortunately, the area here also dried out, making the going relatively easy. Once on the other side, I walk just a few feet inside the treeline, to remain out of view of anyone who might be looking from the farm or along the opposite track.

Soon the target and the pond, from which I would carry out my own observation post, comes into my view. Unlike the other three, I don't have the advantage of a previous recce of the location to uncover a suitable site for my OP. Will do this when on target.

Close to the far end of the woods, a dirt track about three metres wide runs across my front, leading to the farmhouse. This is something I will have to make my way across after the bend. This will ensure I stay out of eyesight from people standing at the gate of the property.

In the planning stage for the OPs, Steve mentioned concealing myself in the bullrushes on the pond's edge. Well, it appears like, for once, he fucked up. I'm now at the rear. The vegetation he referred to is, in fact, in the centre of the water. As I didn't bring a boat or a drysuit, I will have to find an alternative spot.

The ground at the back slopes away from the lakes up into another treeline. Halfway up, a vast patch of brown brackens and bushes are situated between a few tall trees. This will make an ideal OP location, as long as it overlooks the farm.

Time is now running out. First light will soon be here, so speed is now essential. I need to approach the OP from the back. So I head up among the trees until I'm directly behind the area of the potential observation post. A simple case of moving stealthily, using the most available cover, slowly move to the clump of bracken.

Take off my Bergen, resting it on the ground to the rear, carefully part the ferns one stem at a time until I am entirely inside undercover. Through the few lengths of ferns I purposely left in place, I got an uninterrupted view of the farmhouse, yard and buildings on each side of the courtyard. So perfect. All that is required now is to set up the OP for the next 36 hours.

While talking to George back at Steve's place over a few beers, he gave me some good advice, one of which is to ensure I erect some type of protection from the weather. As he put it, 'a cold and wet squaddy is a bad soldier who is ineffective at best'. With his words in my head, erect a shelter from the poncho borrowed from Steve.

Pull my Bergen in, take out the binos and notepad, placing them next to the SLR now pointing in the direction of the farm. So that is me all set up, and just in time as the first radio check is in a few minutes.

Reach inside my pack and grab the mic, ready to transmit at dead on 08:17. Over the short time with the boys, I have learned that if you mess up, the others don't let you forget it for some time. So being the new bloke to the group, I need to prove myself and get everything correct and on time.

Glance down at my timepiece, it is time. Take hold of the transmitter, "DR, OK."

Seconds later, George replies with, "GD, OK."

The last person to broadcast his call sign is Simon, "ST, OK," comes loud and clear over the airwaves.

One of my roles is to keep communications going with Steve over in Cowes via SMS. So I save the text, 'All, OK', on my phone. At 08:18, I push the send button and wait for the reply. a few moments later, the following message, 'S3, OK' became visible on the screen.

Must stay focused after the check-in. If there are any movements in the courtyard, there is no way this new boy is going to miss anything. My focus pays off. One man comes from inside the farmhouse via the front door. He joins his colleague down the stone steps, leaning against an old green Land Rover parked on the far side of the yard close to one of the outbuildings.

My first task is to send the message to inform George and Simon that they have people approaching their locations. Pick up the mic with my left hand and press the transmit button. This is something I better get right as I'm the radio expert. Remembering my training, spoke with a 'Clear, Loud, as an order with Pauses' or 'CLAP' as we used to call it.

"DR, Out Two."

While I wait for confirmation, they head towards Dennis' place. Check Mickey, it is now 08:34. Grab the notebook and record the exact time along with a description. Both men are dressed in black jeans with black jackets, supporting a military-style haircut.

A quarter of an hour passes before it is verified by George they go past him.

"GD, F Two."

"ST, In Two," is broadcast 10 minutes later, as the two men enter the property.

Once more write this all down in a section of my pad I earlier sectioned off and named 'Radio Log'. I am not sure if this level of detail is required by Steve, being the planner, but I will note down the timing from all messages from myself, Simon and George.

All seems quiet over on the target. I use this inactivity to pour a brew from the flask. While sipping the sweet tea, a message comes over the radio.

"ST, Out Two."

Five mins later comes, "GD, D Two."

Eyes now back on the track leading from the woods, watch and wait. Do not have to wait long before two people, a man and a woman dressed the same as the others in black, appear and enter the farmhouse. The woman is about six feet tall, with a curvy body rounded off with long blonde hair tied back into a ponytail.

Again after sending, "DR, In Two," I wrote down everything, including, for some reason, a more detailed description of the female.

With two sets of people moving between two locations—maybe this is a sign of a changeover? Then, while making notes, I notice the man who went inside the house 30 minutes ago leave, to take up a position near the long building that stretches across the back of the yard. Very smart, as anyone walking past would not see an armed guard on the front gate.

If proof was needed that this is a working farm, an old red tractor complete with rusty metal and, like most farm equipment, has seen far better days emerges from the back right corner, pulling a flatbed trailer. After a short stop to converse with our man watching the gate, he exits the property and turns right along the road. I lose sight once it rounds the bend, but the rough running engine could still be heard.

As the tractor is not heading in the direction of the others, I simply make a note of the event and time, no point in sending a message.

Time is definitely going fast, as it is now time for the 11:17 radio check.

George is the first to call in, "GD, OK."

Next is Simon with, "ST, OK."

I am the last one to check-in, "DR, OK." So next job, send a text to Steve, 'All, OK'.

Seconds later, the phone vibrates, 'S3, OK'.

There is plenty of activity in the courtyard, with people walking around and cars coming and going, everything you would expect from a busy farm. But there is nothing at the moment worth sending over the airways. So instead, make notes, as they say, every bit of information can help build up a bigger picture, no matter how trivial. Finish writing when the radio crackles into life.

"ST, Four Out."

The group should reach George in 10 and be with me in 20 minutes—that should give me time for a bite to eat. Unwrap a sarnie from the red serviette taken from my Bergen. Whilst eating, I scrutinise the whole area to my front, alternating between the farmhouse and the track. There is something wrong. Thirty minutes pass, with no confirmation they are coming my way from George.

Another 10 mins went by before, "GD, D Four," comes via the airwaves.

Right, they should be here soon. Another 15 more mins went past with still no sign of them on the route. The question here is, where are the fuckers? There is something that is not going as expected.

At last, they are seen again but not at my location, with Simon checking them back into Dennis' place. More details to be noted down.

Meantime, on the farm, a grey Mercedes car pulls into the yard. The driver climbs out, dressed in a black suit. Pauses for a moment to check the area around him before walking around the vehicle's back to open the rear passenger door. With the head jumping to conclusions, I expect Dennis to clamber out as this is his car. But, instead, a young lady, I would guess, is in her early thirties, wearing a pink dress that came to her knees, with long brown hair flowing across her shoulders, climbs out of the car.

As she turns, I catch a full glimpse of her face. Sure, I recognise her from somewhere. Now I may be crap at remembering names but never forget someone's mug, especially the good looking ones... Got it... The woman is one of the ladies I was talking to in the office of the boatyard. Either she's come into lots of money or somebody, ie. Dennis is playing home and away!

As I view her enter the house, Simon initiates the 14:17 radio check, "ST, OK."

I followed with my own call sign, "DR, OK."

Just George to check-in. He's late. Several minutes pass before he transmits, "GD, OK."

Not like him to be delayed, wonder what went wrong—I will ask him tomorrow. That only leaves a message to Steve in Cowes, 'All, OK'.

With Steve's text coming through seconds later, 'S3, OK', all is OK with everyone.

Mid-afternoon of my first OP with the group, and so far, everything is running smoothly, but this is not the time to relax. Still need to prove to others I can earn my place in the team.

As I sit in my own self-worth, I catch the noise of someone moving down near the bullrushes. Inch forward to the leading edge of the OP for a better look. Down by the pond, three kids are throwing stones at the ducks paddling on the water. As they didn't come from the farmhouse, where did they fucking come from? Scan the area for evidence of their point of entry. Find it—lying on the concrete road are three bikes. Looks like the boys soon became bored as the ducks flew away and moved on.

Time is indeed passing us by, as the 17:17 radio check-in goes with no problems. With nothing happening in regards to movement down the track and not much on the farm complex, apart from the change of the person on sentry changing every two hours, the time goes fast. In fact, if I wasn't sitting in an OP, this would be a pleasant afternoon sat by a pond with the sun shining brightly.

Glance down at Mickey to check the time, it's 18:00. As I glimpse up, the young lady from before is now climbing back into the Mercedes, via the back door being held open by the driver. The vehicle is swung around in the courtyard a few moments later, then departs towards the road.

Last light will be here soon—time to prepare for the nighttime routine. This involves making sure everything I will not use is packed away correctly. Then, with the equipment I may need, where I can automatically find it without any hassle.

Reach into my Bergen, grasp something that shouldn't be there. Shit, totally forgot about the rear defences. This is now a matter of pride, as the others wouldn't know I omitted to do this. This is something we used to call in the army 'attention to detail', where every aspect is essential, little things can cost lives. For example, they could be killed if I need to take a shot to protect someone and forgot something as small as taking the rifle's safety catch off. And it would be my fault.

Still kicking myself over the fuck up, I grab hold of the rifle, placing it in the firing position and take a dry shot at the guard crossing the yard, for nothing more than fun and frustration.

I'm virtually in open ground apart from the few numbers of trees and bushes scattered about, the last rays of sunlight don't fade until about 19:50. Then, over at the farmhouse, small incandescent lights mounted on buildings and one either side of the gate burst into life, illuminating the place like a high street at Christmas.

The next 30 minutes bring no noticeable activity. The only thing to do is wait for the 20:17 call. While I wait, I tuck into another sandwich and a fresh brew. The moment the second hand of the clock landed on 12, I press the transmit button and send, "DR, OK."

"GD, OK," comes next.

Simon checks in last, "ST, OK."

As before, pick up my mobile, find the saved text 'All, OK' and broadcast this to Steve. Roughly 60 seconds later, the return message reads, 'S3, OK'.

Not done that many OPs personally. As the Commanding Officer's radio operator, I was usually back at the rear in the tactical HQ or the A2 Echelon. I remember when a platoon was missing a radio operator for an ambush, and I was kindly volunteered to take his place. Spent two days laying in the undergrowth on the border between Southern and Northern Ireland, waiting for a group of known terrorists to appear. After 48 hours of staring into nothing, in the end, we bugged out as they didn't arrive.

Mind back to the present OP, which is now in complete darkness. The only sounds are the strange ones coming from the woods to my right and behind, including some wood pigeon that hasn't shut the fuck up for the last hour.

One of the bits of advice the boys gave me back at Steve's place is, if you hear someone creeping up on you in the darkness, always take time to really listen, as it is probably the mind playing tricks on you.

Over at the farmhouse, several lights in the downstairs windows penetrated the glass, illuminating parts of the yard, with the occasional glimpse of the security guard walking backwards and forwards along the edge of the building. On the top floor, through the massive window on the side of the house, a landing light could be seen coming on. A few short moments later, a naked woman momentarily paused before disappearing as quickly as she appeared.

The woman would have my full attention any other time but thinking back to the forgotten war, Northern Ireland, the IRA uses this tactic to disguise moments of weapons. The terrorist would use females to prance naked in windows in flats that overlooked army bases and sentry sangers. They knew men who are away from family and girlfriends for six months, wouldn't miss the opportunity of seeing nude women, even through binoculars. In the meantime, they would be moving weapons and explosives below you.

Not falling for this old trick, return my gaze to the guard in the courtyard. The man is still walking around with no other movements visible for now.

Just after the 23:17 radio check comes and goes, my eyes start to feel heavy, need some energy boost. Reach inside the pocket of the Bergen and grab the can of Red Bull. Brought this along for just this moment.

As noise travels further at night and this idiot didn't think this through, I would need to muffle the sound of the ring-pull opening the can. Decide there is only one option. Place the can inside my jacket and close the zip, leaving sufficient room to remove the ring pull. Hopefully, it is not under pressure, soaking me in the process.

Excellent success, the can is open — more importantly, I stay dry. Take seceral sips while observing the sights, sounds and smells of the night. Thankfully our friend, the wood pigeon, at long last, shuts the fuck up, leaving the area in a blanket of silence.

The time now is 01:35, with nothing happening, even our remaining guard over at the farmhouse must be bored or feeling sleepy, as I witness him abandon his post and enter the house. Maybe he will wake his replacement. I continue to view the space to my front, as this should only take a short amount of time before he reappears. But, nope, 45 minutes went past and no sign of either of them. The lazy git is probably getting a brew. Now that's a good idea.

Still with eyes on the target, I sip the lukewarm tea. The act of the man entering the property gets me thinking, mainly why I decided to help the others on this mission. I came to England to see family and a holiday. Now I am not rich by any stretch, but there again, I'm not skint either. Managed to sell the bottle of Domaine de la Romanée-Conti Grand Cru Steve gave me on St Halb for £250,000 to some idiot collector.

I have a beautiful wife and home back on the sunny Caribbean island. Definitely not that I miss this type of operation, as I've only done one before. Spent the next 15 mins trying to find the answer. In the end, I decided that I am looking for a change in routine due to boredom. The crackle of the C350 interrupted my chain of thought.

"GD, OK," comes the message from George.

Pick up the mic and reply with, "DR, OK."

Seconds later, Simon transmits, "ST, OK."

Reach in my jacket pocket, pull out the mobile, search for the stored text, and send it, 'All, OK'. It isn't long before Steve's reply, 'S3, OK', appears on the screen.

Making sure I enter the detail and time, 02:17, into the radio log.

That's what I love about being a radio operator. You can be half-asleep one moment, then you receive a radio call, and you are alert again. Need this boost as nothing happens for the proceeding three hours, with the 05:17 going without any problems.

As the first signs of first light start to appear over the horizon, I think to myself, I have made it through the night of my first real OP, and I'm still alive. But better not get complacent. This part of the mission still has several hours to go yet.

Our guard reappears over on the farm — it appears he spent the night in the warm farmhouse. This will come in handy as most attacks go in just before first light, and our friends will be inside. Make a note of the time he appears, 06:30.

Time for brekkie. Pour the remaining tea from the flask into my black mug before grabbing one of the two sandwiches still left from my Bergen.

Right, let's see what today brings. Scan the farmhouse and the surrounding area through my binos. All looks normal with nothing to concern me at the moment. Over at the farmhouse, both guards are now patrolling the courtyard. A few people are going in and out of buildings. Guess they're doing whatever farm people do at this time of the morning.

Stuffed what is left of the sarnie in my mouth, when Simon initiates the 08:17 radio check, "ST, OK."

Tried to eat as fast as I can, when George sends, "GD, OK."

Finally manage to get the sandwich down, but 60 seconds late, I send my own call sign, DR, OK," so that's cutting it fine.

If yesterday is anything to go by, we should witness a changeover of people. My assumption is correct. At 08:45, Chad's men leave the farm then head towards the track.

I call it in, "DR, Out Two."

Wait, holding the mic for the next 10 minutes until "GD, F Two," comes loud and clear over the radio.

This follows up with, "ST, In Two," a quarter of an hour later.

Not long before Simon signals, two people are leaving Dennis' place. This is definitely a pattern. Confirmation by George and then check in by me.

Things are starting to get busy with several things happening. At the farmhouse, Dennis' grey Mercedes pulls into the yard, stopping close to the house. The big question is, who will get out of the vehicle today, the same woman as yesterday or Dennis? Through my binos, I can see the shape of two people sitting on the rear seat. Once the car came to a stop as before, the driver exits. Then after a quick scan of the area, walk around to the back passenger door and opens it.

This time, Dennis clambers out. Without stopping, enters the house while the other man remains seated on the rear seat. It must be a flying visit as he emerges after five minutes, climbing back in the Mercedes. My question here is, who is the other person? The car pauses for a second as it exits the farm—my question is answered. The person who stayed in the vehicle is Chad.

Pick up the notebook and enter all the relevant information. Pulls in at 09:45, waits for Dennis to do something in the house and leaves again at 09:52.

At the 11:17 check-in, three other people are seen leaving Dennis'. The standard interchange of radio messages follow, with Simon checking them out.

"ST, Three Out, OK," a combination of movements and check-in.

However, maybe they used the track that George and I came down and bypassed him for some reason. This is confirmed when I witnessed them entering the farm about 40 minutes later. Called it in, "DR, In Three."

To my front, several people pass the farmhouse and head in the direction of the woods, probably a group of ramblers. Apart from them and one of Chad's men having a sneaky cigarette while on duty, after that, very little happens until about 13:00, when two cars full of people turn up. Only one person gets out and enter the house with them, leaving half an hour later carrying a small box, plus, from what I saw, a large envelope with a blue strip down the middle. Still working on my theory that every bit of info is significant, so make a note.

After the 14:17 radio check goes without a hitch, all messages are sent, including the text to Steve. My mind turns to preparing the observation post for bugging out after the 17:17 call. The place needs to be spotless, with no signs that anyone has ever been here. I've still got something to prove, so I will check several times before leaving. The last thing I needis for some person to discover the location and fuck up the mission if I want to remain in the group.

It was similar to yesterday afternoon, not much happening apart from more people going for a walk, but they're not critical to our task. Saying that, the death of innocent civvies will need to be considered as much as possible. From what I know about Steve, he is likely to say, 'if they are in the kill zone, then unlucky'.

About 25 minutes before bug out, I take down the rain protection, grab my Bergen and pull it outside, placing it to the rear. Then, crawl back inside, grab my rifle and inch backwards, replacing as many ferns as I could back to the upright position.

One last glance at the area, I'm happy it appears like nobody has been there—time to head for the RV. The plan is to go back following the same course I used to the OP. The very last thing to do is ensure the rifle is covered to keep it out of view. Wouldn't want to scare the shit out of any civvies.

No issues back to the RV, didn't encounter anyone on the route. The road is clear of vehicles, making the crossing straightforward. I'm standing just short of the rendezvous point within no time, wondering how many are back already.

As instructed, stand off for a while, listening for any movements or sounds. Only when I am confident it is safe, I move into the position. Can't see anyone. I must be the first back. Go to conceal myself in an extensive patch of bushes, when a voice cries out.

"No room here, fat boy."

"Who's that?" I ask."

"It's your worst nightmare."

I now recognise the voice, it's Steve. "Hi Steve, are the others back?"

Simultaneously, two voices echo out from different locations, "Yep, been waiting for your lazy arse to get here."

Chapter Fourteen – Rest and Recuperation

Glad to see nobody interfered with the lodge while we've been away. Once inside, I dump my kit in the bedroom, except for my notebook—I need to go through it. Meanwhile, the other three plonk their Bergens on the floor and are now sprawled on the sofas with several cold beers.

"Before you idiots become too comfortable, I suggest you each go through your notes to ensure everything is written down, and pass me one of those beers."

"Anything else, your majesty?" George replies, passing me a beer.

"No, thanks, peasant, that will do for now."

The place is quiet for the next half an hour as all four of us read, write, and double-check our individual notes. With zilch being omitted, no matter how small the bit of information, nothing can be left to chance on the attack phase of our mission.

At last, I'm happy with the info in my notebook, confident I've missed nothing out. Close the book, sit back and wait for the rest to finish. Shortly after, both George and Simon completed their reports, leaving only Derek.

"What you doing, writing a fucking novel, Derek?" Simon asks, launching another can of cold beer in his direction.

"Making sure I don't miss anything out. Would hate for you lot to have something to take to piss out of me for, being the new guy."

"No need to worry there—we will always find things to take the piss out of you. Besides, we are used to you REMFs bring up the rear."

"Remind me again what a REMF stand for again, Simon?"

"Rear Echelon Mother Fucker."

While waiting for Derek to finished his report, grab a handful of pasties from the fridge, take one myself and place the rest on the coffee table in the centre of the room.

"Help yourselves, gents, before George eats them all."

"Fuck off, Steve," comes the instant reply from George.

"The time now is only 19:30. Does anyone else fancy parking the plans and sorting out our kit until tomorrow? The pub down the road serves food until 21:00. I believe the pub's got an extension on its opening hours to 01:00 hrs."

"Now that sounds like a fantastic plan to me," Derek says, putting down his notebook at long last.

"Perfect, shall we say be ready to leave at 20:00? As I didn't hear any objections from you lot, I'm off for a quick shower."

"Make it snappy, nancy boy, so the rest of us can get cleaned up as well. And remember what you said to me in St Halb, washing it fast more than 10 times is classed as a wank."

Walking to the spare room to sort out some clean clothes, "I'll bear that in mind, George."

The boys must either be hungry or thirsty as everyone is ready for the boozer smack on 20:00. Don't remember getting barred after the minor incident with the youths last week, so we should be OK.

When we arrive at the Barleycorn, the place is packed with people having a good time. As before, the stools along the front of the bar are occupied by a mixture of people. The majority of the wood and metal tables to the left are also full. This included two women accompanied by three men, who are sitting on an extended bench-type seat towards the back of the room, near one of the exits.

To the right, the fire roars away in the brick fireplace. This half of the room is filled with four tables identical to those on the other side. Unfortunately, the brown leather sofas I wantd to sit at on my last visit are taken up by the same idiots as my previous visit, who are now starting to fidget nervously in their seats.

"We're not going to get any trouble from you numpties tonight, am I?" I say, warming my hands by the glowing fire. There is a silent shaking of heads to confirm they must have learned not to mess with me last time.

"Friends of yours, Steve?"

"Not really, Simon. May have given them a beating on my earlier visit."

"Any particular reason… no, forget that, I don't want to know."

I rejoin the others, "If you grab that table near the warm fire, gents, I will buy the booze. So take it you two will have your usual beers. What about you, Derek, what you having?"

"I'll have a Guinness, Steve."

After a few minutes, I manage to squeeze in an opening at the wooden bar. Lucky for me, Gary is working tonight behind the bar.

"So what can I get you, Steve."

"Three John Smiths and a pint of Guinness, please, Gary." Well, at least he remembered my name and isn't calling the bouncers over, I think to myself as he pours the drinks.

When I return to the table, the rest are already studying the food menu. One of the conditions of my PTSD is I can't stand people close behind me, something both Simon and George knew so always when possible left the chair along the wall for me. So place the beers down and take up the empty seat against the back wall facing into the room.

"Anything good to eat?" I enquire, picking up the spare menu.

"I fancy the mixed grill," George answers, pointing to it for some reason on the menu.

"I'll have one of them as well. What about you two?"

"Me, too," replies Derek.

"Come on, Simon, it's make your mind up time. Will ask if they do a kiddies' version for you."

You know what you can do, Steve… but on this occasion, I will have a kid's mixed grill."

"Don't go anywhere near there, Derek. It's a long story," George stated, on seeing the puzzled expression on his face.

Like most public houses that serve food, you are required to remove your fat, lazy arse from the seat and order with the staff behind the bar. I'm standing ordering the food at the counter, thinking to myself, I'm sure I got the beers in last time. Oh well, might as well order several rounds of shots—this is going to become very messy.

Return to join the others, with a tray full of a mixture of full shot glasses and a pack of playing cards. "Thought we could have a quick drinking game while we wait for our food."

Arrange the glasses on the wooden-topped table and open the box of cards, placing them on the table. "The game is simple, gents. The person who is dealt the lowest card needs to pick a shot and down it in one. By the way, aces equal one."

Hold the pack in my left hand and place one card face down in front of each person. Turn over my card—it is a nine. Next, Simon turns his over to reveal a king, George has a four. With a two, Derek loses the first round.

"OK, mate, pick your drink and knock it back," I say, collecting the used cards.

After six rounds and Derek losing every hand, he starts to appear a little sick. " I know I'm the new boy, but it can't be a coincidence I keep losing. You bastards must be cheating," he declares, slightly slurring his words.

"Of course we aren't. It is the luck of the cards, mate."

Fortunately for him, Simon loses the next hand with a five, followed by George turning over an ace.

"See, told you no one is deceiving you."

Didn't have the heart to tell him that I've been cheating when he failed to obtain high cards in the previous four rounds. Evey low card I held on the bottom of the pack to be dealt to him. A silly grin develops on my face as I remember something my dad always stated, 'You're a Barker, so when playing cards, cheat'. Eventually, he sees me take the card from underneath the pack.

"You bastards, that's it. I'm not playing another round," as he slams a half-filled glass down on the table next to the other empty ones.

"Just our way of saying welcome to the team, Derek," I pass him the cards, "you deal."

At that point, three vast plates of food that would make any meatatarian proud arrived, plus a smaller kid's version for Simon, arrive. One day I will have that idiot eating a proper man-sized meal. With the food consumed, our minds turned back to the liquid refreshments.

"Don't look at me. I got the last few rounds," I push the empty glasses in front of Simon.

"No problem, I can take a subtle hint."

While Simon is away buying drinks, my attention shifts to scanning the room for potential threats. Yes, I know it's a night off, but this is a condition of my hypervigilance and something hard to break. Besides, it came in handy on more than one occasion. Thankfully tonight, all seems quiet, with people minding their own business and mainly staying in their own social groups. Even our idiot friends on the sofas are keeping to themselves.

My scanning of the room is disrupted when Simon returns with a tray full to the brim with beers. "You get carried away," as I grab a beer in each hand.

"Nope, saves us going back again in 10 minutes."

As the alcohol and conversation flows, Derek makes his first rooky error and mentions the mission. On hearing this, George quickly changes the subject. "Forget that crap. We have more important things to talk about. For one, take a gander at that woman over on the bench table near the back door, the one with the blonde hair tied back in a ponytail?"

We all turn to take a sneaky peek but fail miserably; even a partially sighted person would have seen us staring in her direction. So after a mouthful of beer, "what about her?"

"Are you fucking blind or just stupid, Steve? She hasn't taken her eyes off you since we came in. Maybe she fancies you, mate."

"Can't see no guide dog with her," Simon says, nearly choking on his drink.

"Go chat to her, you never know she might be desperate, and you could get laid tonight."

"You know what, George, I will go and strike up a conversation. But, I need to finish this beer first."

"Well, here's your chance, wimp." Then, with one big shove, George pushes me out of my chair. "She has gone to the far end of the bar."

Haven't done this sort of stuff for many years. And no way I'm going to let the others know that this person, who can stare any danger in the eye without flinching, is indeed scared of chatting up women.

Take a large swig from my glass, looking for the last bit of alcohol-related courage, place the glass down and head towards her. Only one thing for it, treat this as any other mission. The first task, scan the area around her any other threats. Next, find the best opportunity to place myself beside her. In the final part of the task, find some reason to talk to her.

The first two parts went without a hitch. I'm now standing next to her, desperately trying to think of something to say, when she turns around to face me. "Hi, my name is Lorna—what's yours?"

"Funny that I was about to ask you the same thing," I half mumble, being thrown off track, "Hi, I'm Steve. Can I buy that drink for you?"

"Tell you what, let me take these drinks to my friends," she points to the table by the door, "Then I'll come back, mine's a Southern Comfort with one lump of ice."

"Sounds like a perfect plan to me. See you back here in a moment." Carry the beers back to the boys.

"Well, what's her name," Derek asks, taking his drink from me.

"Lorna. I'm going back to speak to her, so carry on without me. But don't fuck off home and leave me behind."

By the time I return, Lorna is already sipping on her drink. The conversation flows easily for the next 10 minutes as we discovered more about each other.

Turns out she is a single woman who lives in Southampton but over on the island for work for the following two months, working for a private security firm.

Even though we are getting on, she even got me laughing, which is something that had eluded me for a long time — apart from when I'm with the idiots over there. But that's usually sarcastic humour — no way I'm telling a woman I just met what line of work I'm in, not that drunk. So instead said to her that I am writing a series of novels called 'Covert Ops', and Simon, George and Derek are here on a short holiday.

Been chatting for what seems like ages, when a voice shouts across the room. "Drying up over here, loverboy, and it's your round," followed by a hail of peanuts.

"No problem, Simon, give me a minute."

Move a little closer to Lorna, "I need to go back to the boys, any chance of getting your number? Would love to meet up again, this time without them idiots?"

"That sounds good to me as well, Steve, let me borrow a pen and paper from behind the bar. Tell you what, once I have written my details down, why don't I come over and say hello to your mates?"

"Perfect, another Southern Comfort?" Lorna nods and kisses me tenderly on the cheek.

Grab the tray of drinks and head back to the table. "OK, boys, this is Lorna, be nice."

"We're always nice," says Simon shaking her hand.

"By the number of empty shot glasses, you have been enjoying yourselves," Lorna points to the glasses.

"Yeah, it is a game made up by Steve, but don't play, the bastard cheats."

"I'm sure he doesn't, Derek," she gives me a knowing smile.

"How about another game, gents. You in Lorna?" George announces, getting out of his chair and heading to the bar before anyone has any chance to object. About five minutes later, he comes back with a mixture of drinks concoctions.

"This time, I will deal, so we don't have a repeat of dealing cards from the bottom of the pack."

Derek gives everyone a card face down. I turn my card over first. It is a two of hearts. Shit, I've lost, I think to myself. This is followed by the rest, in turn, leaving Lorna to turn over her card last. It's the ace of clubs.

"Wow, an ace, do I win?"

"If by a win, you mean lose, then yes. Aces only equal one." I hand her one of the shots. "Sorry, down in one."

"Cheers, boys," Lorna throws back the drink.

The game goes on for another half an hour, with us all taking it in turns to lose, when Lorna's hand squeezes my right leg just above the knee. While the others drink and deal the cards, her hand caresses the inside of my thigh. Turn to face her and give a quick smile and a wink to indicate this feels good. Not sure if this is a tactic to make me lose, I'm definitely not complaining.

This goes on for several more minutes before her hand inches up to the top of my leg and grasps and caresses my manhood. Then, while trying every trick in the book to prevent a situation from developing, she turns, smiles and whispers in my ear.

"My car is out back. Want to go outside and fuck me?"

My mind is saying no, but the building pressure in my trousers is telling a different story. So I move in closer, in a quiet whisper, "You lead, I will follow you out."

After one last squeeze, she stands up, turns and walks to the back door. Wait until she is outside, I give the boys a knowing glance, "Back in 20 minutes." Pull my jumper down as far as it will go and go to join Lorna outside.

A scan of the car park finds Lorna standing at the rear of an estate car parked in the far corner, void of any lights and away from prying eyes. After a quick survey to ensure nobody else is around, I walk over to her. While my hand reaches insid her jumper to grab her ample breasts, Lorna's hands fumble frantically, attempting to undo the belt holding up my jeans. Without saying a word pull her in close, planting a passionate kiss fully on her lips.

With one hand, I open the tailgate of the vehicle, lay her on her back inside. Both hands reach up inside her green dress and ease her knickers inch by inch down her slender legs. Can feel the excitement building up, my body tingling with expectation as she looked up at me. I reach down to pull my pants off when two hands, one on each shoulder, grab me and pull me backwards.

The next thing, I double over in excruciating pain from the result of two simultaneous punches to either side of my ribcage. Several more blows follow as I hit the deck. Absorbing the now frequent hard kicks, I curl up in a ball, trying to grasp the situation. What the fuck is happening? Why are these men beating the shit out of me? As far as I'm aware, I didn't annoy anyone inside. It can't be Lorna's boyfriend and his mate — she said she is single.

Whoever this is, I can't take much more of a thrashing, I need to react. Open my eyes, draw a deep breath. Take stock of my surroundings, then land a well-aimed kick just below and upwards on one of the men's kneecaps. With a loud, clear snap, his kneecap dislocates. He lands on the ground, screaming in agonising pain.

The sight of his mate in pain momentarily stuns the other, giving me a second to stumble to my feet and put a little distance between myself and the attacker.

Now facing the man, through the blood dripping from my head, I recognise him. He is one of the people who was sitting with Lorna in the pub. As I turn towards the car to witness Lorna sitting in the driver seat, the man on the floor finds some more courage and grabs the ankle of my left foot.

Raise my other leg up several feet off the ground before slamming my boot down hard into the side of his head. Once more, the sound of cracking bones drown out the obscenities coming from the person standing in front of me.

By now, I recover my total composure as I observe the other man remove a long knife from inside his black jacket. "Come on, you little prick, let's see what you're made of," he barks at me while throwing the knife, one hand to the other.

Reach for my 9 mm, fuck it's in my jacket pocket, and I've left that inside with the boys. Need to think fast, so I scan the area looking for a weapon to defend myself, still keeping an eye on the blade-wielding idiot to my front. Sod it, nothing is at hand, will have to kill the bastard with his own knife.

The plan is rapidly formulated in my head. I will go in hard, hopefully knocking his arm holding the weapon away from the danger zone. Wait until he throws his knife to the other hand, then launch at him, striking him hard, knocking him to the deck. Before he manages to recover.

Right, time to act before the arsehole launches his own attack. With one swift movement rush at him, my left arm knocking the knife from his hand. At the same time, with my clenched right hand, I land several fast, forceful punches in quick succession to his face. The resulting force and momentum resulting in us both hitting the ground hard.

With one bent arm trying to protect himself from the blows, the other scours the loose dirt to find the dropped knife. Seconds later, with outstretched fingers, he grasps the bony handle. I lurch backwards as the knife enters my shoulder. Then, with the sharp blade still sticking out, in excruciating pain, I stumble to my feet. This man is starting to piss me off. Need to end this, and quick.

As I stagger backwards, I trip over the dead man on the floor, now with deep red blood oozing from the giant gaping hole in the side of his head. While lying in the dirt planning my next move, I turn my head to observe others standing near the door. Finally, I yell out, "Any time you fancy helping will be fine by me."

"You're doing great, Steve," George shouts, as he reaches into my jacket pocket, takes out something and launches it in my direction. It is my 9 mm pistol. With an outreached arm grab it just as my attacker mounts another attack, coming at me with yet another knife.

The moment he leans forward, intent on stabbing me with one well-aimed shot, I pull the trigger. Like the scene is playing out in slow motion, the bullet leaves the barrel in a puff of faint white smoke, recoiling the pistol upwards. A nanosecond later, the round strikes the centre of the man's face, followed almost instantaneously by fragments of skull and brain matter as they exit the back of the head.

Before his body slumps to the ground, I roll on my side to escape the fat bastard landing on me. The first thought when getting up is to turn towards the car to make sure Lorna is OK. The vehicle has disappeared.

As I turn to make my way to where the boys are standing, the sharp pain in my right shoulder reminds me I still have a knife lodged in me.

Take hold of it with my left hand, bite down hard on a small piece of wood I found on the floor, then with gritted teeth, I withdraw the blade with one swift movement, letting out a cry of pain as I do.

But with little time on our hands, this is not the time to think about pain and the blood pouring down from the wound. The two dead idiots are messing up the back of the boozer. We need to dispose of them before anyone sees them and connects them to us.

By this time, I am joined by Simon, Derek and George, "Thanks for the assistance, gents," checking the person I shot for any ID.

"You're welcome, mate—we didn't want to interrupt your lovemaking. It wasn't until Derek suddenly realised he had seen the woman you departed with before," Simon says, turning over the other man lying on the floor.

"Yeah, for some reason during the OP, I paid particular attention to her, maybe it is because she is an attractive woman. She is one of the people moving between the farmhouse and Dennis' place."

"You could have mentioned that a little earlier, before I went outside with her, Derek."

"Ooops, sorry it didn't come to me until you left. That's why we came outside, to warn you."

Parked near the building are several huge wheelie bins. Even though they are not ideal, they are the only place to dispose of the corpses quickly. Inside the containers are loads of full black plastic bags.

"Help me remove the sacks. We need to place our dead friends here at the bottom, so they are not found instantly when someone brings out more rubbish." I kick one of the bodies.

After removing the contents from two of the large bins, now for the disposal of the dead men. About to throw in the second guy when the lights at the pub's back door come on.

227

We all dive for cover behind the mound of bags. Observe as a young man carrying even more rubbish walks in our direction.

Shit, if he comes any closer, he will have to be blind not to stumble across us. This must be our lucky day, as the lazy bastard launched the bags from halfway onto the pile we just made, one landing directly on George.

We wait for five minutes after the young man goes back inside, just in case he comes back out with more rubbish. Then, one more check of our friends to double-check they don't have any identifying ID on them, before dumping them in the dustbins. The police, of course, will find out who they are and discover their identity, but the longer we can delay them, the better.

Once all the sacks are piled back in the wheelie bins on top of the men, my attention once more turns to the blood still dripping from my shoulder. So far, the adrenaline has kept me going, but now I need to arrest the bleeding. Now back over in the location where Lorna's car was previously, I remove my jumper and t-shirt to reveal a two-inch wound.

As I tear up my top, "Give us a hand, Simon, to bandage this up until we are back at my place."

"Sure, that looks nasty, Steve. Think we may have to take you to a hospital for a few stitches."

"Nothing a little bit of super glue can't fix," I say, holding some padding as Simon fastens it tightly in place.

We arrive back at the lodge at about 00:30 hrs. There is no point in doing anything now. It can all wait until the morning. So after pinching the cut together and dabbing a generous amount of superglue over the wound, I go to bed. I am knackered.

Chapter Fifteen – Mission Preparation

Last night was an exciting night, or it would have been if I didn't have a banging headache, a mouth like a camel's flip flop and a hole in my right shoulder. This boy needs several gallons of strong coffee to clear my head, so turn on the machine and plonk my arse on the sofa.

We've still got seven days for the weapons to be back at Mark's warehouse, minus two for getting from here to the mainland. This means the attack on Dennis' gaff needs to be launched in the next five days. One key issue is that of Stuart. I'm positive he will know what day the military inspectors are showing up for the inspection. And inform the relevant people.

We are not dealing with amateurs. Chad will no doubt have worked out the timing for himself. So he will know when the weapons are required to be back. I will have to try to recover them, at the very latest, five days from now. For now, I really need to start planning, but first, my caffeine intake.

One bit of the puzzle that still needs putting in place is more information on the layout and strength of people at Dennis' home. With our OPs and recce, plus data provided by Mark, we are almost there, but with a few more holes to fill, I want to speak to or interrogate Stuart, as some people call it.

The question is how to lure him to the Isle of Wight. Thinking about it, he may still be here as I watch him walking around at the boatyard two days ago. Only one thing for it, ring Mark and ask him to come over today, making sure Stuart is with him.

The clock on the wall tells me it's 07:00. For a split-second, thought it is too early to call, but fuck it, I'm up, so everyone else can drag their lazy arses out of bed as well. Dial Mark's number on the mobile, it starts to ring.

After several minutes, Mark answers the telephone. However, from the sound of his voice, I can tell he is still half asleep.

"Morning, Steve, what's the problem?"

"Nothing much, Mark. So far, most things are going to plan. But, I need you to come to the island today, and it's vital you bring Stuart along. Will explain why once you arrive at my place."

"Can you give me a few hours? Need to contact him and catch the ferry. Should be at your place around lunchtime."

"Perfect, Mark."

Place the phone down, get up and walk over to grab another brew from the kitchen, when Simon's ugly mug appears in the doorway. "Morning mate, help yourself to a coffee and food."

"Cheers, I will. So what you been up to this morning?"

"Not much. Called Mark. He and Stuart will be over here today. My shoulder is OK, thanks for asking."

"Stop being a cry baby, Steve – It's only a knife wound."

I need to start making plans for the attack phase, so I grab my notebook with the OP's findings and the other notes made so far on the mission. Plonk the info down on the dining table and start to read. Forming some sort of an outline of the plan in my mind, but of course, I still require the other three's conclusions.

Manage to get halfway through my notebook when two more sorry looking figures, looking worse for wear, come from the direction of the bedrooms. Both Derek and George have at last put in an appearance.

"Morning, gents." A faint noise resembling a grunt comes back from the pair.

"Once you've grabbed a brew and returned to the living, we must go through the notes from our individual observation posts.

Plus, all the explosive IEDs need to be checked to ensure they are in working order still. Then there is the matter of a plan—remember, the failure to plan is a plan to fail."

Give the boys time to read their notebooks and get themselves sorted before reaching for my own notes. Then, each of us will take turns to discuss any information we believe to be helpful and relevant to the mission's planning. Starting with myself.

"OK, to start with, I believe Dennis is more than an arms dealer but, to use a cliché, he is a triple threat. So first, we know about the weapons, plus he is into people smuggling. I witnessed them return with a load of immigrants on both mornings of the OP. Simon went on the same grey boat when we checked the boatyard

"They were later packed into a back of a 20—foot articulated container vehicle and driven off. Unfortunately, one of the potential slaves mustn't have come up to the standard required by the buyers, as Chad's second in command, Jackson, shot the man dead before placing his body on the boat, possibly to be dumped at sea."

"Observed a box lorry turn up at the property mid-afternoon," Simon interrupts.

I resume, "The third threat would appear our man is also into drug smuggling. I also witnessed several packages wrapped in green plastic tied up with blue nylon rope, loaded and unloaded from the boat. Anyone else notice the bundles?"

"Sure I didn't come across any plastic packages but did witness a man turn up at the farm in a convoy of two cars. He went inside, exiting minutes later, carrying a cardboard box and holding a large envelope. Remembered the envelope as it had a distinctive blue strip down the middle," Derek comments, flicking through his notes.

"Funny you should say that, the fat truck driver, which I must add had a massive trucker's belly to be proud of, left with a similar envelope. Think about it, gents. Where else have we seen these before... Yep on St Halb, it is the same type Henry always used," Simon interjects again.

"You're right, Simon. So I guess you're not just an ugly bastard."

"Do one, George."

"From what I witnessed, the speed boat goes out around 22:00 every night, loaded with some packages and returns early morning with the unfortunate immigrants, ready to be sold into slavery, and even more boxes; would make a guess these are drugs." I continue reading from my notes.

"One last thing before I hand it over to Simon. Yesterday at 11:17, Chad and Dennis appeared on the pier. Not long after this, I left and made my way to the RV."

"What's wrong? You get scared all on your own, bloody part-timer," comes the sarcastic reply from Simon.

"Not going to dignify that with an answer. Over to you, Simon, let's learn what you got up to."

"Unlike that waster," he points to me, "spent the required time in my OP. Found the perfect place, which overlooked the grounds, house and outbuilding. It would make an excellent sniper position. As for the manning strength and the rotation of Chad's people, it would appear at the property at least a two-hour cycle. Seems they alternate from the gate to patrolling, then disappear into the barrack block. Couldn't tell you what happens once they are inside.

"However, all changes of manpower are in groups of two, not including those travelling to the farmhouse at 09:00 & 18:00 who change every 12 hours rather than two, unlike the others. This can be backed up by both Derek and George."

"Sure can. Being an ex-radio operator, got used to writing down every message that came over the airwaves. So my timings can verify what Simon said. Plus, the call log from George will confirm which route they took."

"Thanks for that, Derek," Simon carries on. "We also had four men leave Dennis' place, speculating as they didn't reach Derek, they were sent out to patrol the woods, probably looking for us."

"I can confirm this as when they reached my location, they were spread out walking in a straight line through the undergrowth. In fact, one almost stumbled on me. Would like to add, they are clued up. One person spent time looking under the wooden bridge for any traps or explosives. So if plan is blowing up the thing, hide it well, Steve," George eventually says, after being quiet up to now.

After checking his notebook, Simon resumes, "At 10:00, Dennis arrives in his Mercedes and enters the house. The same routine as earlier continued till 15:00 when a taxi arrives, driving up to the house. Three screaming brats, I guess the oldest being about 11, clambered out and go inside. I'm mentioning this because there may be children on the property. Sure everyone here, apart from Steve, has an issue shooting kids."

"That's not fair, Simon. Defending myself. I hate killing children when it's not required. But I will justify the ones that got in front of bullets this way. How many movies have you seen or on our missions, for that matter, in which that innocent kid is actually the lookout for the organised group?"

"If that's what you want to tell yourself, Steve, fine by me. Anyway, back to my findings, to prove Chad is a mad man with a slight weakness. At 21:00, he hit one of his own men forcibly, striking him on the side of his head with the butt of a pistol. This is while being held on his knees by two more of the group.

I can confirm he is one of his men and not some random person they dragged up from somewhere, as once he composed himself, he staggers to the barrack block.

"Nothing happens until 02:31, an old army-style Land Rover turns up at the gate. Speaks to someone, then drives to stables, unloads 4 bundles wrapped in plastic, and takes them inside. The man was there no more than 20 minutes.

"A relatively quiet night followed, until 09:30 when Dennis leaves in his car. Then at 14:17, the truck we spoke about earlier arrived, leaving soon afterwards. One last thing before handing over to the next guy, why were you so late for the 14:17 radio check, George?"

Shuffling in his seat, George looks up sheepishly, "Easy, I was having a shit."

Trying my best not to burst out laughing, "Over to you, George, let's discover what you have."

"Thanks, Simon. Well, not much to say that hasn't been said before, as I spent most of the time staring into the empty woods with very little going on. Besides confirming the people who left either the farmhouse or the property, the only thing happening was civvies walking about. Almost forgot. There was one patrol at about 23:20, that walked along the ridge to the rear of my location, rather than take the route through the woods.

"My conclusion is that we need to be careful of civilians spotting us, even early in the morning. Although, in my professional opinion, as a sniper, this location is not suitable for a firing position, I suggest we scrap this. So I set up where Simon had his OP."

"Your judgement in these matters is always valued, George. I agree, when I make plans for the attack, I will locate you overlooking Dennis' place. That leaves you, Derek, to go through your observation post findings," I state, turning to face him.

"Thanks, Steve. I've not done this type of thing for a while. So best I start from the front of my notebook. To begin with, during the day, there are two guards always in the farm courtyard. From what's been spoken about and from what I witnessed, these are changed every 12 hours. This includes the attractive lady with blonde hair tied back in a ponytail which you met last night, leaving you a reminder of your encounter." Derek points to Steve's shoulder.

"This is a working farm with lots of activities throughout the day, with farm vehicles and cars coming and going all day. At 14:00, Dennis' grey Mercedes turns up, but instead of him climbing out, it is one of the women from the boatyard. Remember talking to her while everyone else explored the yard and buildings. She leaves again at 18:00.

"Depending on Steve's plans, what could be helpful are the lights around the farmhouse do not come on until 19:50 and go off again just after first light. This leads on to the guards in the courtyard. So it will appear that at night there is only one person in the yard. If the other night is anything to go on, this goes down to zero as I observed him go inside the house at 01:30, not coming out again to 06:32.

"The same activities occurred on the second morning as the previous day, with Dennis and Chad arriving in his car at 09:45. They didn't stay long and left seven minutes later. Guess he was collecting something. Think that's everything the rest been covered already."

"Thanks for that, Derek. I've taken notes on the information provided. All I need to do now is start on some sort of plan. While I do that, fancy making some nosh, Simon?" I point towards the fridge.

"No problem, what you got in the cupboards?"

"Not sure, help yourself, better make extra as Stuart and Mark should be here within the hour."

With some ideas formulating in my head, I start to break up the mission, planning into several parts.

1. Planting of Vehicle IED.
2. Route to starting points.
3. Launch of the attack.
4. Clearing the grounds.
5. Clearing the barrack block and tunnel.
6. Assault on the main house.
7. Recovery of the weapon system.

I need to break each section into smaller components to ensure I don't miss any vital elements. Once a rough plan for the first five parts is down in my notebook, I turn my attention to the homemade explosives. Unfortunately, I can't go much further, as I still need more information and confirmation on the house's layout from Stuart.

"Can you two help me with examining the explosives while Simon is busy in the kitchen?"

Both Derek and George follow me into the garden. A quick look around confirms that nobody is watching. Then proceed to walk over to and under the bush to the front of the lodge and lift the grass section covering my underground metal crate. Next, unfold the heavy lid, resting it on the ground.

Once all the packages are removed and taken inside, I make alterations to the box's lid, as I'm planning to use it for something later.

Nobody used any of the claymores on the OPs, so this means the total explosive counts is:

4 x Homemade Claymores

4 x Vehicle IEDs

8 x Mobile Phone Detonators, 2 are in place at the boatyard.

10 x Explosive packs.

My planning earlier calculated that four explosions would be detonated remotely, leaving a few spares. However, the four-vehicle IEDs now need to be rewired to have a chain reaction, if any one of them is set off. Plus, as these will be buried the night before, and we don't want them detonating prematurely, a safety device will need to be added.

Several packs will be attached to internal lights, especially in the tunnel. Switching on the lights will cause an electrical current to flow to the detonators, setting off the explosives. In addition, several of the claymores will possibly be put on tripwires.

After finishing putting the packs into groups and thinking that there is enough explosive here to light up a small village, my phone vibrates. It is a text from Mark. He's disembarked from the vehicle ferry over at East Cowes.

Thirty minutes later, Mark arrives at the lodge. "Come in, Mark, good to see you brought Stuart along with you."

"Thank you, Steve. We were fortunate Stuart was on the Isle of Wight visiting friends."

"That is lucky," comes out of my mouth, while thinking what a lying bastard—you were at the boatyard in Cowes two days ago. "Before I explain why I brought you over to the island, Simon managed to knock up some scran. Would you like a brew or a beer? Not sure if you've met that ugly git over there. If not, this is Derek."

"Nice to meet you, Derek, and coffee will be fine."

"Tea for me," Stuart replies, taking a seat at the table.

"Coming right up."

Meanwhile, Simon lays out two trays of assorted sandwiches, cold meats and some green stuff which reminds me of rabbit food on the dining table. "Tuck in, boys."

With the food and drink finished, it's time to start on why we are all here. Plonk my arse down close to the door, and in a position where I can keep an eye on everyone without having to constantly turn my head or shoulders, as the knife wound is still throbbing in my shoulder.

"The reason I got you both over here is I need more information on Dennis' place, as the recovery of the weapons goes in seven days." It isn't. It will go in two days from now, but I need to feed Stuart as much false data as possible, knowing that he will inform Chad of our plans once I let him go. "As you two have actually been inside the estate, who better to fill in the gaps."

Mark turns to face Stuart, "Of course, Steve, we would be happy to answer any questions." Stuart gives several short nods of his head to confirm.

"First, we need to go over the drawings you gave us when we met in Southampton. Want to clarify the entry points." With my right hand, I gesture to the sketch.

Over at the table, Mark points to the drawing. "As far as I'm aware, like I told you last time, the only entrance locations to the grounds are here at the gate. The house can be accessed by the wooden door at the front of the house. Plus the one around the back. If the patio doors are open, you can go that way. The only other way is via the tunnel that leads from this outbuilding." Again, Mark points to the map.

Simultaneously, I move to prevent anyone from getting to the door while Simon and Derek edge closer to Stuart, leaving George to block the exit from the kitchen and the back door.

"Right, on to the movements of Chad's people. This is where you come in, Stuart, bearing in mind you spent some time with him. If you could answer a few questions for me, that would be helpful."

You can see Stuart start to become fidgety, and nervously altering his position as he glares at us in turn like a rabbit caught in the glare of a set of headlights. "Sure, Steve, no problem." However, his voice now hesitates as he speaks in a quieter voice than usual, like he is trying to hide something.

"Cheers. first, how many men are there at both Dennis' place and the farmhouse? Second what is their rotation?" Questions I already know the answers to. All part of the technique of making him believe we are the good guys and his friends.

After taking a sip of his tea, "I think there are around 20 people altogether employed by Chad. On my very last visit before leaving and going back to work for Mark, I noticed two guards in the cellar and two armed sentries at the gate. I'm not sure how often they are changed. What I do know, all personnel use the tunnel between the house and the building in the grounds where they are billeted."

"That's valuable information, Stuart—thanks. Just a few more, if you don't mind."

"OK, no problem," comes the reply from Stuart, relaxing in his seat.

Make sure the boys are in position and ready before I ask my final questions for now. "Only two more. What can you tell me about Dennis' drug and people smuggling operation? And my last one for you, what were you doing with Dennis on the pier at around 11:17 yesterday? Yes, someone was watching you. Sorry, I lied—one more question, where did you go in the speedboat?"

As I finish, he realises that we know what game he plays, pretending to be employed by Mark while being employed by Dennis, feeding back information.

Then, Stuart leaps to his feet with one movement and hurtles at the door leading to the bedrooms, trying to escape via the rear exit. What he forgot is I anticipated this, and George is down the corridor.

Seconds later, the sound of two people grappling in a tight space can be heard, followed by a loud crack and thump as George lands an uppercut to his chin. The sound is Stuart hitting the floor. A split-second later, Simon and Derek race to restrain him.

I turn to Mark, who is looking perplexed at what had occurred. "Sorry about that, Mark. Couldn't tell you before, as you never know if your phones have been tapped. We've known about Stuart's activities and his employment for Dennis, and not you for several days. From the intelligence we've managed to gather, he never stopped working for Chad and Dennis. He only came back to feedback information on yours and our movements."

By now, the boys have Stuart all tied up with a dark blue bag placed over his head and sat him on the sofa. His breathing is now heavy, with urine trickling down his left leg. Unlike the rest of Chad's men, he is not a professional. Instead, we have a young man now physically shaking with fear, as he doesn't know what is coming his way.

"I'm going to ask you some questions, then, if you give me the right answers and don't fucking lie to me, we will let you be on your way. Nod if you fully comprehend what I said." Stuart nods slowly.

"Let's start with an easy one to get you warmed up. Even think about making something up, and George, who is next to you, will inflict a lot of pain, understand?" Stuart nods again. "What can you tell me about the envelopes people are using, the ones with a blue s

tripe?"

"Not much. I believe the envelopes are a family trademark. It was reintroduced by one of Dennis' relations after they took over the wine business on a Caribbean island, after his father was attacked and murdered in an alleyway in London, as a sign of respect."

Stared directly at George and Simon and mimed, 'What the fuck.'

"Second question, where are you taking the people loaded into the truck?"

He hesitates to answer, so George reminds him to respond with a full-force punch to his ribcage. Doubled up with agonising pain, Stuart mumbles something incoherent.

I whisper in his ear, "Unless you want another reminder, I suggest speaking up."

" Somewhere in the Midlands, I believe," comes the mumbled reply via a scared, trembling, just about audible voice.

"Next question, how are the weapon systems transferred from the property to the boatyard in Cowes?"

"I don't know," Stuart responds through gritted teeth, his voice now starting to become angry, like most people once they've got over the initial fear.

"My final question, for now, is regarding the drugs. Where do you collect them from in the speedboat?" Again he takes too long to reply, so once more, George punches him several times. Silence was the reply.

"This is not the time for you to be stupid, Stuart. Perhaps a stint in my dark underground metal box may knock the stupidness out of you. Grab the arsehole and bring him along with you." Derek and George reach around the back, grab one arm each. Lift them vertically, forcing Stuart off the sofa, screaming in pain as his arm is put in an unnatural position.

Then, Stuart is dragged outside while he tries frantically to escape. The boys raise his arms even higher, nearly breaking them to keep him under control. I open the metal box in the ground by the time they reach me.

"Throw the little shit inside. I will lock the box before backfilling the top with dirt." Saying this loud enough for Stuart to hear, I require him to be in panic mode.

To prove I'm not always a psychopath, the modification I made earlier was a pipe to let air in for him to breathe. I don't want him dead, well, not yet anyway, need him to answer questions.

Chapter Sixteen – Planning

While we wait for Stuart to become familiar with his new surroundings for a few hours —with any luck, this will ensure he answers questions in a little more detail —might as well go over some of the strategies I'd already formulated in my head.

"If you don't need me for this part, Steve, I need to head back to the mainland. Got a business meeting at 16:00 today."

"No problem, Mark. Thanks for coming over. Will see you soon with your equipment; hope the trip back goes OK."

"Cheers, Steve, see you later," as Mark left the lodge.

For the first task, I need a model of the property, as this is where the attack will commence. First, move the coffee table to give me more room on the floor to construct a rough layout, with the aid of some household objects.

"When you're ready, gents, will go through some of the plans.

"Phase One — Planting of Vehicle IED.

"Even with our best efforts, we can't dig up the track and plant the vehicle IEDs on the night of the assault. Therefore I have an alternative idea. Not far from here are several sets of roadworks, with conveniently placed red and white plastic barriers—these need to be liberated for our own use. Once the hire depot opens tomorrow morning, we take the car back and exchange this for a white van.

"The next stage relies on people paying no attention to what's happening right under their noses. In the afternoon, we drive towards Dennis' place dressed as workmen. Plenty of hi-vis vests for us, all in my store.

"Once we are parked up, we can use our liberated barriers for cordoning off half of the track, while digging a trench sufficiently deep enough for the IEDs. Once the explosive devices are in place, backfill with earth, leaving only the electrical wires exposed.

"The barricade will be left there until the morning of the attack on the property. Then, we simply move the barriers to the other side on our way to our start positions, forcing any motor vehicles to drive over the IED. Any questions on stage one?"

"What happens if some nosey bastard from Chad's group of people comes asking what we are doing?"

"That's an easy one there, George. The cover story is we are laying fiber optics. It should be believable as Wight Fiber are digging up the roads all over the island for broadband."

"Just one suggestion, as you three GRUNTS are used to digging holes in the ground, I will do the bit regarding the movement of any vehicles."

"OK, as you're a lazy arse Donkey Walloper, Simon, you can be traffic control. So with no more questions or comments, we can move on to the next part of the plan." So with shaking heads from Simon, Derek and George, I continue.

"Phase Two — Route to Start Points.

"This stage involves us all getting to our starting positions. For this, we will take the route down the Red Squirrel way until we come to the concrete road near the houses, the same one you lot took to your OPs. Then traverse the main road into the woods, following the trail to a point just short of the target area.

"From here, we will make our way to the dirt track leading to Dennis' property to swap the barriers over, then on to where Simon had his OP. Apart from you, Derek, I got a unique task for you.

"Along the perimeter wall is a hole, large enough for you to clamber through. Once you enter, proceed to the stables located here and dispatch anyone you find inside. If you wait for 60 seconds after the initial shots are fired, most people will be heading for us, giving you cover to enter the outbuildings.

"If something goes wrong on route, RV back here. Any questions on stage two?"

"How will I find the hole in the wall?"

"Don't worry, I'll point it out on the way to the road leading from the property, Derek."

"Phase Three — Launch of Assault.

"Right, on to initiating the assault. As we will need the cover of darkness to make our way to our start positions, we need to be ready and in place before 05:20. At 06:00. Simon and I will move down and take up a concealed location on either side of the entrance to the grounds. From here, Simon will place the first remote homemade claymore close to the brick upright nearest to the guardhouse. This will be detonated to cover our withdrawal, killing anyone who might follow us out of the gate.

"The assault will begin dead on 06:30, when Gorge has taken the first shot from his firing position and killed at least one of the two guards on the front gate. Plus, you are to follow this up with the detonation of the package under the bridge in the woods. The aim here is to hinder any help coming from the farmhouse.

"However, if Simon and me are in place and the guards have not appeared after five minutes, I will initiate the assault into the grounds. Once we have our first dead bodies, with the help of Simon, we will start to clear the area in front of the main house.

"As already mentioned, give it one minute before you start making your way through the opening, Derek. Make double sure that all the telephone numbers for the detonators are stored in your spare phone, George, and for fuck sake, make sure it is fully charged. Questions?"

"If you could take my wind indicator with you and place it on the wall, this would give me a more accurate kill ratio."

"No problem, George.

"Phase Four — Clearing the Grounds.

"Simon and I will systematically start emptying the grounds between the gate and the house of any of Chad's people. If you see people moving around after this, George, it is your responsibility to dispatch them. Also, remember to keep a lookout for any children on the property. Simon hates you shooting them.

"After we've cleared the exterior, our next task will be the barrack block. Once the stables are free of anyone you find, Derek, join us near the bridge close to the house. Again, this is straight forward so you lot shouldn't have any questions."

"Not true, Steve. I would like to make one vital comment. Make sure you don't take a fucking pot shot at me, George."

"What? You're my first target, Simon," George responds with a big, stupid grin.

I continue, "Phase Five — Clearing the Barracks and Tunnel.

"As they will not be expecting an attack from this direction, the best way is by the tunnel. After entering via the escape hatch halfway along and making sure we turn off the lights, I will attach two explosive packs with electrical detonators to light fixings. If any person comes this way and turns them on, they will detonate, giving them a terrible day.

"Once inside and up the spiral staircase, I will clear the room to the left if you take the other half of the room, Simon. If anybody exits the building alive, again, George, this is your responsibility if you can get a kill shot. Furthermore, once Derek is free, he will assist you.

"After rigging up an explosive pack, George will detonate it, but only once he can see we are well clear of the area. Then Simon and I will make our way to a location on the far side of the bridge, close to the house and wait for or join George and Derek. We can go over this in more detail later. Questions?" Once more, confronted with three shaking heads.

"Phase Six — Assault on Main House.

"After entering the rear door, we will carry out our standard operating procedure for the first and upper floors. If Derek and George take the top floor while we," I point at Simon, "take the bottom level. Only when they are clear will we proceed to the cellar where all the work is being completed.

"Our primary mission here is the recovery and return of the L115A3 sniper rifles and associated accessories. So not knowing the strengths, we will need to play this by ear, clearing rooms individually. Once in, try not to damage any of the equipment. This includes their stuff, which could come in handy later. This leads me on nicely to the final phase.

"Phase Seven — Recovery of the Weapons Systems.

"Our last task is to collect all the stuff to be returned to Mark's depot on the mainland. The van we hired will be used, if we can't find any vehicles available at the property we can use. You are our transport guy, Simon, so this will be down to you to organise."

"No problem, Steve. I'll sort something out."

"Part of the initial assault, George would have detonated the devices I attached to the pier over at the boatyard in Cowes, separating it from the shore. The purpose is to prevent Chad's people from leaving in the speedboat with any of Mark's stuff that might be on site. This means once all equipment here has been recovered, we must make a bolt for Cowes to recover what's there. I'll work on how we return them to Mark later. Before I move on to the emergencies, any more questions?" All three shake their heads to indicate they have no questions up to this point.

"Emergency Plans.

"We discussed what happens on the route, but to confirm if something goes badly wrong on this part, RV back here. If we have any weapons failure, especially yours, George, ensure you take an SLR with you. For the rest of us, make sure a 9 mm pistol and plenty of spare magazines are taken with you for the house clearing.

"If anyone gets injured and can't continue, try to return to the front entrance and wait for us to come to you. If not, stay put. We will find you.

"If you find more than you can handle at the stables, Derek, shoot two rounds in quick succession into the air. Simon and I will come over once the grounds are cleared.

"If everything goes tit's up, come back here. Any further questions on the rough plans, before we grab our friend from the pit?"

"One from me, what if all goes wrong while setting the vehicle IED into the road, ie. Chad's people are clued up and on to us."

"If that happens, Simon, we will depart and then it will be up to George from his location, to do his best to kill the driver of any vehicle that approaches during the mission to block the track. If no more questions, let's fetch Stuart.

"Remember, gents, once we've got Stuart inside, everything we say about the purpose at hand is fake information for the benefit of Stuart, as we know it will be fed back once he is released," I say, walking out the door.

A quiet sobbing can be heard as I approach to unlock and remove Stuart from his prison. As I open the lid, his tightly bound arms shoot up, covering his head, revealing scarred and blood-stained hands, from where he had been hitting the roof of the container, trying to free himself.

"OK, stand up so we can get you out." Speaking in a calm relaxing voice, I crouch down. Frozen in fear of what might come next, Stuart stays utterly motionless.

"If you will not come out the easy way, we'll drag you out." As I speak, Derek jumps in and grabbed his arms, forcing them upwards. Then, taking one arm each, George and I drag a heavy, stiff body from the metal box.

While Derek and George escort our friend inside, I ensure everything is recovered and out of view from passerbys. Meanwhile, back in the lodge, Stuart is put in a stressful position. His untied hands are placed on the painted wall as far up as he can reach above his head. Both legs are spread out as much as physically achievable and away from the bottom of the wall, forcing him to stand on the balls of his feet.

With nobody saying a word, Stuart remains in the uncomfortable position for the next half an hour. This allows his mind to cover every possible life-threatening scenario, not knowing what will happen next. The few times his hands slip down a few inches, George lands a hard punch to the area of his kidneys to remind him we are still here.

I give the signal to start feeding him false info by opening and closing my right hand.

"If I can have your attention, gents, finally managed to put together a plan for the recovery of Mark's equipment."

Again, speaking loud so Stuart can hear every word. "Our first task will be to launch an attack on the boatyard, to collect what's any bits of kit on site. This will go in at 06:30, two days from now. Our approach will be from the sea, making our way up the gangway from the pontoon." Hopefully, when he feeds this bit of information back to Chad, they will concentrate his men around the pier close to where we will detonate our explosive. Therefore reducing his manpower for when we assault the property. "Any questions?"

"Yes, once everyone is up the ramp, will we head for the shed or the building first?" making up the question as he goes.

"Great one, Simon. The boatshed will be our first target."

I continue with my fabricated story. "This equipment will be returned back to the mainland by ferry boat. Once we return to the island, the principal assault on Dennis' place will be in seven days, at last light, again after the recovery of all equipment, we will catch the vehicle ferry from East Cowes to Southampton."

We continue for the next 20 minutes feeding Stuart just enough information to remember and report back. "I think that's more than adequate planning. There is plenty more stuff to do today. I will fill you in with more details later."

"What do you want us to do with this idiot, Steve?" as George touches Stuart's back, laughing as he flinches uncontrollably, expecting pain to come his way.

"Not sure yet, might as well put him back in the hole."

Once more, I remove the cover, our friend starts kicking out, trying everything to stop being thrown back down in the ground. After a few minutes, we eventually manage to get Stuart inside, and I attempt to close the top cover.

This time I place a piece of wood between the lid and the brim. Set the unlocked lock by the rim of the metal box so it can be seen unlocked from inside. We need Stuart to escape. It's crucial to our mission.

It must have taken Stuart 30 minutes or so to regain his composure and realise the box he is in hasn't been secured, and he could escape. Through the gap in the curtain, we watch as the heavy top is flung open. Then with one swift movement, a figure clambers out and sprints as fast as his legs could carry him, off down the track leading away from my lodge.

"That's the first part of our plan underway," I report to the boys.

"How fast did the arsehole move?" Derek asks, sipping on the can of beer.

"Not sure, but there was a flash of light," I reply, while chuckling to myself. "We might as well relax for the next few hours, gents, nothing to do except checking your personal equipment. The barriers we need can only be obtained later tonight under cover of darkness, and the workmen have buggered off."

Chapter Seventeen – Pre-mission

In case this idiot falls asleep, the alarm on my phone is set for 01:00, and it is now ringing in my ears. So guess I did fall asleep. Drag my fully clothed sorry arse off my pit and head for the coffee machine. After pouring several mugs of the wide awake juice, it is time to wake the boys from their slumber.

"Right, come on, you lot, you can sleep when you're dead. We need to go and borrow some barriers on a permanent basis."

"The second word is off," comes the half-coherent reply from Simon.

My third cup of coffee is half-finished by the time the other three are slouched on the sofa, mugs in hand. "Once you've finished your brews, let's make a move. Best we fetch this stuff when there are few or hopefully no nosey people about. By the way, you're driving Simon." I throw him the car keys.

"As for us three, like any task, needs to be a plan of sorts for it to go without a hitch. So while George and me grab the plastic barriers, I think we will need a minimum of six. If you can, you find a couple of those yellow diversion signs with the arrows, Derek."

"Any idea from which set of roadworks we will be nicking, sorry 'borrowing' these from?"

"Yep, there are several major sets of works not far from here, Derek."

After driving slowly past the first location to check for people, Simon turns into a small side road close to one end of the barricaded-off area, turns off the headlights and parks up. The moment the vehicle comes to a stop, everyone climbs out without saying a word and goes about the task at hand.

The plan to limit time at the location is to collect half here and the rest from a different site on the other side of Shanklin. Load the first two barriers onto the roof rack, securing them with webbing belts, while Derek drops the first diversion signs in the car's boot.

"Let's drive to the next scene to liberate more, Simon."

Once more, after an initial drive past, we stop on a side street, wait for a couple of minutes with the lights switched off. "Can't find a sign this end, will try the other end."

"OK, mate, be quick," I say, turning to help George place two more plastic barriers on the top of the car.

Release the straps and toss the loose end over to Simon. As I do, the cuff of my jumper catches on one barrier sending it sliding off, hitting the tarmac road with what sounded to us a loud crash, enough to wake the whole street. We both stand frozen to the spot. In the house close to our location, a light blazes through a downstairs window. I turned gradually to check if anyone might be looking out in our direction through a gap in the curtains.

On seeing the bright lights come on, Derek takes cover behind a green hedge that runs along the front of the property. Several agonising minutes pass before the incandescent lights go out over at the house. That's our clue to hurry up and get the fuck out of here, just in case this do-gooder contacted the police or tried being a hero and come out to tackle us.

Back home, the barriers are stored under a bush, ready to be loaded into the van once we've swapped vehicles later today. "Might as well put our heads down a for a couple of hours, gents, until breakfast. I've volunteered Simon for this job."

"Don't have any problem with making scran."

"Good man, Simon," I head back to my room to catch a few hours kip.

Wake up to the smell and the sizzling sound of bacon being fried, with the aroma of freshly brewed coffee filling the air. In the kitchen, Simon is hard at work making a full English breakfast.

"Well played, mate, how long before it's ready?"

"About 10 minutes, go and kick the other two out of bed."

While I wait for brekkie, I make most of the time and go through my plans for the assault on Dennis' place tomorrow. With all the information gathered and info provided reluctantly by Stuart, everything will go to plan. Plus, I'm positive all the false info given to Stuart would have been passed on to Chad by now. Knowing the others, they would have done the same. However, it never hurts to go over plans more than once to confirm they are in your head.

Put the books down and join the rest at the table, now tucking into the excellent food cooked by Simon.

As we eat, I say, "The hiring company opens at 09:00, so Simon and myself will make our way to the office for when the doors open to exchange vehicles. If you two can check the equipment one more time, to be double safe."

Pull up outside the rental facility at 08:50, in time for them to open. Want to make certain we are the first in the queue to make sure vans are still available. Plus, I don't have an alternative plan if they haven't. Right on time, I witness the identical lady who served us last time unlock the door to the reception area.

After a final check inside the car, to ensure no evidence linking back to us can be found by the next renter. For safety reasons, once I reconnect the equipment, I chang the home address in the sat nav to some other poor sod's home.

Once we are in reception, the young lady dressed the same as on the last visit in a black skirt and a pink polo shirt with a blue jumper joins us at the counter. "Good morning, gents. Are you bringing the motor vehicle back early, or do you have an issue with the vehicle?"

"Hi, there is no problem. I'm moving house," I lie while flicking through the leaflet on the stand. "Would simply like to change it for a large white van if that's possible?"

"Fortunately, you're in luck. We have one left, a Ford Transit, will that do?"

"Perfect," I hand over my credit card for payment of the difference between the van hire and the car coming back several days early. In the meantime, Simon gives the new vehicle the once over to check for damage.

"Is everything OK, Simon?"

"She'll do for what we need it for," while climbing into the driver seat.

When we arrive back at the lodge, Derek is busy making adjustments to the radio equipment laid out on the dining table. Plonk my arse next to him, "What are you doing?"

"Just made a few modifications to the walkie-talkies, so we can use their hands-free along with the earpieces during the assault on the target."

"This is why I'm glad you tagged along, Derek. Our very own radio expert."

Time is now getting on. So with the barriers loaded into the back of the van, we head for the road leading to Dennis' front gate. The location has to be close enough to the entrance, but be out of eyesight as well. Plus, the last thing we want is to draw attention to ourselves, driving up and down looking for the best spot. So our first stop will have to be where we set up the IEDs.

Fortunately, the track bends to the left before it enters the property. Approximately 20 metres before the bend, Simon pulls over, stopping close to the woods.

While we unload the equipment, George disappears into the treeline and walks towards the main gate to check on the guards. We need any vehicle that comes this way tomorrow to drive over the device and block the route into the grounds. Therefore, leaving just enough room for cars to squeeze past on the right, we barricade off an area one barrier width by two deep. Need to ensure they stretch back in the direction of the trees as much as possible.

By the time George returns, we have started to dig, starting from the middle. "See, you're making this look authentic, with one man working while the others stand around observing what is going on."

"About to give him a hand, George, while Simon checks down the road. What about our guard friends? Are they standing at the gate or patrolling?"

"I believe you, Steve, many wouldn't. At the moment just one person is walking in front of the entrance, couldn't see the other one. Guess he is in the guardhouse."

All the years of being driven over have made the ground rock hard-going. So grab the long wooden-handled pickaxe, ready to break up the hard, firm ground in the trench, ready for Derek to shovel out. Hold the bottom of the handle with both hands and swing the pickaxe over my shoulder, my right hand sliding along its length to the top as I did so. Then, I swing it back with my whole force, striking the solid ground, breaking up a small area of the soil. Do this several times before allowing Derek in with the shovel.

Repeat the same procedure until a trench half a metre across and 30 centimetres deep, stretches halfway across the cordoned-off area. A few minutes after, George takes over swinging the axe when a call comes from Simon.

"There is a car coming your way," Simon cries out.

Wait for the vehicle to inch through the narrow gap left to the right of where we are working. Of course, we have no way of knowing who is in the car. So Derek and George bend forward and look down into the hole, while I hide to the side of the van in case the occupants recognise us.

The instance it drives off around the curve in the dirt track, we continue to dig. This is taking longer than anticipated, and the longer we stay here, the more chance of one of the idiots coming to investigate. No sooner than the thought enters my head, when ambling along with a rifle slung over his shoulder, one of Chad's men heads in our direction.

Whoever is in that car must have told him to come and find out why people are digging up the track. No need to panic yet, but shit, if he recognises any of us, our mission may have to be scrapped. Or I could save the whole thing by possibly giving him a tap on the top of his head with the point of the pickaxe. But that's not a viable option, as his mate would probably come looking for him.

Wait patiently with my eyes fixed on him until he comes closer. Then I pull up the collar of my polo shirt and smother my face with mud in some sort of attempt to disguise my appearance. The others follow suit. The man is now only five metres from our location. Only one thing for it, try to blend into the background. The moment he is next to the barrier, I raise my head to talk to the man when I'm beaten to it.

Cleverly, Simon waits until the person is close before he approaches him. Then while talking, he manages to have the bloke turn and face away from us. So I watch as the man constantly turns in every direction but ours, making sure he doesn't look him directly in the face by slightly spitting as he speaks.

Soon after, the man heads back to the property, Simon shouts out, "Remember, call me if you want free broadband."

"That was a pleasure to see," I say as Simon comes over and leans on the barrier.

"Thanks, Steve. It would seem you three GRUNTS are making progress in digging your trench. So I will go back to my traffic control. "

Another 35 minutes pass before, at last, the trench is ready for the homemade IEDs. One explosive device at a time, the four devices, with as much care as I can muster, are placed each in turn in the newly dug trench, separated out enough that they drive over an IED at least one wheel.

"You're the explosive expert, Steve, so we'll leave you to connect them up."

"Makes sense, Derek. That way, if anything does go wrong, it's my fault. In the meantime, can you and George collect some thin twigs, long enough to stretch over the hole and some leaves?"

This requires a short amount of time and cannot be rushed if all the wires of the IEDs are to be correct. So they would all go off, even if only one device is activated. Once I have them all set up, I run two extended cables five metres into the woods from the one nearest the road. The wires will not be connected to complete the circuit until the start of the attack on the property.

Return to the roadworks to find both George and Derek clutching hands full of vegetation and short, thin branches. "Thanks, gents, chuck them on the floor for now. Then help me pack the soil hard against the barrels."

Once the dirt is around the edges of the four IEDs, I stamp the ground down with my feet. The earth needs to be packed hard, so that the explosion is directed upwards and not out.

Before backfilling, the last task is to span the gap with the wooden branches, then cover them with the vegetation. This way, the lids and plungers inside will remain open and not closed by the weight of the heavy soil on top of them.

With one half-filled shovel at a time, we ease the loose dirt no more than a few inches deep over the buried IEDs. With my hand, I then do my best to camouflage the newly-dug ground to look like the rest of the area.

"OK, gents, another task complete, someone fetch Simon."

"I'll go and fetch the lazy git," George replies, heading off down the track to find him.

"No need, George, I'm here."

"Nice of you to turn up now all the work is done, Simon," Derek interjects.

" You know what you can do, radio geek. Been looking for a place to hide the van, just in case we need it tomorrow."

No way can we afford to risk the noise driving here in the morning, so we may as well hide it now, saves coming back later. So Simon climbs in and makes a slow three-point turn, trying not to leave too many tracks in the dirt, then drives 100 metres down the road before coming to a stop. By the time we reach him, he is has started pulling back the undergrowth to clear a path. Once we understand Simon's plan, we assist in making room for the vehicle to pass through.

Soon the way is clear, and Simon reverses in and parks between several thick, towering trees and under an extensive clump of foliage. To remove any chance of the glare reflecting off the windscreen if the sun happens to penetrate the woods, several branches with as many leaves as possible are laid against the screen. The same goes for the side and rear windows.

After confirming the van is well camouflaged, we start the trek on foot back to my place. The walk back is uneventful, and we arrive back within 35 minutes.

"Yes, I know I'm a pain in the arse, gents, but before we relax, let's go through our equipment one last time and share out the explosives."

Grab my kit from the bedroom and empty my small pack containing spare ammunition, radio, tripwire and explosives on the living room floor. Only after checking everything twice, do I start to repack, this time ensuring everything is put away so there would be no noise of parts hitting each other as I run. Keep the radio out, as this will be in a pouch on a webbing belt around my waist. The plan is to drop the pack near the house before clearing the principal target.

Next, my attention turns to my weapon, the one thing I can't afford to fail. So I take it apart, clean each part, then reassemble it again, ensuring each piece works as it should. Once I finish my own kit, I look up to see the boys doing likewise and double-checking everything.

After waiting for everyone to finish, "I've been rethinking the order of the remote detonations. They should now go in this order. First will be the bridge in the woods, to hinder any people rushing from the farm to assist. Then, at 07:00, George will detonate the one on the speedboat. It will have left the boatyard by then and will be out at sea with only a couple of people, including Stuart onboard.

"Next is the barrack block, if required. Then to cover our retreat, or reinforcements are heading towards us from the house, will be the bridge crossing the lake. Finally, that leaves the explosives at the gate, which will be detonated once we leave the property.

"This only gives us the ones I placed on the pier in Cowes. Given this some thought. Now believe that if we set this off too early, by the time we arrive at the boatyard, it will be swarming with police, fire engines and other emergency services. Therefore, it will not be detonated until we are ready to recover any equipment on the premises.

"If, by any chance, we find all the weapons and associated equipment at Dennis' place, then as we depart, the devices will be set off just to piss him off and delay his other activities. Remember, George, you are the one who will be dialling into the separate devices."

"Is there anything else of the plan you want to change, you fucking idiot?"

"Nope, everything else is as planned, George. Does anyone want a cold beer?"

"Might as well, I might be dead tomorrow," says Simon, heading for the fridge.

As always, on a night before any mission, the next few hours are spent relaxing, drinking beers, talking about anything but the task.

Chapter Eighteen –Assault Phase One

Don't know why I even bother trying to get some sleep on the night before a mission, as my brain never shuts the fuck up. With its constant rolling over of every stage of the plans, plus the added worry of being the planner, it all goes wrong. Of course, it will be my fucking fault. The last thing I need is for one of the other guys to get injured or, worst, killed. But hey, they knew the risks when they signed up for the mission.

Turn over in bed to see the bright illuminated light of my phone burst into life, a split-second before the alarm starts to ring. The time is now 04:00, and we need to be in position, by the latest, 05:45. OK, let's get this part of the operation underway. By the time I enter the living room, the other three can be heard as they get dressed, collect their kit and make their way to join me.

"Good morning, gents. Once we've completed a final check of our personal equipment and radios Derek modified the other day, I suggest we make a move."

"Sure, no problem, Steve, just let my body catch up with the brain, and I'll be right with you."

"Not an issue, Simon, once we are all ready, we can make our way to the point where we intersect the main road. When we leave, I will lead, if Derek, you file in behind me, as I will have to show you your start point when we reach the property. Simon, if you can take up your customary position at the rear. George, slot yourself between Derek and Simon."

Dead on 04:30, after implementing the standard safety measure to secure the lodge, I lead off through a deserted park along the small dirt track towards the Red Squirrel trail. As I turn right, I look behind to check on the rest of the patrol. Everyone is entirely in assault mode and are spaced at 20-metre intervals behind.

It isn't long before I approach the houses near the concrete path, close to the tarmac road. Perfect, they are in complete darkness. Unlike last time, when the other three crossed on their way to the OPs, we will stay separated. The last thing we need at this late stage is for some nosey bastard to see a group of men bent down by the side of a highway.

Pause for a few moments before making my way to the edge of the roadway, finding cover in the long, damp grass. For once, I confirm the area is void of any signs of vehicle headlights approaching. So take a deep breath, leap to my feet and sprint across the road into the undergrowth on the other side.

Look across to see Derek now paused, ready to make his own way over. Once he has joined me, I make my way just inside the woods, find a place to conceal myself and wait. Everyone else follows the same routine. Once the next person crosses, they also come to join me. Finally, George enters the woodlands.

Without saying a word, stand up and head off down the dirt track. There is no point in me counting the number of paces, been here many times and know the place well, even in the pitch dark. While crossing the wooden bridge, I turn back to ensure the boys are still behind me. This is something every recruit learns in basic training, pointless arriving at a battle if you've lost half your men because they went the wrong way.

The red brick wall surrounding Dennis' place is just ahead of me, appearing through the trees in the moon's dim light. My first task is to show Derek the gap and his start location. After concealing myself by the side of the trail, I signall for him to close up on me by pointing at him and then placing my right hand on the top of my head.

"OK, Derek, to your front," I point to the small bush that conceals the hole in the wall, "This is your start position. Remember to wait for at least 60 seconds after the shooting starts before you enter."

"Roger that, mate. See you later in the RV near the house."

Give it a few minutes after Derek leaves before indicating to Simon and George to follow me. There is still one more task before heading to the roadworks we prepared yesterday. The homemade IED needs placing under the wooden bridge, if nothing else, to hinder people running along the track from the farmhouse once the fun starts.

Once I reach the location of the crossing, I stand off for a while to watch out for any movement of Chad's men. You never know, they might be around at daft o'clock in the morning. Then, out of the corner of my eye, I spot something moving, with the faint sound of an electric motor strapped between two branches of a tree that overlooked the bridge.

It would appear like people have been watching for anyone coming this way, including us. Might explain why both George and Simon reported people patrolling through the woods on their OPs. This makes putting the remote IED in the correct position a more tricky, but not impossible task. So bearing in mind that time is not in our favour, call Simon over, him being the tallest.

"Grab that branch over there, the one full of densely-packed leaves, then start waving it in front of the camera. By the time anyone watching their monitor realises what's going on, I will have planted the explosive, and we will be on our way."

The best place to blow up this type of bridge will be where it joins the far bank. So wait until Simon is wafting the branch, before sprinting down to the other side. Once there, reach underneath, securing the IED on the thick wooden beam that spanned the gap. The entire operation takes no more than a few minutes. After signalling to Simon, he can stop waving the dead foliage like a demented forest elf and head back up the trail in the direction of our vehicle IEDs.

To confirm our progress, I glance down at Mickey to check the time. Shit, we only have half an hour before we need to be in position, and we still have to rearrange the fences used to protect the IEDs. Luckily, first light is not until 06:30, so we have some wiggle room, but I don't want to use this, so we open up the pace.

The prepared roadworks are 50 metres further down, to our left when we arrive at the road. Once more, we stand off for five minutes to watch for people or cars moving in any direction.

"Here is the plan, gents. While George and I drag the barriers across to the opposite side of the track, Simon, you keep a look out and warn us if anyone comes close."

Due to my experience in dealing with terrorists in different locations worldwide, I start checking the area around where we buried the vehicle IEDs, for any signs of tampering or interference. Only when we are satisfied, do we begin moving the plastic barriers to the other side to force vehicles to drive over the devices, therefore resulting in a satisfying explosion and a blocked road, preventing reinforcements from assisting the people on the property.

Once they are all in place, and with George covering down towards the target area, I connect the electrical wires I left trailing into the treeline yesterday.

"All set, Steve?

"Yes, George, better call Simon to join us."

A few seconds later, "Best come this way, Simon, as we all know you tankies are attracted to landmines."

"Fuck off, George, before a put a bullet up your arse," pointing the SLR in his direction.

"No time for that now, gents, but you know it's true, Simon."

"You can do one as well, Steve."

As the start point and George's sniper position will be where Simon carried out his OP, he will lead from here. As our present location is around the corner from the entrance to Dennis' property, we head off into the trees on the far side.

The undergrowth in this area is more compact than the rest of the forest. So the going is much slower than before, as we very gingerly manoeuvre our way through the woods, trying not to make the slightest sound.

If we detect or make any louder noise than a mouse scurrying through leaf litter, we will freeze instantly to the spot, daring not to twitch a single muscle until the only thing audible is the exhaling of our own breathing. But we are in luck, Simon knows where he is going, and we are soon within 10 metres of his former OP.

Only after observing the area for a short time do we move in on the location. Time is now back on our side. We now have 15 minutes till the assault on the property gets underway.

While George sets up the sniper position to ensure he uses it to his advantage, I check my rifle. With my left hand, pull back on the cocking handle a few inches, to ensure a round is up the spout. Give the magazine a firm shake to guarantee it is located correctly and not likely to fall off. Over to my right, Simon is doing the same thing.

"Ready, mate, time to get to our start point on both sides of the main gate. Do you have the IED?" raising myself off the floor and into a kneeling posture.

"Once you say go, remember fat boy, no fucking shooting at me."

"Now that takes the fun out of things, Simon, But on a serious note, both of you stay alive. It's Steve's round at the boozer."

"You're all fucking heart, George," I whisper, getting to my feet.

The next phase is probably one of the most important, get this wrong, and everything else goes to shit. So once more, keeping low and moving with caution, trying not to make any resemblance of a sound that might be detected by the two people operating the gate, both Simon and I moved to a position on the forward edge of the woods.

Our go positions are now 10 metres away, on the other side of the road. No point in crossing and risk being seen until it is time to launch the assault. Instead, we will watch for a gap in the guard's routine, for the best time to make a sprint for the opposite side.

It isn't long before the perfect opportunity occurs, when one man starts to amble in front of the entrance. Turns and makes his way back to a small building being used when not patrolling. Glance over to Simon, raise my left arm, swing it down sharply to indicate: move now.

Instantaneously we both spring to our feet and launch ourselves towards the protection of the perimeter wall. A tense few moments pass as Simon unscrews the clear glass shade hanging from the light attached to the brick pillar. Then, remove the bulb before placing the IED inside and screwing it back into position.

This is now the point of no return. Once any person exits the gatehouse and strolls across the gateway, it will be their last walk ever as George puts a well-aimed shot into their head. Spattering bits of brain matter, thick dark red blood and tiny fragments of bone over the gravel driveway.

Shit, that fucking reminds me, George wants his wind indicator thingy placed on the top of the wall. So unzipp my jacket to retrieve the device from the inner pocket. Lucky for me, standing on my toes and reaching up as high as possible with both arms, I can just about reach. Let's hope no fucker is looking this way. Take a deep breath and reach up as far as I could, and ease the wind device into place.

Meanwhile, back up the OP position, a piece of camouflage netting is hanging in front of the sniper rifle, placed there by George to help conceal any visible muzzle flash from the barrel, as the bullet exits on its way to the unfortunate person on the receiving end.

To the rifle's right lay the mobile phone containing the preprogrammed number for each remote explosives package. The first will be detonated seconds after the first round strikes home.

Nearly time to start the killing, George thinks to himself as he picks up the butt of the rifle and pulls hard into his right shoulder, the index finger now tenderly touching the hairline trigger. Along the top barrel, he could see a soon-to-be dead man emerge from behind the concrete pillar to the left of the gate, walking carefree on his final walk.

With his eye now staring down the sights, George begins to control his breathing. One breath in, exhale, then repeat, holding the next out-breath while taking up the first pressure on the trigger. Eventually, the target arrives at the other side, turns, and starts his last walk on earth back towards the gatehouse.

As he reaches the middle, George's finger is squeezed all the way home. A nanosecond later, the firing pin strikes the base of the brass casing in the chamber, igniting the power contained within, in turn, forcing the bullet out of its casing to spin in the barrel, as the rifling grooves take hold as it travels down the entire length.

In the meantime, the gasses from the explosive events are expelled to the right, allowing the weapon's recoil to move straight back into George's shoulder, with no deflection in any other direction.

The distinctive crack can be detected as the round leaves the long barrel, travelling at 2,350 fps heading for its target, then striking the man's head a split-second later, with the second of the two sounds a bullet makes when fired.

The one you always want to hear, a thump, as it means the shooter missed you. Finally, the side of his head explodes as the spent round exits, shooting brain tissue, crimson red blood and bone fragments across the gateway.

George reaches for the mobile without pausing, finds the number for the IED under the bridge in the woods, and dialls. Several long seconds pass before the asymmetrical wheel of the phone, bundled with the explosives, starts to vibrate, sending an electrical current down the wires to the detonator. Then, milliseconds after, the whole package explodes in a massive fireball, throwing segments of the wooden bridge along with parts of closeby trees several metres into the air.

Back at the gate, Steve and Simon sprint to the gatehouse to take down the remaining person, who is probably still hazed and trying to work out what the fuck just happened seconds ago. Simon flings the door wide open without saying a word, as I stand facing the open doorway with my rifle already in a firing position. Inside, the guard is upright, frozen to the spot, back leaning against the rear wall with both hands reaching for the ceiling.

There is no way I could afford to leave anyone who might shoot back later, so I squeeze the trigger, sending a 7.62 mm round hurtling towards the centre of his face, blowing the back of his head through the glass window, onto the gravel track behind.

There is no time to hang about here. There are still two guards patrolling the grounds to kill, before they start to return fire. Within minutes, the whistling sounds of bullets could be overheard as they whizz too close for comfort, striking the ground behind and to the side of me. Well, it would appear they have spotted us first.

As I look in the direction of the incoming shots, Simon screams out at the top of his voice, "They're near the bridge."

"Roger, that," I yell, running in a zig-zag pattern, heading for the new target.

Got within 20 metres when, in quick succession, both attackers lay face down in the dirt, blood oozing from large gaping holes in the place where once their faces used to occupy. Find the radio mic and press the transmit button, "Good shooting, George." George has managed two perfect heads shots from 400 metres.

"Cheers, mate, but forget that, a man is heading with some momentum in your direction from the house."

He isn't the only one to spot him. Look over to Simon, who is in the kneeling firing position, with the sling wrapped around his arm to give support, and taking aim. A moment later, another one of Chad's men is eating dirt.

Once more, I squeeze the mic again, "You two cover me, while I plant the explosives underneath."

"Don't panic, Steve, I've got you covered," comes George's voice over the PRC-350 radio.

Safe in the knowledge the boys had my back, I sprint as fast as my legs can carry me, to the centre of the wooden bridge. Now, I can do the same as the majority of people destroying a construction like this, and go for the embankment on this side. But with only one chance of blowing up the structure, I can't afford for it to explode, only to come back down and rest on the far side. So it will have to be the middle to cause the most damage.

Once there, lay flat on my belly and remove the package and black tape from my day pack. Use this to secure everything to one of the small wooden beams stretching from one bank to the other. This should separate the back of the bridge, preventing people or vehicles from crossing.

Arrive back to join Simon in time to spot three men exiting the barrack block rushing in our direction, firing from the hip. A promising sign that these people are still in confusion mode, but now is not the time to panic, not that I ever do. So instead, raise the rifle into the shoulder and let off two rounds, hitting the person closest to me. Simultaneously, Simon takes down another while the third is killed by our friendly sniper.

At the stables, Derek climbs through the gap in the brick wall and is now heading for the first of two long stable blocks, one on either side of a grey concreted area about eight metres apart.

Right, the one on the left seems the most substantial from here. This is where I'm more than likely to find anything or someone, Derek thinks to himself as he takes cover in the shadows behind the building. From this dark, concealed spot, he can hear gunfire as the rest start to clear the grounds, time for him to enter the action and do his part.

Takes several deep breaths to calm himself down, as adrenaline starts pumping through his veins. It's been a long time since he did anything like this, but there is no way he will let the others down. So with his left leg, he kicks open the first door and races inside with the SLR at the ready.

A quick scan confirms the first room is empty, apart from bales of hay and other horsey-type stuff piled up in a darkened area towards the back of the stall.

Derek turns on the balls of his feet, heading to the next room to be cleared. En route, he detects a half-incoherent voice cry out, "There are two men in here."

This is followed by the sound of a heavy object coming in contact with someone. Moments later, a loud distinctive thud as a body hits the concrete floor.

With the rifle raised up and the butt held firmly in his right shoulder, he is fully prepared to let off several rounds in quick succession, into whoever is in the adjoining room. A brown, wooden full-length door, close to the wall hinged along the right side, is now the only thing standing between him and the armed person on the other side.

As he composes himself, waiting to kick the door down, a hail of bullets fly through the partition off to his left, in turn sending tiny splinters wildly through the air, narrowly missing him. Thank fuck I didn't stand to the left of the door, Derek thinks to himself, while barging through the door. On the other side, he is confronted by one of the men working for Chad, charging at him.

Derek fires off two rounds before he gets within striking distance, dropping the man to the floor. The man's body lay motionless in the used straw and horse shit on the ground, while he scans the area for the other man.

A metal cage has been constructed adjacent to the rear, and now housed around 20 people; a mixture of men, women, and children.

From the far end, a man roars out, "Drop the weapon, or this bitch gets a bullet to her head." With the rifle still held tightly, ready to fire, Derek turns to face the voice.

Standing just outside the cage, close to the opened metal gate swinging noiselessly on its hinges, a man dressed like the rest of Chad's men about six feet tall, with his arm wrapped around a young woman's neck. By the looks of her, she can't have been more than 30 years of age, somewhat smaller in height than the assailant. With his other hand, he holds a 9 mm pistol to the young lady's head.

For some reason, time appears to run in slow motion, as Dereks's brain rolls over all the plausible scenarios. Finally, he is confronted with two options, lay down his weapon to save the woman or shoot, with any luck missing her and killing the man.

As his subconscious wrestles with the consequences of taking an innocent person's life, the mind makes the only possible decision for the mission. Two rounds are fired, the first hitting the man in the head, throwing his lifeless body against the rear wall before slumping to the ground to join his colleague. The second hits the woman, resulting in deafening screams as she falls to her knees, with blood pouring from the gaping wound just below the top of her shoulder.

With still more of the stables to clear, he must get a move on if he is to meet up the guys at the front of the house in time. But not being a heartless bastard like Steve, he checks on the woman now being attended by others from the group before moving on. "By the look of the wound, you will live but stay here until the whole shooting stops or the next five hours, whichever is the longest."

Time to check the horse stables on the other side. It shouldn't take too long because if anyone else is over there, they will have come over when the firing first started. So, with the same procedure as before, Derek kicks open the half-length wooden door to the first stall. It's empty. Like the building across the yard, this one is also divided into two halves.

As he moves cautiously, faint sounds of movement can be heard from within the room behind the stable wall. Once more, with the rifle ready to fire, he rushes through the door, prepared to kill anyone who wants to put up a fight. Through the dim light from the white bulb dangling from the ceiling, the shape of a horse can be seen frantically kicking out. All the shooting must have scared the crap out of the stupid thing.

With all the buildings cleared, Derek heads to the RV near the house to join the others, ready to clear the house.

Back on the grounds, Steve and Simon are running towards the concealed emergency exit from the tunnel. The metal hatch is hidden behind a square hedgerow in the garden, close to the principal house. Reaching the area first, Simon jumps to clear the shrubbery while diving for cover on the other side.

"Good move, mate, or it would have been if you hadn't tripped over the hedge."

"You can take the piss later, Steve," Simon replies through gritted teeth, as he adopts a kneeling firing position facing the barrack block.

As Mark predicts, the cast metal cover is unlocked. While grabbing the handle with my left hand, I listen for a few seconds for any indication that people might be making their way in either direction. Perfect, all sounds clear, so I gradually start to lift the massive lid to gain entry to the steps and the platform below. Must have got the damn thing nearly open when someone appears near the opening.

Instinct automatically kicks in. Seize the person by the collar and drag the top half of the man's body through, before slamming the cover down hard, pinning him between the lid and the rim.

As I do, I shout at Simon, "Give us a fucking hand, before this bastard escapes."

With one swift movement, Simon turns where he stands and rushes over to assist me. There is no time to fuck around with words on what to do next. As I hold the man in position, Simon places the end of the SLR on the back of the gentleman's head.

A nanosecond passes before the rifle recoils as the round accelerates down the barrel, leaving with a slight puff of white smoke and enters the skull; only to exit a split-second later, painting the freshly cut grass a dark crimson red as the contents of the person's head spilt out from the giant gaping hole.

The now limp, lifeless body is now blocking the way down, so I fling open the massive metal lid before both Simon and I grab the torso then, with one single action, pull the dead body out and discard it over in the bushes to our rear.

There is no time to worry about someone else being below, so I make my way down the small iron steps until I reach the one-metre square wire mesh platform. On one side, attached to the painted wall, a dim white light gives off just enough glow to see the steps leading down the rest of the way.

To be effective, the IEDs will need to be placed in the electric lights lining the tunnel wall, as per the plan. As I start my descent, Simon enters and takes up a position on the platform. He will follow me down, once I confirm it is safe for him to do so.

The emergency exit has been cut into the wall, to keep the route clear. This gives sufficient space for me to stand near the bottom of the stairway without protruding into the passageway. With the rifle tucked in along the length of my body, I stand in silence and listen for a few minutes.

Then, I am about to leave the stairwell, when to my left, the sound of someone running towards me has me trying my best to blend into the blackness, remaining motionless, frozen to the spot, not daring to move or even breathe too loudly. From the safety of darkness, I watch as the woman runs past, heading to the barracks, or once Simon and I finish planting the IED, the killing room.

After a glance around the corner into the brightly lit tunnel, to confirm nobody is around, I go back to the ladder and give it a gentle tap, only just audible to Simon, to start his descent to join me.

Once I'm joined by Simon, "OK mate, the first of the two lights for the explosives is opposite. If you try to cover me from here, I will set up the first one."

Simon takes up a firing position facing the house without saying a word, as this is more than likely the direction any help might come from.

Before doing anything else, I need to locate the light switch or primary power circuit board to turn off the electric lights, thus preventing any electrical current from running through the wires setting off the device. After a quick scan, I locate what looked like the control panel mounted on the right wall close to the entrance, leading to the barrack block above.

So, Simon knows my plan, I bend down next to him and tap his shoulder before whispering, "The controls for the lights are down the end," I indicate down the tunnel. "Will turn the power off from there." To show he understands, Simon gives me the thumbs-up signal.

Once he knows the plan, I sprint down the tunnel, doing my utmost not to make too much noise as my boots hit the floor. The last thing we need is for Chad's men to pour out into this tunnel from either end.

Looks like they're not expecting any issues down here, as the box is unlocked. After releasing the two catches on the side, I ease the door open to expose the fuses and electrical wiring. Thank fuck the person who wired the whole place up was a professional, and all the fuses are labelled, so finding the one I need will be easy.

With the index finger of my right hand running along the top lines of circuit breakers, I read out the name on each label in my head, until I reach the final one of the row.

The white printed tag has the words 'tunnel lights'. I press down on the switch, after a final glance to ensure Simon is still covering the house. The place is now in darkness. Pause for a moment, to become accustomed to the change from the faint glow of the electric bulbs to the blackness that now engulfed the area, before turning and sprinting back to the stairwell.

Now time to set the first of the two IEDs. Take off my pack, placing it down on the floor right beneath the light and touching my legs, so I won't have to fumble about to retrieve the device. Take my multi-tool from my jacket pocket, unfolding the screwdriver attachment. I locate the tiny crosshead screw with my finger, guide the tip into position, and effortlessly remove the fastener from the bottom of the fixture, prising off the glass cover, and place this by my feet.

Next, I unscrew the lightbulb, also laying it on the deck. Next comes the dangerous bit, attaching the explosives. Reach inside my bag and take out the first of the IEDs adapted back at my place. Rather than being connected to a mobile phone, I attach the wires to the metal fixing of a bulb after the glass is removed.

When preparing the IED back at my place, I am faced with a choice of two types of fixings — bayonet or screw. Fortunately, I go with the latter, so the adapter isn't required. Next, while holding the explosive package with one hand, I twist the cap and wires with the other. Hopefully, this will prevent the cables from becoming tangled when I screw in the connection. Now with everything connected, replace the cover and screw.

Seems like setting the first IED has taken far too long, but a glance down at Mickey on my wrist confirms the task is completed in less than a minute. Time to push on to the second one close to the fuse box. Perform the same procedure as previously, and the final device is set. Time to collect Simon and move on to the following phase of our mission.

When I reach Simon, he is already getting to his feet, "You could have turned the lights back on, Steve," with a big stupid grin.

"All I can say to that is you're a fucking idiot, Simon," turning around, before heading back along the dark tunnel towards the entrance at the end, which leads to the spiral staircase and the barrack block.

The only thing standing between us and the subsequent assault phase, the clearing of buildings, is the heavy cast iron door that leads to the accommodation above. With all the movements on the ground, plus the fact I've forgotten the number of Chad's men who have been killed so far, I haven't a clue on the number of people we will encounter, if any, upstairs.

Chapter Nineteen – Assault Phase Two

One thing for sure is, space will be tight. Even though it's an excellent weapon, the SLR's not that good in confined spaces, so the pistol will have to be used instead. With the rifle slung over my shoulder, pulled the 9 mm from its holster on my belt and wait for Simon to do the same.

I grab the handle of the door, while turning to face Simon, "You ready, mate?"

"Whenever you are."

On that, I push down a few centimetres before opening the door a few inches, to listen for any sounds from above. Can't detect anyone, so with one single action fling the door open the rest of the way and start to make my way up the spiral staircase, with Simon following behind.

Pause momentarily, just below floor level and listen again to try to detect people's positions with relation to the room. From what I can perceive, we have movement coming from both sides of the room. Turn to Simon and point to my ear with the index finger of my left hand, then with an outreached hand indicate to each side. No need to explain more, as he will understand what I mean.

A second later, we simultaneously, with my 9 mm in the firing position, burst out into the middle of the room, both covering different parts of the rooms, as discussed in the planning stage. To my front, a woman dressed in black is bending over a long wooden table collecting sheets of paper.

The noise of our entry must have alerted her. As she turns, facing the direction of the disturbance, I send two rounds in quick succession down the short barrel, both striking their target, her head.

Her lifeless body hit the tabletop hard before unhurriedly sliding to the floor with dark red blood oozing from the two holes I just put there.

Behind me, the sound of gunfire as Simon dispatches another. After a scan, I can't see anyone else in my target area, but that doesn't mean there isn't any of the fuckers hiding here. Still with the pistol raised, ready to fire the next round, move forward cautiously to the sleeping quarters. Seems like the place is clear, so I move to join Simon, clearing the other side of the room.

As I do, the distinctive crack of a weapon being fired, followed a nanosecond later by showers of tiny wooden splinters, as the bullet strikes the bunk bed close by. Spinning on the balls of my feet, I am confronted with a stocky man charging at me, his rifle firing from the hip. With no time to dive for cover, the option is to compose myself and fire at the moving target.

Time seems to stand still, as I pull back the sweaty metal trigger of the 9 mm. The events in front of me ran in ultra-slow motion, from the gas igniting in the metal casing to the recoil as the bullets leaving the barrel. Finally, both fired shots, now slicing through the atmosphere on their short journey to the target.

Now, only metres from me, my assailant is diving through the air when the rounds stuck home, entering the man's head then leaving via the rear a split-second later, in a shower of blood and brain matter. Again in slow motion, his body falls to the floor, bouncing twice as it did so. With the last act of defiance, his finger still gripped around the trigger, fire off his final deadly shot.

From behind me, I detect the sounds of a man screaming in pain. Glance over to see Simon sitting on the deck, blood dripping through a hole in his trousers, yelling at the top of his voice, "The cheeky little bastard."

On reaching Simon, "You OK, mate? Let me take a look." I roll up his trouser leg with care, revealing a deep gash on the bottom part of his calf.

"You're lucky, Simon — it only grazed you. So you will live, plus remember, pain is the only thing in the world that is free, so you might as well enjoy it. Can you walk?"

"You're all fucking heart, Steve, and yes, let's make a move."

One more task before we leave here, set the remote explosive for George to detonate once we are clear. While Simon bandages up the wound, I remove the electrical IED, marked 'three', from my pack and head for the cooker in the kitchen area. Thank God Dennis hasn't equipped the joint with mains gas. So instead, Chad's people have been using a 25 kg propane bottle to power the stove.

Perfect for what I have planned. The first task is to secure the package to the cannister with black masking tape, followed by the mobile. As soon as everything is in place with the cables connected, I turn to check Simon is ready to go before turning on the phone.

Observe as Simon hobbled to the doorway. Once there, I turn back to the IED and turn on the telephone. After checking there is a signal, I run over to the door, grab Simon. Then make our way around the side of the barrack block and across the grounds to the RV point in front of the house.

Back up in the sniper position, George observes the whole area, killing anyone who comes into my view through the optics. If things are going to plan, Steve and Simon should be exiting the accommodation block very soon, swinging the rifle to his right.

Well, that's one bit of good news, the two idiots are still alive, picking them up as they run from the building. Better keep the optical sights on the outbuilding, in case they are followed. They may have missed someone, unlikely, but you never know.

A few moments later, a figure appears from behind the block heading towards Simon and Steve.

With the weapon held tight in my shoulder, place the crosshairs on the centre of his target, press the button on the side and wait for everything to realign.

While they move, I take up the first pressure on the trigger and start to control my breathing. The moment the cross in the centre of the sights stops moving, the trigger is pulled back fully, setting the sequence of deadly events in motion.

Within the rifle, the firing pin strikes the bottom of the cartridge, igniting the gunpowder in the brass metal casing. This, in turn, causes a miniature explosion hurtling the 9 mm bullet down the barrel heading for its victim, twisting as it goes due to the riffling. As the round leaves the end, the recoil forces the stock hard, back against my shoulder.

Over on the target, the soil around the man's feet explodes into the air. He is now sprinting and catching up with the others.

"Crap, I've fucking missed," I say quietly through gritted teeth, and takes aim once more. The bullet hits its mark this time, and the man drops dead onto the freshly-cut grass.

Now moving the view to the rendezvous location at the front of the house, just in time to see Steve and Simon closing in on Derek, who is already there. Right, one more thing to do before shutting down this position, blow up the accommodation block. Pick up the phone and scroll through the numbers, until I find the correct preprogrammed number and dialled.

Over on the gas bottle, the small glass window of the mobile springs into life, followed by the tiny vibration of the asymmetrical wheel, sending a slight electrical current along the wires to the detonator. Inside, the Nichrome 80 starts to heats up, igniting the match head and the gunpowder, resulting in a small blast that ignites the primary explosive.

Within less than a second, a giant ball of superheated gas and explosives shoots upwards through the ceiling of the block, followed a nanosecond later by the deafening sound of an explosion as the building explodes, shooting shards of wood, metal and fire high into the morning air.

With debris falling and striking the ground in all directions, wait until all has settled before collecting the remaining bits of equipment and heading to join the rest at the RV.

Back on the grounds of the property Steve and Simon reach the rendezvous point. Derek is already there, covering their approach. "What the fuck happened?" pointing at the blood dripping through the bottom half of Simon's right trouser leg.

"That bastard George shot me... OK, not really. It was a stray bullet in the barrack block, but nothing to worry about, Derek."

"Not worried, mate, just wanted to know if I needed my blunt penknife to hack it off for you."

"You have been around that psycho too long," Simon points in my direction.

While waiting for George to meet us from the sniper position, we each cover different areas of the grounds; me facing the gate, to cover his sprint across the open ground to join us. As I scan the treeline beyond the entrance, George emerges from the woods. With only a brief check of the area, he starts racing towards us, zig-zagging, making it harder for anyone to get their sights on him.

Two minutes later, we are all in the RV, ready to kick off the next phase of the operation, clearing the house. Best I change the magazine on the 9 mm just to be safe. So I take one of the spares from the pouch, attach to the webbing belt wrapped around my waist, press down on the topmost round. It doesn't move. Perfect, this means I have a full mag of 13 bullets.

Glance over to the others. They are doing the same and using the pistols for any close quarter battles we may face once inside.

Without turning around, "Right, gents, George and Derek go around to the back, then clear the top floor as per the plan, while Simon and myself take the front and bottom level. If everyone is ready, entry starts in three mins from now." With that, Derek and George leap up from their positions and run towards the back of the building.

I turn to Simon, "OK, mate, let's go."

I Don't wait for a reply. Spring to my feet and head to the house, with Simon close behind me.

Now standing to the right of the massive wooden door, I sling the SLR over my shoulder, double-check the Browning 9 mm before checking the time. We have 30 seconds before we go in. I count down in my head. Once I reach one, I stand in front of the door and fire two shots in quick succession, before seeking protection back to the side.

Grasp the door handle and turn — perfect, it isn't locked — so push it ajar just a fraction. This is the signal for Simon to kick the door down, as I stand with the 9 mm Browning ready to kill anyone standing inside.

Moments later, the door is flung open. I rush into the hallway under a hail of gunshots, from a person 10 metres away down the other end, taking cover behind a massive teak unit.

My eyes scan the area for protection; fuck, there isn't any, only one possible action. My legs now moving as fast as I can muster, I hurtle towards him, firing several shots as I go.

I'm now within one metre, close enough to detect the breathing of a desperate man as his pistol makes the distinctive sound of an empty weapon being fired. Out of desperation, he launches his tall, stocky body at me, knocking me off-balance. I swiftly compose myself, and through the barrage of punches coming my way, I manage to wrap my right forearm around the man's neck. The man is fighting to set himself free, with my stomach receiving several blows from his elbow.

As a last-ditch attempt to release my grip, he runs backwards, slamming my back into the unit. The pain is agonising. Better end this now. With my left hand, I reach behind his head and the side of his face. With my arm squeezing his neck, preventing air from being taken in filling his lungs, I jerk his head sidewards, breaking the top half of his spine.

Once all movement fades away, I release my grip and let the lifeless body slump to the floor. I pause, before turning to see Simon dispatching a woman close to the entrance to the living room. As I run over to join him, two more shots can be detected from the back of the house. George and Derek are also in the building.

Without any words being spoken, we've done this far too many times before, preparing to enter the front room, I take the right of the door closest to me while Simon places himself on the opposite side. While looking across at Simon, I quietly count down, three, two. As soon as I reach one, we both burst into the room, our 9 mms following the precise movements of our eyes, as we each cover opposing sides of the room.

To my right is a giant TV showing some type of kids show. Shit, this means the children are still on the property. Over near the patio glass windows, a substantial green leather sofa stands a few feet away from the wall, near the patio glass windows. A perfect place for someone to be hiding. Look over to Simon, point to my eyes to indicate we should check this out, follow by indicating with my arm in the direction of the couch.

As I make my way past the TV and coffee table, I keep close to the outside of the room until I come to the vast patio windows, then pause until we're both in position. With my 9 mm pointing down at 45 degrees, eager to kill anyone, I rush the remaining distance. Sitting huddled together, sobbing with tears running down their cheeks, are the three young children.

I'm now facing a dilemma, waste the brats or not? As I straighten my arms, ready to fire, the voice of reason comes screeching across the room.

"They're just innocent kids, Steve, fucking leave them alone." But, of course, on this occasion, Simon is right.

Instead, I kneel down next to them, "OK, you're safe, just do me a favour. Stay here until someone comes to collect you. If you move, you could be struck by a stray bullet and killed. Nod, if you understand me." I need to scare the crap out of them, so they stay put. All three terrified and now shaking kids gently nod their heads to confirm they understand.

With the dining room void of Chad's men, we re-enter the hallway, making our way to the office-come-library on the other side. Again following the same procedure as before, we take up position by the door. About to give the word to go when upstairs, the sound of a door being swung open followed by two shots in rapid succession can be heard. Either there are bad guys upstairs, or Derek and George are getting trigger happy.

On the count of one, I enter the big, square room, with Simon closely behind. On the far side, a teak desk takes up a fair amount of the space. Guess this is Dennis' centre of operations. Along two of the walls runs shelving from the deck to the ceiling, full of books. Situated in the left wall are more glass patio doors leading to the grounds.

A room scan confirms it is empty, so we move on to the next room on the ground floor, the kitchen. Inside, a cooking station takes up most of the middle of the room. Stainless steel cupboards run along each side. Once Simon enters, I follow suit, making my way to the back, checking all cabinets as I go, looking for any idiot trying to hide.

As we converge behind the cooking aisle, "This place seems clear. Let's make our way to the top of the cellar to meet up with the other two."

"Roger that, Simon."

About to leave when a hand taps me on the shoulder, "Listen," Simon points to the cupboards down and in front. Below, the sounds of someone breathing heavily through clasped hands wrapped around their mouths. With my index finger taking up the first pressure on the trigger, I step back. The 9 mm is now aimed at the source of the noise.

With one hand grasping the handle, Simon throws open the cooker door. Crouched within, a young female with long blonde hair, her knees pulled up tight to her body, held in place with one arm, the other hand is pressed tightly against her lips.

"Right, very slowly remove yourself from out of there and move over here," I gesture with the pistol.

After rotating herself inside, both legs gradually come out, her feet hitting the tiled floor in sync. Struggling to stand up, she holds out her right arm. With my weapon still pointing at her, I grasp her now wet hand with the tiny droplets of water from her heavy gasping. Standing next to us is a well-shaped youthful lady with all the curves in the right place. Looks to be in her mid-thirties.

With Simon's 9 mm resting on her forehead, "Let me start with two simple questions. First, who are you, second, your connection to Dennis?"

Through a faint trembling voice, "My name is Nicole. I am Dennis' housekeeper. As for his work and what's going on down in the cellar, I know nothing."

With one of the rare moments of compassion coming over me, "No point wasting a bullet on the stupid bitch, just bind and gag her."

Over on the counter is a roll of cling film, that will have to do to stop her shouting out. While Simon binds her hands with a cable tie from his jacket, I wrap several layers of clear plastic around her head, making sure it covers her entire face. Not wanting her to suffocate, I kindly make two slits below the nostrils and insert a couple of straws to prevent the holes from closing up. This should help her breathe. If not, I don't know her, so I don't care.

A gentle tap on the back of the knees has Nicole complying and kneeling on the floor. To ensure she stays put, two more thick black cable ties are used to bind her to the long stainless steel handle running along the front of the oven.

Once our housekeeper is secure, I turn to Simon, "OK mate, let's make for the cellar."

Meanwhile, upstairs, George and Derek are clearing the first-floor bedrooms. "If you clear the rooms to the right of the stairs, I'll take the other side."

"No problem, George, meet you back here when I'm finished."

With that, Derek turns around and heads for the first closed door, now on his left. Like most things on this mission, I've not done anything like this before, but how hard could it be? Simply kick the door open and kill any bad guys inside.

Standing opposite the door, listening to multiple shots being fired downstairs, I run through the subsequent actions in my mind. No time to fuck about, I raise my right leg, then with one swift boot, kick the door open and rush inside.

With the Browning 9 mm held out to the front, I sweep the room. No sign of anyone so far, better check the cupboards and under the well-made bed just in case some fucker is hiding there. No way am I'm randomly peeking underneath to be faced with a weapon pointing at my head. So with my left hand, grab the bottom of the double bed, throwing it across the room, while keeping the 9 mm in the other, aiming under where the bed is situated.

Right, that's the first room cleared. Better move on to the next one. Like the first one, the second and third rooms are empty. As I exit the last room, the sound of a single shot comes from George's half of the first level. Without hesitation, spin around and sprint towards the gunshot.

On entering, George is standing over a man dressed in black is crawling along the carpeted floor, inching his way to an open window that leads to a balcony. As he creeps inch by inch forward, two narrow lines of blood stretch out on the new carpet from the position falls.

As if he is torturing the man, giving him some sort of false he will make it out of here a live, George watches and waits until he reaches the opening. Then, as the man's hand touchs the cold marble of the balcony, he casually walks over and fires a 9 mm round in the back of his head.

What is left of the guy's blood, now oozes from the gaping hole and unhurriedly seeps over the black and cream tiles.

Out of the corner of his eye, George sees the shape of an armed figure in the doorway. With one swift movement, he turns with the 9 mm leading the way, his red blood-stained finger ready to squeeze the trigger.

"For fuck sake, Derek, let me know you're there — nearly bloody shot you. But as you're here, check the room behind me."

"Will do, lesson well and truly learned," Derek says, getting to grips with the situation and heading for the bedroom behind him.

A few minutes later, both Derek and George are descending the stairs, making their way to join the others at the entrance to the cellar.

Once everyone is in position covering all directions, ready for the final part of this phase, "Before we head down to the basement, has anyone seen Dennis?" while changing the magazine on my 9 mm.

"Not yet, mate, but when we do find the arsehole, do we take him alive or kill him where he stands?"

"That's an easy one, bearing in mind the suffering he's caused a lot of people. With the selling of people into slavery and the misery inflicted by the drugs, shoot on sight, unless you are planning on taking him on a date, Derek."

"Here's me thinking you would like to torture him a little first, before delivering an agonising death, Steve," Simon responds, also checking his ammo count.

"I can live with that. Once we are downstairs, I'll head for the biggest room. You lot clear all the smaller rooms before joining me.

Our primary aim here is to kill Chad's people and recover the weapons. So if you're ready, gents, let's make a move."

There is no point in creeping down the stone steps, as they will be aware we are coming their way from all the gunshots and radio chatter. With me leading, we rush down to the cellar to be confronted with one of Chad's men emerging from one of the rooms to my right. From behind me, the sound of a 9 mm being double-tapped by George, followed a split-second later, the guard's head exploding in a shower of blood and tissue as he falls to the floor.

Now entering the most significant room to my front, two people, a man and a woman, are closing down computer screens and packing them into boxes. To their right, another man is loading the weapon systems into wooden crates.

Over on my left, from behind a stack of containers, a man is shooting wildly in my direction. As a bullet strikes the wall, sending fragments of brick into the room inches from my head, I grab the massive metal desk in front of me and turn it over on its side and dive for cover.

Shots are still coming my way, so wait until he fires, then once he disappears back behind the containers, I leap to my feet and race over to his position. As I round the corner, a single shot skims my arm, ripping through the flesh. A moment's loss of concentration, due to the agonising pain coming from the wound, gives him the advantage; something he takes full advantage of and hurtles at me like a raging bull.

The full force of the guy's body hitting mine, knocks me to the painted solid floor. As I hit the ground hard with him on top, the 9 mm comes free from my hand. My assailant's hands are held firm around my neck, as he tries to squeeze the last remaining breath from my body.

In desperation, my right arm sweeps the deck, searching in vain for the pistol. At last, my hand feels something cold and hard. My fingers take hold, then, with my full strength, the object is swung up and into the side of the man's head, knocking the bastard clear.

With adrenaline pumping even faster through my veins, I straddle the man, sitting on his chest with my knees, pinning his arms to the floor. I raise my hand, still grasping the heavy object above my head, before bringing it down with my whole body force into the person's skull.

Repeat the actions several times, until it is impossible to recognise the person from the flattened remains of bone fragments intertwined with brain tissue and dark crimson blood now spreading across the concrete floor.

From behind, over near the small kitchen, I hear Simon crying out, "Clear."

I turn to face him, to see Derek and George racing towards the computer screens. Within seconds, the first two of the three people lay motionless on the ground.

The third, not wanting to end up like his mates, grabs a rifle, aiming at Derek, ready to fire. A distinctive crack from the back of the room comes from Simon's SLR, as the bullet exits the barrel in a tiny cloud of smoke, striking the last of Chad's men in the chest. He falls to the deck, twitching uncontrollably as he takes his last remaining breath.

With the whole team together in the biggest of the rooms, all uninjured apart from a few flesh wounds, it's time to start collecting all the equipment that needs to be loaded and taken with us to the boatyard.

While the others are packing Mark's stuff, I turn my attention to the rows of computer servers located behind thick glass walls. We can't afford to leave the code-breaking software and any progress they will have made, on cracking the complicated programming of the weapons systems. Thankfully, the door to the enclosure isn't locked. Once inside, I switch off the main power, before smashing open each server in turn, to remove the hard drives. We didn't need them. I just need to ensure they are made inoperable.

Once they are all out and stacked up, I removed the SLR from my back, load a full magazine of 20 rounds, then proceed to empty the mag into computers. That should fuck them up.

As the last round strikes home, a figure darts out from a stack of crates at the back of the room, sprinting towards the tunnel door.

"That's Dennis," Simon yells out, while firing several shots in Dennis' direction, narrowly missing.

"Grab the bastard," I reply, running after him.

By the time I reach the entrance, it is too late, the door is swung open and he disappears inside. I turn and dive for cover, knowing what is coming next.

The idiot must have turned on the lights to see as seconds later, an electrical current is sent along the wires to the IEDs I placed there earlier. As the power runs up the tiny cables of the detonators, they ignite, causing a small blast. This, in turn, causes the principal explosive package to explode, sending a shower of nails, fiery mixture and flames everywhere in the long tunnel. The full force of the detonation sends shock waves throughout the cellar, knocking objects smashing to the floor.

Eventually, the room stops shaking, and no more sounds of falling debris can be detected from inside. "Better make sure the arsehole is dead, George."

"Will do, if he is alive, I'll drag his sorry arse back to you, Steve."

A few minutes later, what remains of the door is kicked open, and George emerges, dragging Dennis' body. "He's been a lucky sod. He was down this end, not the other end where you planted the IEDs. Apart from many puncture wounds from the four-inch nails you added for good measure, the twat is still alive."

"Dump him over here, George," I say, kneeling down next to Dennis.

He appears to be unconscious from the looks of him, but better check the slippery little bastard. With Derek's SLR barrel resting on his head, I place my right hand over his mouth. With the other, I pinch his nose. Almost imminently, Dennis starts to cough and splutter as he tries to breathe. The sneaky little fucker has been trying to fool us. With that, I remove my hand, clench my fingers into a tight fist and slam it hard against the side of Dennis' face.

"That's just because you... No, just because."

Once Dennis is sitting up and thoroughly with us, "From what we've seen, you've been a bad boy and caused misery to lots of people, from your activities, selling innocent people into slavery. Let's not forget the drugs, then there is the reason we are here, your venture into arms dealing. Because of this, you do not deserve a quick, pain-free death, so I'm going to make it as painful as possible. Pull him over here." I walk over to what is left of the server room.

"They say, 'never kick a man when he is down', but in your case, I'll make a huge exception," George lands several hard kicks to Dennis' stomach, before he and Simon grab him by the collar and drag him over.

"Put him in here, gents, fetch me the last remote IED from my pack, Derek," as my right foot helps Dennis inside.

After securing him to the computer wreckage, I place the explosive package and mobile telephone just out of his reach. Make sure the screen is facing him.

"Look here, Dennis," I indicate with my finger to the phone, "when the light comes on, you have a second to say goodbye to whoever you like, but then you are on the way to hell."

After scanning the room to ensure we hadn't left anything important behind, we start to ferry the equipment up the stone steps and place them close to the front door.

"Did you locate any vehicles, Simon that we can use, or are you heading for the van?"

"Been with you the entire time, Steve, so I'll go and fetch the truck."

Before exiting the building into the grounds, Simon scans the area, especially near the front gate. His professionalism pays off, as laying on top of the gatehouse is a person looking this way, possibly a trap.

At that moment, George appears, entering the hallway from the stairs leading to the cellar. "Got a dilemma where your skill may help, George." Simon points towards the gate.

"No problem, mate, I'll dispose of him for you," taking the rifle from his back.

George pulls the stock hard into his shoulder, with legs of the L115A3 on one of the boxes, he takes aim. Simon observes as George's chest goes in and out from the cover of the doorway, as he starts to control his breathing.

No more than two seconds pass when the recoil from the small explosion inside the brass casing explodes, forcing the rifle's stock backwards in a straight line into George's shoulder. Then, on the business end, the bullet strikes home, the person falling to the ground with no audible sound.

"OK, you lazy bastard, jog-on and fetch the fucking van," picking up the sniper rifle.

"Cheers, George, back in five minutes."

With that, Simon races out of the house and sprints for the gate. Then, with only a brief stop at the entrance to ensure nobody is coming down the road, continue towards the roadworks and the hidden vehicle. Rounding the bend near where we had buried the vehicle IEDs, the remains of a Range Rover smoulder away.

This must be why people didn't come from the farmhouse to assist the rest of Chad's men. We must have not detected the explosion from the cellar.

Not sure if anyone is still alive in the car or in the vicinity with the rifle at the hip ready to fire, so approached with caution. Inside, four people lay motionless. After seeing Dennis try to bluff being dead, he raises the SLR and empties a 7.62 mm round into each of the bodies, just to be on the safe side.

A sweep of the area around the white van confirms it hasn't been interfered with, so climb behind the wheel and drive back past the burnt-out vehicle to the house. After reversing up to the heavy wooden front door, Steve appears in the doorway.

"Any problems, Simon?"

"Nothing I couldn't handle, plus the vehicle IEDs worked. We have a burnt vehicle half blocking the road."

"Roger that, mate, get the van open."

Once all the equipment is loaded, Derek climbs in the back while I close the rear doors before joining Simon and George in the front.

"OK, Simon, take us to the boatyard. Need to arrive before the people there start to build up too much of a defensive position. Let's face it, they know we might be becoming."

With that, Simon slams the accelerator pedal to the floor and speeds off towards the gate, passing remains of the Range Rover and its dead occupants.

I turn in my seat, "Do you have your mobile handy, George?"

"Yeah, why."

"Then give Dennis a call."

George knows I don't mean his usual number, but the one attached to the IED. Once he finds the right one corresponding with the figure on the package, he presses the green button. A few seconds later, the screen on the phone lights up as Dennis looks up to his fate.

Chapter Twenty – Assault on Boatyard

Thirty minutes later, we reach the edge of Cowes, making good progress towards the boatyard. After sliding the small metal hatch in the rear bulkhead, Derek can hear what is being said.

"Right, gents, this next phase will be in broad daylight, and civvies might be roaming about the place, so only take well-aimed shots. Plus, we need to be in and out of here as fast as possible, because mayhem undoubtedly will follow once George blows the pontoon. So while Derek and I recover the weapon systems, you cover the river and dispatch any of Chad's people still kicking about. If you can stay with the vehicle, Simon and tackle anyone leaving the office, that could be a threat. Is everyone clear on what to do?"

"Any idea of when should I set off the IED, Steve?" George enquires, playing with the mobile phone.

"The moment we drive through the gate."

As we drive down Newport Road entering into Cowes, Simon checks his mirrors. "Fuck, I think we have a bigger problem to deal with. We have a police car 20 metres behind us with its siren and blue lights flashing. The copper in the passenger seat is swinging his arm to the right. Think he wants me to pull over."

"No need for panic. Ahead, on your right, is M&S. The local buses use this to swing around. Suggest you do the same," I say, leaning forward to peer in the mirror.

A minute passes, Simon slows down, makes a sharp right turn, and parks in front of the shop. While we wait, my head runs through several reasons why the back of the van is loaded with stolen military weapons.

Moments later, the police vehicle shoots past us at some speed and disappears out of our line of sight. "Definitely do without that shit today. When you're ready, mate, drive to the boatyard."

Not far to go for the mission's next stage to get underway. Derek can be heard in the back, cocking his SLR as we approach the yard. Makes sense, so grab my rifle from the side of the seat, where it's been since leaving Dennis' place and check it is still loaded — it is.

Simon drives into the target area without stopping or glancing in any direction but forward, driving straight to the wooden boat shed where the weapons are being stored. On route, a loud explosion and a ball of bright light shooting into the air is coming from the pier area. George has detonated the IED. Seconds later, the deafening screams as people flee in all directions like headless chickens, once they comprehend what just happened.

We need to make the utmost of the confusion. So we all jump out of the vehicle and sprint to the shed. Once our feet are on the ground, George proceeds to the water's edge to watch the pontoon floating away, out into the waters of the Solent. Several dead bodies are bobbing about nearby. At one end, two men dressed in the uniform of Chad's people and carrying some type of weapon, are climbing into a small boat.

George adopts a kneeling position. With his elbow resting just past the kneecap of his left leg and the sniper rifle pulled tightly in his shoulder by his right arm, he takes aim a tad to the right of the first person to compromise for the gentle breeze blowing across the bay. The first pressure on the trigger is taken up, followed by the second, sending the bullet skimming a few feet above the sea at 936 mp/s.

The first guy falls backwards into the ocean as the round strikes its target, George reloads and resets the sights once more. Moments later, both of Chad's former employees are floating face down in the water, being taken out to the middle of the Solent shipping lane.

Meanwhile, Derek and I are about to enter the shed to search for the altered weapons systems. "Here is the plan, Derek. I'll go in first, been in the building before, while you cover me from the door. Are you ready?"

"Yeah, let's go for it," Derek replies, taking up position by the side of the door.

As I enter with the SLR raised, I am all ready to open fire. The interior is in darkness, apart from the light coming from the window in the ceiling. Scan the room for any of Chad's men. Can't see any in the gloom, so I shout for Derek to join me.

If the missing equipment is here, it should be over in the wire-mesh cage to my right. With Derek still covering the rest of the inside, I walk over to the enclosure, grabbing a metal crowbar to break the lock. When I reach the gate inside, instead of the weapons we came for, are a mixture of 20 men, women, and children huddled in the back corner. After what I witnessed during my OP, I'm not surprised.

"Come over here, Derek. We have an issue," while inserting the crowbar in the loop of the padlock, I point to the people on the floor inside, "We can't afford to take them with us, plus they've seen our faces. So the question is, do I kill them all or leave them here for the police, hoping they don't describe us to the coppers?"

"Don't know about you, but I, for one, am not into murdering innocent people. Best they stay put, uninjured and wait for a policeman. Sure none of them speaks English anyway," Derek says, looking at the small group, who are now inching closer together.

"Maybe you're right," I displace the bar from the lock.

The exact moment I start to turn away, an older man dressed in rags, "I speak a little."

"In that case, my friend, tell everyone to stay here and not to move until the authorities arrive to collect you, nod if you understand me?" I say, with a combination of words and hand gestures. He nods before sitting down with the rest of the group.

The big question now is if they are currently occupying the space, where the fuck is the stuff we came for? While I check the area around the cage, Derek investigates the other side.

Over in the far corner, buried under a massive white sailcloth, are the missing rifles and the control boxes. "Steve, I think what we came for is over here, plus some of the huge green bundles we talked about."

"Yep, that's them," tearing open the edge of one of the packages. "We are in luck. This one is full of cash! Start loading them into the van, especially that one. Might as well make a few quid extra for our troubles."

"That's a bonus and should keep my missus on St Halb happy for a while," making sure he takes the money out first to the vehicle.

With only one left to load, "If you can take that one, Derek, I want to check around the back of the cage, to see what else is about. I'll be out in a moment."

Manage to reach halfway to the back when someone lands on me from above, knocking me face down to the wooden floor. In a confined space, the person sat on my back is grabbing my head, doing their best to wrap an arm around my neck. Only one course of action is open to me. Place my hands palm down, close to my chest. Then, with a single movement, I push with all my might until my arms are straight and my legs are bent under me, succeeding to rise to a standing position.

While feeling several agonising punches into my kidneys from my assailant, I move backwards as fast as possible in such a tight space.

Once free from the confines, I grab the man's arm while immediately bending forward, throwing him over my back and to the floor to my front. To give me time to comprehend the situation and what the fuck is happening, I put a little distance between us.

My attacker rises to his feet and lifts his head in a slow, menacing manner. I recognise him. It is Chad. With his reputation, I can't afford for him to seize even the slightest of an upper hand. So without pausing, I launch myself in his direction, driving him backwards until his back slams hard into the cage's wire mesh.

With my left forearm pushing against his neck, pinning him to the cage, I frantically search for my 9 mm with the other hand. Shit, in the scuffle, I must have dropped the bloody thing, time for plan 'B'.

Bring my right knee upwards with speed, but before it makes contact with his bollocks, sensing I'm now off balance, Chad's well-placed leg makes me lose my footing, resulting in me dropping to the ground again.

A fraction after my arse hits the floor, I am up, launching at him again, this time with a long knife. As I sink the blade deep into his chest, slightly above the heart, I feel another excruciating pain, this time in my side, forcing me to stumble back a few feet. Glance down to see blood oozing from a deep-seated wound. The bastard stabbed me.

While I stand motionless for a second or two, looking in Chad's direction with time seeming as if it ran in slow motion. "Would appear you're not that hard, Steve, seen women put up a better fight," comes the voice leaving his lips and echoing in my ears. "Thought it would be a lot more fun killing you."

"I'm not fucking dead yet," I reply, falling to my knees, frantically searching for the pistol. When I glance back up to face him, I relocate my own 9 mm. Chad must have found it, and now my own weapon is pointing at my head.

"Time to say goodbye, Steve."

Feels like my greatest fear of dying alone is now laid out in front of me. Where are the others when you need their assistance? Still feeling the excruciating pain rise up inside me, I close my eyes and wait for the fateful moments of my life to pass before my eyes. At that precise moment, the unmistakable sound of the crack of a weapon being fired comes from above the wire cage.

As I open my eyes, Chad is lying in front of me, face down in the dirt. Red crimson blood is oozing from the exit wound on the side of his face. What the fuck just happened? Turn to the door to see if the boys have come to my rescue.

Nobody is there, so I look up to the platform several feet higher than the cage to observe Lorna holding a rifle, pointing towards the body lying face down.

Through gritted teeth, due to the pain, I say, "Thanks." With that, she descends and rushes to my side.

"Here, hold this against the open wound. It should help arrest the bleeding a little, while I make sure Chad doesn't have anything interesting on him."

"Thank you, but why, I thought you worked for Chad?

"Well, I did until about five minutes ago when I thought I was about to lose you. The funny thing is, I haven't stopped thinking about you since the night in the pub."

"You drove off and left me to fend for myself in the car park," I reply, while taking a deep breath.

"Yes and no. One of the others climbed in the vehicle and made me drive off, while his colleague tried to finish you off. At this stage, I had no comprehension of who you are."

As I hold the rag over the wound, Derek runs in, "What's been keeping you...?" then caught sight of Lorna and goes to fire his weapon.

"Don't fucking shoot, Derek—she just saved my life while you idiots waited outside."

"Well, you better get your lazy arse off the floor. The emergency services are starting to arrive, and we need to leave now, or you can be the one explaining why we have a van loaded with weapons, cash and drugs."

"Give us a hand then, Derek," staggering to my feet.

Outside, Simon is standing near the van's back doors as Derek and Lorna help me to the waiting vehicle. "Would you want to clarify why the young lady is assisting you?" says Simon, a very puzzled appearance spread across his face.

"Will explain on the way, mate, where is George?"

"He is still around the back, covering out to sea in case any idiots come that way. I'll go and fetch him."

By the time everyone is in the vehicle, a considerable crowd has gathered outside on the road, kept back by a couple of police officers. The question now is how do we get out from the boatyard. The last thing we need is to be stopped and questioned, and worse, held back to be interviewed on the events that have occurred.

"Play along, Steve," as she removes the bandage from the knife wound.

As Simon approaches the main gate, a policeman is standing in front with his right hand raised, indicating that we should stop. As he approaches, Lorna waves her hand for the person to come to her side.

"Sorry, you can't leave yet. We may need to take some information regarding what you know about the explosion," comes a stern voice through the open window.

"I understand, officer, but this man is injured and trust me, we don't have time to wait for an ambulance," Lorna points to the blood dripping from my side. "Here is my phone number," she hands the policeman a piece of paper with a made-up set of digits. "Will come straight back, but this man will die if I don't take him to a hospital." With that, he waves us through.

"Where to next?" Simon says, turning right out of the gate.

"Anywhere out of Cowes, so we can bandage up this wound better with bandages from the first aid pack in my bag."

"No problem, Steve, I know just the place."

A few minutes later, Simon turns left onto the empty Isle of Wight county grounds. Once I manage to scramble out of the front of the truck, I go around the back, open both doors, and grab my Bergen. Reach in and remove the medical kit. After removing my jacket and t-shirt, I take out some super-glue. "Can you do the glueing, Lorna? Those three idiots will only make it worse, and on purpose."

"Stop winging, you wimp—it's only a knife injury. Positive you will live."

"You can go forth and multiply, George."

"What do you want me to do, Steve?" comes Lorna's tender voice.

"When I push the skin together, pour the superglue down the cut to seal the wound. You ready?"

"Yes, Steve."

My left hand pinched both sides while clenching my teeth due to the pain. "Now, Lorna, before I let go."

"If you're sure, you could have internal injuries," with that, she spread the glue along the two-centimetre gash.

Inside the van's rear, Derek opens the green bundle of cash we liberated from the boatyard. "How much do you think is in the package?" I grab a handful of the used banknotes.

"Not sure, mate, but I would estimate at least a million."

"He is right, Steve. Dennis sent it along with the speedboat to France to purchase the drugs and collect those poor people to be sold into modern-day slavery," Lorna interjects.

"Always good to have a work's bonus," says George, putting the money back.

"To be safe, we better stay away from my place tonight, so when you're ready, Simon, drive us to Sandown airport in Lake. I will be flying us back to the mainland tomorrow."

"Just one tiny question, Steve, when did you obtain a pilot's licence?"

"Don't be so picky, George," I reply, smiling through a stupid grin.

Chapter Twenty One – Weapons Recovery

After turning right onto Scothelles Brook Lane, "Keep driving, Simon, there is a holiday camp up the drive on the left opposite the airfield. Let's see if we can book one night's accommodation, far better than us all sleeping in the van."

On arrival at the park, Simon parks in one of the parking bays running along the right-hand side. On the opposite side, is what seems like the office, "I can't go in due to this hole in my side, so best if George and Lorna go over and try to make a booking."

"Any excuse, Steve, you sit and relax while we go in to book us a room. Come on, Lorna, let's see what we can get." With that, George grabs a handful of the used notes from the bundle of cash and walks over to the small brick office building on the other side of the road.

Inside, a counter runs along one side, separating customers from the several wooden desks. To the right, numerous seats are situated among the tall wooden stands, stuffed to the brim with stupid leaflets of every possible type imaginable.

The moment Lorna and George approach the counter, a smartly dressed young woman, probably in her late twenties, welcomes them, "Hi, welcome to the Copse Holiday Park. Do you have reservations for tonight?"

"No, sorry, we've just arrived on the island and decided to visit for a while, and your place was highly recommended to us," Lorna replies with a feminine smile.

"That's not an issue. There are still some caravans available. How long would you like to stay with us?"

Before leaving the van, it is agreed that there is no point in asking for one night as this might seem suspicious, so Lorna replies, "Three nights would be good."

"Not a problem, the system is showing a silver grade caravan is free at £210 plus £50 security deposit against any damages."

"Perfect," Lorna says, handing over £260 in cash.

After several forms to complete, we are handed the keys along with a map of the entire park, on which our accommodation is circled.

Back at the van, the others are on the other side of the hedgerow, looking in the direction of the airfield. "What you looking at?" George enquires.

"Debating if we help ourselves to one of the aircraft parked over on the airstrip, or hire one using my pilot's licence. How did you get on with booking somewhere to stay tonight?"

"All booked, Steve, and you do actually possess a licence then?"

"Yes, George, I obtained it a few years back."

The caravan looks simple, but all we require for one night. Tomorrow we will be taking the weapon systems back to Mark. This reminds me, we still need to develop a plan to make our way from Popham airstrip to the premises and, most importantly, receive the money owed. After the problems getting compensated by Henry after the last mission, there is no way I'm handing over all the weapons without some sort of payment first.

While everyone else sorts themselves out, I spend the next 15 minutes running several scenarios through my mind, until I thought I process some type of plan.

"OK, folks, if you give me a minute, here is what I came up with for tomorrow. First, need some kind of diversion in case some of Chad's people are still around and try to follow our movements.

"To that end, Simon and Derek will take the van once we unload it at the aircraft, then drive to Popham airfield near Basingstoke, via the Red Funnel Ferry."

"So you want Derek and me to act as bait while you take a leisurely flight to the mainland," Simon interrupts, in a sarcastic voice.

"Stop moaning, pretend you're in a tank, and you'll be fine."

"The rest of us will fly with the weapons and cash, then meet you at the airstrip. While it is on my mind, Simon, can you contact Mark and get someone to join us when we land? Plus, it goes without saying that a stag needs to be placed on the vehicle. Suggest a two-hour rotation. Any questions?"

"Not got a problem driving but will need dosh for the ferry, and what do you want us to do if some idiot follows us?"

"Help yourself to the cash, and if someone does follow you, Simon, I recommend you lead them down some excluded road and deal with the matter."

"If nobody's got any question on the plans, I'm making a brew — anyone else fancy one?"

"Yes please, mate, and by the way, Simon and myself will take the room with the two small beds, Derek you're the new boy, so the sofa is all yours. Why don't you two love birds take the double bed? If you are thinking of continuing what you started in the car park the other day, keep the fucking noise down as the remainder of us will be trying to sleep."

I look over to Lorna, sitting near the dining table and is now starting to blush slightly, "Ignore them idiots."

To stop the usual moaning from George about always getting the very last stag, we give him the first, I will take the last one. Once George is patrolling the area between the caravan and the vehicle, the rest of us catch up on some well-deserved sleep. Its been a hard few days, but as they say, this operation will not be over until the weapons are handed to Mark.

With Lorna's arms wrapped around mine under the warm quilt, I soon drift off into the land of nod to await being woken at daft o'clock for my own time on guard.

"Good morning sleeping beauty, coffee is on the go," comes the gentle message from Lorna, as I open my eyes.

"What time is it and what happened to my stag?" now fully awake.

"Because of your injury, we took your shift. Talking of which, let me take a peek at the dressing."

From looking at the bed sheets, it would appear there was only slight bleeding during the night. "Thanks, Lorna, but it's fine."

Once I manage to get myself dressed and enter the kitchen, Simon, Lorna and George are at the table drinking freshly made brews. "Take it Derek is outside?" I ask, sitting next to them.

"Yeah, I'm just about to take him out a brew," as she rises to her feet and grabs the black mug from the counter.

"Sure, he will appreciate that," I say, sipping on my own coffee.

Soon our conversation turns to the plans for today, going over every stage in fine detail, missing nothing out. In fact, we become that engrossed we don't notice that 20 minutes pass and Lorna hasn't returned.

"Something is up, gents, suggest we all go and investigate," standing up and heading to the door.

"Right behind you, Steve," says Simon, also making for the exit.

At first, there is no sign of her or Derek anywhere between the caravan and our transport. It isn't until we reach the opposite side of the van, close to the hedgerow, we spot that something must have gone badly wrong.

In the open space, connecting the left of the white van and the green bushes lining the road's edge, is a person lying face down, blood still spilling onto the tarmac from underneath the body.

All of us instinctively reach for our weapons, "You go around the other way and come in from a different angle, Simon. George and I will go this way."

As we round the corner of the vehicle on the driver's side, there's a tallish man dressed similar to one of Chad's men, but it can't be, sure we disposed of all of them. Whoever this fucking person is, he now holds one arm around Lorna's neck and a pistol barrel resting lightly on the side of her head.

"OK, mate, keep calm, nobody else needs to be killed today. What are you after?" holding my 9 mm out to the front, pointing at his head.

"Come on, Steve, you're not an idiot. You know what we want. Where is the flash drive with the coding for the weapons systems you took from Chad at the boatyard?" comes an aggressive reply.

"Not sure what you're talking about, but put down the weapon and let her go and we can discuss the issue like two grown men."

While Lorna does her best to release herself from the attacker's grip, he drags her towards the driver's door. As he reaches for the handle, the sound of a gunshot echoes past, very close by my head. A nanosecond later, the man's face explodes in a cloud of blood and brain matter, the force sending him hurtling backwards, before hitting the deck. I turn to see our marksman has taken the shot.

"What? Someone needs to end the situation, plus it was an easy shot. The question is, where the fuck is Derek?" while lowering his weapon.

"Not sure, George, better try to find him," I say, walking in his direction.

"Found him. The idiot is tied up in the back. Luckily, the weapons and the money are still here," Simon shouts, as he flings open the back doors of the van.

By this time, Lorna has joined me, a slight tear in her eyes, more to do with frustration that she let the man get the best of her, more than anything else.

"Back at the boatyard when Chad was taken down, you were the only other person in the shed with me, Lorna, so do you know anything about the flash drive?"

"Yes, Steve, I have it," she lifts the device from her pocket. "Removed it when searching his pockets after I killed him, forgot about it until now. At least we now know what's on the memory stick."

No point in hanging about now. Might as well get the final phase underway, so once everyone's kit is collected from the accommodation and packed in the vehicle, Simon drives to the airstrip.

Did consider stealing a small plane but thinking logically, this would cause more issues than we need, due to having to contact both control towers during the flight. Instead, we will try to rent an aeroplane for me to fly or, if that fails, hire a plane with a pilot. Fortunately, as we enter the airfield, on the right-hand side are several black buildings, one of which has its doors wide open. Inside are three light aircraft, perfect for what we want them for.

Above the door of one of the hangers, a giant sign stating all visitors should report to the booking office located below the signage. While George and myself go in, the rest wait in the van.

The interior consists of a few desks behind a makeshift wooden counter. Along two of the internal walls, generously-sized windows give visibility into the hanger. Beyond the office, a pile of crates are being loaded onto an aircraft. It isn't long before a man dressed in black trousers and a white, neatly-pressed shirt spots us waiting and enters via the back door.

"Good morning, gentlemen. How can I help?"

"A good morning, sir, wondering if you have any light aeroplanes for hire for a couple of days?" I place my pilot's licence and logbook on the counter.

"Afraid you are out of luck — rented the last one yesterday. Is it for just you two, or do you want to shift equipment?"

"I'm hoping to transport three people and some gear to Popham airfield first thing this morning, an urgent delivery," I lie.

"In that case, that plane," he points inside the hanger, "is going up to the Midlands half empty. If you act as the co-pilot for the first part, I can shift you and your kit for £1,500."

"Sounds good to me. I'll get the van driven indoors and fetch you the money."

While I introduce myself to the pilot and check over the plane, as I will be acting as co-pilot, I will be jointly responsible if anything goes wrong during the flight, affecting my licence. With that, George goes and grabs the dosh and directs Simon to drive inside and park near the aircraft.

"So what's in the boxes? Need to add them to the manifest. By the way, the name's Allan," asks my new flying partner.

"Just some boring electronic equipment needed for an inspection at a factory in Basingstoke."

"They resemble rifle cases to me," he points at the sniper boxes.

Time to think on my feet and hope the man can take a bribe and not report us, "£2,000 says they are electronics," hoping he will take the money.

"OK, electronics it is then," holding out his hand.

About 30 minutes later, and everything is loaded and all monetary requirements settled, we are all set to depart. One last thing to do before we take off, I turn to Simon and Derek, "Once we land, I'll unload our stuff and wait for you near the control tower. Make sure you confirm with Mark that someone will be at the airport to meet us. Have a safe journey." With that, they drive off into the distance, heading for the ferry.

The aircraft lines up at the start of the main runway, carries out pre-departure checks and waits for the tower to give us clearance. As I will be flying the first leg, I pick a point at the far end of the runway and position myself, ready to commence takeoff.

Through my headphones, a voice comes over the airways, "SABH, you're clear for takeoff."

I repeat the phrase to confirm I understand, then release the brakes and smoothly apply the power until full power is obtained. Then midway down the grass runway, with me keeping the light aircraft aiming at my reference point, the nose wheel gradually lifts up off the ground.

At 200 feet, I place the ailerons in the neutral position, fly level for a few minutes until the plane picks up speed, then continue the climb.

Sandown to Popham aerodrome is only a short hop in flying terms, so we soon approach the landing field. "Popham control tower, this is SABH now on downwind leg."

"SAHP, on downwind leg, proceed to final approach," comes the reply from the tower.

A few moments later, "Popham tower, SABH, on final approach."

With that, I pick a spot halfway down the runway and point the front of the aircraft towards it. Then with the use of power, airspeed, and the elevators controlling my descent, make the perfect landing.

As we taxi off the landing strip to our designated parking bay, "There is a lot more to you than meets the eye, Steve," George declares through a 'thank fuck we are down' type of expression.

I turn to face Lorna, a beautiful smile now spread across her face.

All we have to do now is unload our equipment. "Grab that old metal trolley, George, while Lorna and I start unloading the kit," I say, pointing in the direction of the tall tower.

Once all the equipment is loaded securely, we pull the cart over towards the central vehicle park and wait for Simon and Derek to turn up with the hire van.

We don't have to stand around too long before George shouts out, "Here they come, down the road at your 11 O'clock, Steve."

Turn my head slightly to my left, to see the white truck emerging from the treeline and driving down the path in our direction. We have come too far to make the rookie mistake of waving down the vehicle and approaching too early. You never know, something could have gone wrong, and a nasty surprise could be waiting for us in the back of the van.

Watch as Simon drives past down to the end of the narrow road, before turning around the control tower. He will be doing the same as us, and making sure everything is OK before entering the car park.

The vehicle is reversed up to the waiting equipment, with both Derek and Simon clambering out moments later. "Morning gents, any major problems on the journey to deal with?"

"Nope, no issues at all," replies Derek, as he plonks his arse on the front edge of the kit.

"Perfect, the flight went without any problems as well, so this is turning out to be a good day. But before we turn the equipment over to Mark at the factory, we better add a safeguard."

"That makes complete sense, especially since on our last mission, Henry tried to swindle us out of our payment for the job completed. What do you have in your twisted mind, Steve?"

"As we have in our possession the flash drive with the new coding, George, let's unlock one to prove they still work and keep the rest and the codes to ourselves until Mark coughs up the funds."

"Sounds like some type of plan to me, mate."

While George unlocks one piece of kit, I grab my mobile from my inside jacket pocket and dial Mark's number. After several rings, Mark answers the phone.

"Hi, it is Steve. Your man hasn't shown up at the airfield yet, is he on his way?"

"Hi Steve, yes, sorry been a hectic morning here, as the military turned up unannounced for an inspection of the equipment. Do you have everything?" Mark replie in an apprehensive voice.

"Yep, we have the lot. Give us the location of your factory — we will bring the stuff to you."

"Thanks, Steve, you might have just saved the company. While I'm waiting for you, I will stall the army top brass as long as possible. Once you arrive, go to reception and get the receptionist to call me and I will come and meet you. The address is BASHP Enterprises, Houndsmill Road, Basingstoke. If you drive past the Sainsbury distribution depot, we are the next unit on the right."

"OK, Mark, see you in 15 minutes."

While I have been on the phone, the rest repacked the equipment into the van. With the unlocked one positioned at the rear, it is the first to be unloaded.

I turned to the others, "Change of plans. Seems like we are now not being met here by one of Mark's people, but have to take stuff to the industrial unit instead. So if we are all ready, let's make a move."

"Any idea where it is, Steve?" Simon asks, climbing into the driver's seat.

"Yes, mate, the place is on Houndsmill Road."

"And where is that then, and don't say Basingstoke."

"Can you hear this, George? Our reconnaissance troop hasn't a clue where they are going. Now that's a change, not."

"Never trust a tanky," George yells from the back in between, laughing to himself.

"You pair of GRUNTS can do one," comes the 'fuck you' reply from Simon, as he enters the address into Google Maps on his phone.

As I estimated, the drive only takes 15 minutes before turning right from the main road, into a small side street that forms part of the complex. To our right is a car park located in front of the offices. A security gatehouse is to the right, about 50 metres further down.

Once Simon parks the van close to what looks like the reception area, clamber out of the passenger seat and head to speak to the receptionist, who sits at a single desk inside.

Good morning. Could you give Mark a call, please? He is expecting me."

The oldish-looking lady in her mid-fifties, dressed in a smart grey suit which covered a white blouse, looks up. "A good day to you as well. Who should I say wants to talk to him?"

"Steve."

"What is the purpose of your visit, Steve?"

I fucking hate these gatekeepers. "Just say Steve's arrived with the equipment— —he will know what it's about."

With that, she pushes a button on a comprehensive communication console to the right of her desk. Seconds later, Mark's voice can be heard coming from the speaker, "Yes, Donna, what's the issue and can't it wait? I'm busy with the people from the military?"

"The man calls himself Steve. Says he is here with the equipment," Donna responds into the mic.

"In that case, I'm on my way—can you please tell him to drive through the front gate into the yard? I'll meet him at the first loading dock."

"Of course, Mark."

After closing the microphone, Donna glances up, "Did you catch all of that?"

"Yes, thanks for your help."

As we drive to the gatehouse, Mark must have contacted the person operating the gate directly, as the man raises the barrier to allow us access, without coming out to check for any identification.

Once past security, the rear opens up into a busy transport yard. To our immediate right are several tall, round structures, while over to the left, a truck is being refuelled from a diesel storage tank.

Just past the two towers, Mark can be seen standing in an open doorway. "Over there, Simon, reverse up to the dock," I point in Mark's direction.

"You don't know how pleased I am to see you all again and, of course, the young lady," Mark points to Lorna, who has climbed out of the back of the van with George. "Is everything accounted for?"

"Yep, every last bit of kit is here," as I wave my hand towards the equipment stacked up in the vehicle.

Mark gives a massive smile as stress releases itself from his whole body, to be replaced with relief. "Thanks, Steve. Can you unload it all on here? My people will take it from here."

Apart from the one George unlocked earlier, all the green storage boxes are placed on the metal dock. Once the last crates are unloaded, Mark comes outside to join us.

If for nothing more than to give Mark the impression that he even thinks of stitching us up regarding payment for the work, we all stand in a semicircle around him.

Shaking Mark by the hand, "One last thing before we go, that set of equipment over on the ground, this is the only one that works at the moment, so I suggest that is the one you show to your military friends inside."

" I don't understand," Mark answers, with a puzzled appearance.

"Nothing personal, Mark. All the other equipment will work once I give you this portable flashdrive with new coding," I take the device from my pocket and hold it out for him to see.

Still looking confused, "What's that about, Steve."

"As I said, Mark, nothing aimed at you. The last person who we worked for tried to withhold payment. He is now pushing up grass in some graveyard. So this is our protection. The instance you transfer the money into Simon's bank account, I will have the flash drive delivered to you by courier."

"Now I understand. I will wire the payment, once the people from the military have departed."

"Cheers, Mark, pleasure doing business with you," I rejoin the others who have relocated to the van.

The place is built with a one-way circuit to drive out, so Simon drives to the end of the yard, turns right and heads for the out gate.

With the small hatch that opens to the back open, so Derek and George can understand what is being said, "Well, that's another mission over, with the added bonus that we are all almost still in one piece. Is anyone coming back to the Isle of Wight for some deserved R&R?"

"Think I'll head home, Steve. Best check wifey fed the polo donkey."

"No problem, Simon, let us know when the cash arrives in your bank. As always will leave you to divide the money up. While we are going to the drop-off point, fancy dividing the bonus dosh up into five lots, Derek, so you have some to take back to St Bethanie."

"Will do, mate. Any chance you can take me to the station? Might as well catch a train to Heathrow, spend a couple of nights in a hotel before my flight home."

"Will be off home as well," George interjects from the rear.

I turn to Lorna, "What about you, fancy coming back to my place for a few days?"

"Might as well, I've got nothing else planned, plus it will be nice to spend time with you, without them idiots," she points at Simon, George and Derek in turn, with a playful grin on her face.

With everyone dropped off at their respective places, I head for the Red Funnel terminal to return to the island. As I'm the type of person, thanks to PTSD, that does not trust anyone I do not know, I carry out the same precautions, as I am still on the mission until we reach my lodge.

"Here we are, my little safe refuge. Make yourself comfortable."

"Looks fantastic—I will dump my stuff in your bedroom."

"Sounds perfect to me, fancy a brew?"

"Yes, please," Lorna calls out from the bedroom.

The kettle just boils when the phone rings. It is Simon. "Hi, mate, miss me already?"

"No fucking chance, just to let you know Mark came through with the money. Will transfer the funds to everyone later today."

"Thanks for letting me know. Have you called George and Derek? I will tell Lorna. Is there anything else before I attend to other business?"

"Will call them after you. Plus, make sure your bed can take the extra activity! Oh, I almost forgot, I received a message on the answerphone. Someone has a job we may be interested in.

Glossary

Army Chuckin	Stew
Bergen	Backpack
Binos	Binoculars
Call Sign DR	Derek Radio
Call Sign GD	George Dog
Call Sign S3	Steve 3(RGJ)
Call Sign TS	Tanky Simon
Chimp	Mind / Anger Management program used in the treatment of PTSD
Click	Kilometre
Donkey Walloper	Tank Driver
Dubby Dust	Washing Powder
Egg Banjo	Egg Sandwich
Endex	End of Mission
Escaped Librarian	A term used in the treatment of PTSD
Grunt	Ground Reconnaissance Untrainable

Maggot	Sleeping Bag
Mickey	Cheap Wristwatch
OP	Observation Post
PAYG	Pay As You Go
Pit	Bed
Range Card	A drawing or sketch used in OPs which show potential locations and distance to targets.
RV	Rendezvous – Meeting Point
Shank's Pony	Walking
SLR	Self Loading Rifle
Stag	Sentry Duty
Tab	Walk or Hike

ABOUT THE AUTHOR

In 2017 after many years of suffering, I was diagnosed with PTSD from three life-threatening events during my service. Part of my recovery at Combat Stress someone suggested I should begin writing. During my last two week stay at Combat Stress in Apil 2019, I started to write. Have now published my first ever book on poetry called Poetry from the PTSD Mind which takes you on a journey from the bad times to the good. I have also written two other books called 'The Lighter Side of Cruising" parts one and two.

OTHER BOOKS WITH GREEN CAT BOOKS

Covert Ops: Danger in Paradise

For details of our other books, or to submit your own manuscript please visit www.green-cat.shop

Green Cat Books